HELEN ROW TOEWS

THE
LEGACY

By Helen Row Toews

Runestaff Chronicles

The Awakening
The Resistance
The Legacy
The Secret

Vinci Books

vinci-books.com

Published by Vinci Books Ltd in 2025

1

A CIP catalogue record for this book is available from the British Library.

Paperback ISBN: 9781036701598

The EU GPSR authorised representative is Logos Europe, 9 rue Nicolas Poussion, 17000 La Rochelle, France

contact@logoseurope.eu

Chapter One

"The reign of Erinbourne's king must end, and his line be destroyed," Malahd said with a snarl. "It is well he has no offspring to deal with. Before the full moon wanes, King Larkender will be dead, and *I* shall possess the Gemstones of Erinbourne."

An unwilling sunbeam slanted through the narrow window of the great dining hall in Respiele's forgotten fortress. Two torches burned on either side of a massive oaken door, and by this light, the occupants talked. Snurler, captain of the stronghold's small group of defenders, sat twisting his hands together at a long table recently cleared of some meager meal. Malahd, the sorcerer, paced nearby, his feet making no sound as he moved along the cold flagstones.

He whirled about at the far end of the room. His long black robe swished around his ankles as he paused. He struck the flagstones with the end of a long silver staff to punctuate his remark with barely suppressed glee. Red sparks burst from the tip, illuminating the sorcerer's stringy grey hair, and crooked smile distorted by hatred. Malahd held the smooth rod in his one good hand. The other was not a hand at all, but a gleaming metal claw. He glided back.

"Larkender is a fool. He has no more idea how to wield the power of the sceptre, and its gemstones, than that of an infant." Malahd stopped beside Snurler. "Too long have I waited to rule this land."

Spittle flew from his thin lips with his angry pronouncement. Snurler watched in alarm as the saliva landed on his sleeve with a puff of smoke, singeing a hole in the rough cloth.

"Yes, sir." Snurler crouched a little lower on his stool, surreptitiously wiping his arm down one leg of his breeches. "But are you not forgetting the other—"

Malahd flung himself at Snurler.

"Forget? You fool! I assure you nothing escapes my memory or intellect!" He banged a fist onto the wood beside Snurler's face, sending crumbs bouncing. "What are you saying? Be out with it!"

Snurler opened his mouth and then slammed it shut just as quick. Shifting uncomfortably on the stool, he drew his tattered cloak closer around his thin frame and opened his mouth to speak again. Still, he said nothing.

Snurler's eyes flicked into the dim recesses of the room where a small movement had captured his eye, but it was only a mouse. Malahd always made sure he and Snurler were alone for these conversations. If the sorcerer chose to punish the captain, there would be no one to object.

In any case, no one *would* object to anything Malahd said or did, if they knew what was good for them. People had been killed for less than what Snurler was about to say now. Yet after years of servitude to this cruel master with nothing to show for it except the misery of his body and soul, some part of Snurler wanted to see the sorcerer squirm.

"There…there is one other of Larkender lineage," Snurler said. "Remember the boy who carried the Emerald? I have heard he is grandson of Alainea Ilstyne, one of the ancient Garde of these Araleesh Mountains, and the great-grandson of Respiele Larkender himself."

Snurler ducked his head beneath the strong wooden table beside him in anticipation of the blow that would follow this foul reminder. Yet, he spoke again, his voice thin and wobbly. "You know, as well as I, that if it is true, the boy is heir to the throne of Erinbourne."

With a hiss of rage, Malahd swung his staff through the air, an arc of tiny red coals following the movement. The embers flew high, crackling and snapping, before dropping onto Snurler's unprotected head. The coals sizzled there, filling the room with a choking smell of burning hair and flesh. Then, the sorcerer pointed the tip of his staff, and a ribbon of fire leapt from the silver tip to where Snurler crouched, batting at his head in a frantic effort to rid himself of the smouldering embers. Weaving about the captain's body, Malahd's curling threads of flame lifted Snurler, screaming, into the smoky air.

"You dare to speak to me of this illegitimate child! We have no proof the boy is Respiele's descendant." Malahd extended his arm a little further, slamming Snurler against a spot on the wall near the ceiling. He held him there within a living inferno. "A mere child cannot defeat *me*."

Malahd drew himself up to his full height. "Besides, this…boy returned to his own kind long ago, through the portal that divides our worlds. He cannot return to Erinbourne without aid, and the ill plans I have arranged for the king are known only by me. There is no one to prevent the actions of such a powerful sorcerer as myself." Malahd jabbed the staff toward the helpless Snurler again. "Do you hear? No one! Every inhabitant of this land shall fear me and bow to my desires!"

A liquid blue flame ran from Malahd's staff, merging with the ruby red, and mutating into deepening threads of cobalt. It licked at Snurler's face. Fingers of indigo fire crept about his chest and legs, pinning him to the scored rock wall. The blue blaze lit his eyes with a turquoise terror. Yet it did not burn him, and he slumped against the raging inferno knowing escape useless, but hoping his words might have some effect.

"Release me," Snurler croaked. "Have I served you all these many years to be treated thus? Someone had to remind you. The boy was here once—perhaps he could traverse through the great portal again."

Snurler took a ragged breath, needing to finish the task he had set before himself, despite his own peril.

Malahd relaxed his grip and Snurler slid down the stony wall, his body jolting over the rough surface. Then, impatiently, the sorcerer turned away, lowering his staff, and the blue flame thinned and returned like the thong of a whip to its owner. Snurler dropped to the ground with a sickening crunch and a scream of pain.

Furiously, Malahd marched along one side of the long table, ignoring the gurgling moans that issued from Snurler's crumpled form.

With his tongue, Snurler pushed a mouthful of blood and teeth onto the floor. His suffering at the hands of Malahd would be over soon, and part of him was relieved. Gathering himself for one last declaration, Snurler drew a tiny, rasping breath. He was past feeling fear. Loathing for the tyrant curled in his stomach, and he wished only to inject as much doubt as possible into the heart of the sorcerer he had both served and despised. Unable to move, his body wracked with pain, Snurler spoke from the floor.

"R-remember this—if the boy—does return…" he rasped, stuttering with pain. He paused to take a small bubbling breath, "and if he seeks you out—know that he will find—more of his inheritance—beneath this mountain than he or anyone else alive—could ever dream of."

Snurler's wasted body spasmed. "…A-and if he finds that inheritance, *you* are the one who should be afraid."

Malahd rounded on Snurler to finish him, aiming a bolt of jagged fire at the crushed remains, but all breath was gone from the broken body. The empty shell that once was Snurler, finally lay at rest. Malahd could inflict nothing more upon the man.

In a shadowed corner of the room, the little mouse dropped to all fours before it scurried through an opening in the rock and was gone.

Malahd shrieked with fury. Flinging his cloak behind his shoulders, he lifted his staff and ground it with all his might into the rock beneath his feet. Fire fell around him like blood-soaked rain from the rafters. The mountain that he stood upon rumbled from somewhere far, far below.

Chapter Two

Kayden pulled the uncomfortable bowtie from around his neck. He tossed it onto his bed before shrugging out of his suit jacket and hanging it carefully over a chair. He'd done it —graduated from high school. Resting his hands on the ancient wooden bureau that had been in this room since his father was a kid, Kayden leaned over the littered surface and searched the face reflected in the ornate mirror hanging above. He'd changed quite a bit in the three years since his family had moved to his grandparents' ranch in Southern Alberta.

He'd lost that perpetual look of fear he'd worn back then, and thought he even had an air of confidence about him now. Long gone was the former anxiety of his new life and school. He no longer wanted to return to his old life in Toronto. He'd enjoyed his senior year at school and loved country living.

He stared into the yellow eyes that he and his grand-mother shared and ran fingers through his ginger hair as he straightened. In fact, a lot of the kids looked up to him like he was some kind of hero after the day he'd taken his runestaff to school and dealt with the group that had terrorized his high school. Once he and a group of teenagers stood up to the bullies, all the students breathed easier. There was strength in numbers, and of course, in his magical runestaff.

That was the last time the staff had responded to him in any great capacity. Gran had told him the runestaff wouldn't be able to do much of significance here because it drew its energy from Erinbourne. Now, in Canada, it simply leaned in a corner of his closet. Yet, he thought about the magical staff and his friends in Erinbourne every day.

He turned away from the mirror to finish undressing and hang the rented suit back in its carrying bag. Then, he slid on a pair of well-worn jeans and a t-shirt, tucked his cell phone into a back pocket, and hurried downstairs.

"You're not going to a grad party tonight?" his father asked, as Kayden plopped onto a chair at the kitchen table beside him and poured a glass of iced tea.

The family had come home right after final ceremonies. Gran, his sister Sarah, and his mother were still upstairs changing.

"Nope, I have better things to do." Kayden grinned at his father's surprised expression. "I need to pack and get a good night's sleep, because…if you're okay with it, I want to take a couple days and go hiking into the mountains. I'll be careful."

His father laughed. "That's fine with me. Your mother might disagree. But if that's how my eighteen-year-old wants to celebrate his graduation, I think it's great." He clapped Kayden on the shoulder and held up his glass to clink. "Congratulations, son. I'm proud of you. I know it wasn't easy to move here and start a new school and life, but you did it, and did it well."

"Thanks, Dad." Kayden flushed with pride

It surprised him that his parents had known the difficulties he had when they first moved to the ranch. He'd hated it here then. But after meeting Durgot, the little man who was gatekeeper of the portal between Kayden's world and the alternate universe of Erinbourne, and carrying the powerful Emerald to its king, Kayden had returned a changed person. It had been an amazing adventure. And it was to Erinbourne that he planned to travel now. Of course, he couldn't say that since only Gran knew of its existence.

Fortunately, time passed differently in Erinbourne. If he allowed himself two days to be gone on this side of the portal, he should have ample time to cross through the divide and visit the people he cared about. As long as he could figure out how to do it. He longed to go back, especially to see Rosalyn.

Kayden got up from the table and set his glass in the sink. He knew it was more than just missing his friends. Lately, he'd begun to feel Erinbourne pulling him, as though he were being called from the other side. He placed a hand on his chest and remembered when King Ludwig had done the same. That great man had made it clear that Kayden would know in his heart, when it was time to return.

"I'm gonna get packed then," he said. Coming to stand beside his father he asked in an undertone, "Will you break it to mom for me?"

"I'll tell her and Gran when they get back," his dad said with a smile. "The pup tent is on a shelf behind my old golf clubs, and I think all the sleeping bags are there too."

Scraping his chair away from the table, he stood, and

threw an arm around Kayden's shoulders as they walked to the basement door. "You'll take your bow?"

Once Kayden had turned sixteen and gotten his driver's license, he'd been quick to join the local archery club and begin learning the art.

"Definitely." He left his dad standing at the top of the stairs and clattered hurriedly down to the cement floor below.

Kayden deliberated over what to take with him. The last time he'd passed through the portal he hadn't known what to expect. This time he would be a little more prepared. He grabbed his sleeping bag and fastened it and the small tent to straps that hung from a large backpack. Then he searched for the kit he'd assembled for a school photography trip: tiny frying pan, razor-sharp pocketknife, matches, spoon, first aid stuff, a flashlight, and a lightweight thermos. Shrugging the laden bag onto his shoulders, he clumped upstairs to find the rest of his family assembled in the kitchen.

"Hi," he said, glancing nervously at his mother, who was rinsing a bowl of fruit at the sink. He swung the pack off his back and dumped it onto the floor, bracing himself for her lecture on safety and not going out alone. She dried her hands on a towel and walked toward him.

"Have a good time honey," she said. Reaching up, she held his face and looked lovingly into his eyes before pulling him down to plant a kiss on his cheek. Her eyes glistened. "I was so proud of you today. When you get home, I'll have a special supper for you. All your favourites."

Sniffling, she tucked a strand of light brown hair behind her ear. She stepped back to pull a tissue from a box on the counter and dab at her eyes.

Gran spoke from her seated position at the table. "We're

all proud as punch of the young man you've become, Kayden."

Her face was wreathed in smiles.

"Yeah, even me," Sarah said, poking her head around the corner. "Surprised?" she added, making a face at him.

Chuckling, she disappeared into the living room with her book.

"Thanks a lot. You guys mean the world to me." Kayden stepped around the backpack and whisked his mother into his arms, swinging her off her feet.

"Stop!" she said, giggling. "Do you want to break your back before you leave?"

Setting her down gently, he moved to Gran. Leaning over the elderly woman, he enveloped her in a hug too.

"You're the best family anyone could ask for," Kayden said. He turned quickly before they saw the tears in his eyes. He walked into the kitchen where he opened cupboard doors, removed a few food items like cookies, bread, and peanut butter, and began to prepare some sandwiches.

Later, back in his room, he stuffed extra socks and underwear inside the bag, then stepped to his closet to rummage around at the bottom for the things he'd worn last time he'd been in Erinbourne. Pulling them out, he held up the old-fashioned breeches. They were way too small for him now and he folded them back up. Same with the boots and tunic he'd been given at the Resistance camp so long ago.

The only thing he might take was the cloak, although it would be short. He wanted to fit in with what others were wearing once he got there and not stand out, but he guessed he'd figure out how to do that when the time came. He threw the cloak behind him on the bed to be included.

After laying the other things he'd outgrown carefully inside his closet on a shelf, he reached into the corner for the most important item of all—his runestaff. Pushing aside hangers, he grasped the walking staff that was so much more than what it appeared. It was lightweight, grey in colour, and looked rather unremarkable, but he knew what wonders it was capable of.

He could hardly wait to use it again. He ran his fingers over the images etched from top to bottom along its length. The bed creaked as he moved to sit at one end, holding the runestaff before him and studying each carving.

There was a slight tap at the door.

"Come in."

Gran's grey head appeared in the light of the hallway and Kayden beckoned to her.

"I've been expecting you," he said, patting a spot beside him.

Her eyes flew to the runestaff and then to Kayden before she perched on the bed.

"I was going to make sure you took it along," she said quietly, nodding at the staff. "I know where you are going, my dear, and I wish you a safe journey."

"I thought you'd guess." He smiled at her. His heart warmed, thinking of the common bond they shared.

She reached for his hand and squeezed it tight.

"Please greet them all for me, will you? Especially Durgot and Talbot." Her yellow eyes shone in the light from a lamp on his bedside table. "There are times when I wish I could go back. If Dranich were alive…"

Her voice broke off and then she patted Kayden's knee and said briskly, "But I have my memories to hold onto and I have my family here." She smiled and looked away. "We were quite a pair, Dranich and I. There was nothing we could not do together. I only wish you could have experienced it, my boy."

She sighed deeply.

"You mean—riding a dragon?" Kayden asked hesitantly.

"In part. But mostly I refer to the closeness we shared. We knew one another's thoughts almost before they were thoughts at all. It was a dreadful day when dragons were erased from Erinbourne. It would have been your birthright to be united with such a mighty creature," she added. "And as future king, you would have been powerful indeed."

"Gran. Don't say that. I'm no king," Kayden said. He looked down and brushed imaginary lint from his jeans. "I understand about the bloodlines and everything, but it's crazy to think that *I* could be a king."

"Ah," she said, her eyes twinkling at him, "yet such decisions are not our own. We may neither choose nor decline what fate decrees. There is a reason for everything under the sun and this may well be your destiny, as it was mine to come to Canada. I believe you were destined to be in Erinbourne the last time. Do *you* not?"

She raised her eyebrows, daring him to disagree.

"Yeah, I know you're right. I think I was meant to play a part in saving Erinbourne and King Larkender."

"Your great-uncle," Gran said.

"Yes," he answered. "My great-uncle. But I still don't see how I could ever be a king."

After his grandmother had kissed him goodbye and tiptoed from the room, Kayden's thoughts lingered on what Gran had said about her dragon.

"It would have been great," he said to himself. Closing his eyes, he could see it—a huge golden dragon coiled with massive wings outstretched as it poised on a mountain peak. He yearned for what could have been, but brought his thoughts back to the present, and the urgency he felt within. He was being summoned, but for what reason, he did not know.

Chapter Three

Kayden woke before sunrise. In fact, he had barely slept at all, so great was his excitement. Flipping on the lamp, he dressed without a sound, grabbed his runestaff and backpack, and eased down the staircase to the kitchen below.

His stomach was in too much turmoil to eat. Instead, he filled his thermos with cold water, grabbed an apple, and two granola bars to jam in his pockets. Then he headed to the entry for the boots, coat, and bow and arrows he'd left by the door.

It was just after five a.m. as he stepped outside and closed the back door behind him. He breathed deeply. The sky was taking on the first pink light of dawn.

Kayden looked around with appreciation as he made his way along the back of the house and struck out across the pasture. He knew where he was going, because he'd scouted it out many times before. The only part he was unsure of was where to strike the mountain with his Runestaff to open the portal. Finding the right spot might take some time.

He passed a herd of the Charolais cattle his family

raised. They were lying on a hilltop to take advantage of any cool breezes that might ward off some of the mosquitoes and black flies that plagued them during the summer months. The animals ignored his passage.

Although he had inherited Gran's ability to speak with animals in Erinbourne, he couldn't communicate with them on this side of the portal. He'd tried. And he'd felt pretty stupid when he'd been caught by his Gran, trying to carry on a conversation with a cow, until she explained some things didn't work quite the same way here.

He chuckled, remembering those first days after his adventure in Erinbourne had ended, and he'd returned to normal life in Canada.

Fishing out the apple, he bit into it with a crunch and wiped the juice from his chin with a sleeve. He wasn't planning to stop before he reached the mountain. It would take him about three hours if he hurried. Tossing away the core, he noted that the ground was rising sharply.

He dug his staff into the earth and strode on, imagining the welcome he'd receive when he knocked on the locked gate to Durgot's small realm at the center of what he knew to be called the Ildune Mountain. At least, that was what it was called in Erinbourne.

A forest loomed in front of him, and ducking his head he plunged within, parting the low hanging branches with one hand and gripping his runestaff with the other. He breathed in the pungent scent of the pine. The bow, slung across his back, hindered him a little. While fallen trees and thick, springy mosses slowed him down, but overall Kayden thought he was making good time.

He consulted a watch that had been his father's. There was no point in bringing his cell phone, as it wouldn't work beyond the portal. He'd hidden it in his room, so his parents wouldn't wonder why he'd left it behind. Technology was non-existent where he was going. It was like walking back into the fifteenth century.

Finally, the trees thinned ahead of him and he knew he was almost there. He came out the other side of the tall, straight pines, and was faced with a climb over fallen rocks and thick shale to reach the mountain face. Sliding down, sometimes further than he moved up, he fought his way to the skirt of the mountain and stood panting and leaning on his staff.

Now to find the hidden notch to strike with his runestaff. He remembered there was a huge boulder next to the portal that, if he squinted at it, resembled the head of a dog. It was to that spot that he manoeuvered now. Then, he began searching the mountain face with his fingers, hoping to find the small indentation. Shrugging out of his pack, he let it drop to earth as he moved along the rock, centimeter by centimeter, looking for a needle in a haystack.

Nothing. After an hour of exploring, he flopped against the boulder and wiped his brow. It was noon and the sun was hot. He unwrapped a sandwich and ate it thoughtfully, scrutinising the expanse of rock before him. As he washed the last bite down with a cold gulp of water, he realized what he'd been doing wrong.

He crumpled the plastic wrapping and shoved it into his pocket. Then shouldering the backpack and his bow, he grasped his staff, and held it in front of him. He turned it so he could clearly see the image of a mountain near the tip and concentrated on what he needed, the portal.

The staff came to life for the first time in three years. It shivered, as though waking from a long sleep, and then the image Kayden regarded began to glow with a brightness that was noticeable even in the bright sun of midday.

He smiled with satisfaction, willing the crevice in the rock to reveal itself and allow him entrance into the world beyond its gates.

With a clap like thunder, a jagged fissure split the rock vertically, glimmering as though a bolt of lightning were inlaid in the stone. Moving toward the fracture, Kayden saw the tiny depression off to one side. With both hands, he raised the staff high over his head, lunged forward, and struck the dent with all his might. The fissure cracked wide open, each edge blazing with shimmering light.

Grinning broadly, Kayden stepped through.

Behind him, the aperture slammed shut with a resounding boom. Apart from some dust that sifted onto his hair, everything was still. He was in complete darkness, listening for the distant sounds of the Enchanted River. The water ran around the interior of this mountain to protect the portal from all who might seek to pass without leave.

Concentrating on the rune he could feel at the tip of the staff, he called upon it for light. He was rewarded with the glowing image of a sun that soon grew bright, illuminating the familiar, round cavity hewn from the rock where he now stood.

"It's great to be back!" Kayden said, his voice echoing in the chamber.

He set off along the narrow corridor leading down into the bowels of the mountain. Despite the unevenness of the passage, he strode with a sure step, and soon reached the edge of the Enchanted River. It gurgled at his toes. He raised his runestaff into the air as he had seen Durgot do and focused his thoughts on what he needed at that moment —a bridge.

The staff leapt from his hand, contorting in mid-air, growing and adding to itself as it stretched out across the dark rushing waters of the stream, and fell with a thump to span its width. Kayden extended a foot to test it, since he'd never done this himself. The waters were dangerous, but the makeshift bridge seemed strong, and he hurried across.

Kayden looked down, only for a moment, at the waters that rose in white-capped waves to seek his feet. He knew from experience that if only one drop of that water touched him, every memory he possessed would be blotted from existence.

He stepped onto the other side and turned to stretch out his arm, willing the runestaff to return to him. The bridge reared away from the opposite side and swept into the air, folding onto itself until it was once more the unassuming runestaff.

As it flew into his waiting hand, Kayden realized that he had one last hurdle to jump before arriving at Durgot's gate. He craned his neck to look at the sheer rock wall he must climb in order to reach the marble door high above. Durgot had used his charmed boussole to trigger hidden steps, but Kayden didn't have one. He'd carried the flat silver object for a while, but had given it back to Durgot once they returned from the quest.

How was he going to get up there?

Kayden crouched down, well away from the stream, to think. He hadn't thought to bring rope. Besides, there was nothing to loop it around if he had one. He was stumped and leaned against the cold, damp wall.

Could he get this close and fail to reach Durgot? It was unthinkable.

A sound from over his head broke into Kayden's thoughts. It was the long drawn-out screech of rusty hinges and he stood up to peer into the gloom.

"I shall endeavor to correct that," came a voice from the shadows. "A spot of oil should do the trick."

To Kayden's amazement, steps began to slide smoothly from the rock and move into place.

"Were you *planning* to remain at the foot of my door, young man? Or shall I expect you to ascend forthwith and partake of my evening meal?"

"Durgot!" Kayden scrambled up the steps, pulling himself along the steep cliff until he crawled over the edge and rushed to clutch the little man who waited at the top.

"Mercy!" Durgot said breathlessly, putting a hand up to keep his wide-brimmed hat from tumbling down to the river below. "It is marvelous to gaze upon your visage, Kayden. I am ineffably pleased to witness your return to my humble abode."

Kayden stepped back to follow the little man through the huge door and then waited while Durgot pushed it closed and locked it.

"Same old Durgot," Kayden said with a laugh. "I still don't understand a word you say."

"Ah, I do apologize, young man." Durgot winked at him. "I shall curb my speech while you are here. I only wished to say that I am *most* happy to see you again!"

He bowed slightly, and grinning, led the way down the dirt path to a spindly red house in the distance.

He really hadn't changed, Kayden thought. He was only about four feet tall, and still wore the floppy blue pants and jacket that seemed too big for him. The grey hair and long beard had not changed much either, only looking a little longer than they had three years ago. Durgot's eyes were crinkled at the corners from laughter, giving him a kindly appearance, which Kayden knew was all too true.

Kayden gazed at his surroundings. The place was just as

he remembered it. Sunlight, from somewhere unknown, streamed through the oddly shaped trees that grew in Erinbourne, and rows upon rows of neatly tilled garden plots unfolded across the wide area up to where a waterfall fell from the domelike side. Durgot's spherical domain, lying at the center of the Ildune Mountain, abounded with animals and vegetation.

"We shall talk once we are inside, my dear boy," Durgot said over his shoulder as he scurried along the trail ahead. "But I must say your arrival has been well-timed. There is someone here you must meet. Including yourself, I have received two visitors from abroad today, which is quite remarkable, as few from outside this mountain know of my existence at all."

He stopped dead in his tracks and Kayden was hard put not to bowl him over.

"The visitor's name is Millinworth and she bears ill tidings." Durgot turned slowly and fixed Kayden with his piercing amber eyes. "Evil is rising in the west. Malahd rises against the king and plots to kill him. You must go at once to his aid."

Chapter Four

"Okay—what?" Kayden spluttered.

Durgot wheeled around and marched toward his house once more.

"King Larkender is in danger?" Shaking his head in bewilderment, Kayden followed in Durgot's wake.

"Yes. But I shall explain once we are inside. Let us be swift."

As they drew near to Durgot's house set high on a knoll, Kayden gazed at it. His feelings of pleasure at being back squelched with concern at the news.

Malahd was causing trouble, again?

They came to the first of several flights of stairs to Durgot's front door. Kayden took them two at a time to keep up with the small man, who was clearly in a rush. At the top, Durgot crossed the wide deck, which ran around the entire perimeter of his house, and flung open his bright yellow door.

Kayden had to duck to enter the house, but his gaze took in the oodles of familiar ferns hanging from the ceiling and multi-coloured flowers that lined the hallway to the kitchen. Durgot had already disappeared around the corner.

Kayden emerged into the homey kitchen expecting to see Durgot's informant seated at the table, but there was no one. He pulled the heavy pack from his back and set it, along with his bow, arrows, and his runestaff, under Durgot's coat that hung from one of several hooks on the wall. Kayden peeled off his jacket too and hung it beside his friend's. A fire burned brightly on the hearth, warming the room.

"Please make yourself at home," Durgot called, from inside a large wooden cupboard where he was bent over double, rattling pans. Finding what he wanted, the man hurried to the counter, began to chop something, and throw it into the pot.

"How did you know I was at the door?" Kayden asked. "And how is Talbot? And what can *I* do to save the king?"

"Same old Kayden," Durgot imitated, wheeling about to grin at him with knife in hand. "Still full of questions."

Durgot returned to his work. Kayden felt a little awkward. It had been a long time since he first visited this place and met Talbot for the first time.

"I am the gatekeeper," Durgot said, answering Kayden's first question. "It is my business to know who is outside my realm and who seeks passage through the portal."

Picking up the pot, he shuffled to the sink and began to work the handle of a small pump. After a few moments, water gushed from the spout. Durgot filled both the pot and a kettle, before bustling over to the fire where he hung them both on hooks over the flames. Then he hurried to the table and picking up a small towel folded atop a stack of books, he wiped his hands and regarded Kayden seriously.

"Talbot is well. He is off about on his own business, but I expect you will meet up with him. In any case, he needs to be informed of this dire news." With a sigh, Durgot waved the cloth toward the table and forced a smile. "Sit, for goodness' sakes. Nothing can be done right this minute. We shall have a bite to eat and talk."

Kayden sat. The chair seemed smaller and shorter than he recalled. With some difficulty he shoved his long legs under the table and out the other side.

"Yes, you have gotten tall and filled out nicely," Durgot said, almost to himself. He peered into Kayden's face with his bright yellow eyes in much the same way as he had done at their first meeting.

Kayden felt measured from the inside out. He sat up straighter.

"You are not the frightened boy I brought to Erinbourne three of your years ago." Durgot pulled out a chair opposite Kayden and seated himself. "This is good. Truly, I am most glad you are here."

"I'm glad to see you too, Durgot." Kayden ran his fingers through his ginger hair. "But you say the king is about to be killed? I came to see him, as well as Talbot, Rosalyn, and others. What can I do to help?"

"I have no specifics as to the form of attack Malahd is planning." Durgot folded his hands together on the table in front of him. "I know only what Millinworth said. She was quite upset and desperately tired when she arrived here this morning. I told her to lie down and rest for a while."

Durgot glanced up at what looked like a huge clock on the wall over their coats. Yet Kayden could see it was no ordinary timepiece. It was more like a huge triangular boussole. There were four round dials on the bottom and a larger one at the top. Each dial had hands pointing to strange symbols. Only one was moving at the moment though, and Durgot appeared to consult it before jumping to his feet and rushing from the room.

"She has been sleeping long enough," he called over his shoulder. "I shall wake her."

Kayden was left alone to ponder who Millinworth might be. The last time he sat at this table, he'd been told a great warrior named Talbot was coming. A guide who would also serve as protector on his dangerous expedition to deliver the Emerald to King Larkender.

And then a hedgehog had scampered into the room.

Kayden chuckled to himself. Talbot had certainly turned out to be more than expected.

So, what or who is Millinworth? A striped chipmunk perhaps, or how about a fluffy bunny? Wait—maybe a tiny turtle will crawl through the door?

He was still snickering to himself when Durgot returned. Kayden looked past the little man, watching for Millinworth to appear, but there was no one. Durgot strode to the table and extended his arm. A small brown mouse leapt from his hand and skidded to a halt on the polished surface.

"Hello," the mouse chirped, standing on her hind legs and managing a tiny curtsy. "Millinworth at your service, good sir. How did you get here? Have you always known Durgot? Are you the one folks talk about? Heir to the throne and all that rot?"

She spoke very fast and at such a high decibel that Kayden had trouble following what she said.

"Umm." Although Kayden had been expecting someone quite unusual to appear, he was taken aback and blinked a few times before finding his voice. "My name is

Kayden. I'd like to help, but I'm not now, nor will I ever be a king."

"Ooh," she said and twirled on one foot. "I think you are. You are, you are, you are the next king."

She fell over onto the table holding her head and muttering, "You are, you are, you are..."

"Fine, fine, that will do, Millinworth," Durgot said rather irritably. He caught Kayden's attention and ever-so-slightly rolled his eyes. "I shall finish preparing something for us to eat. You must pick yourself up and tell Kayden what you overheard."

He moved back to the fire and busied himself with meal preparations, leaving Kayden to deal with the giddy mouse alone.

She rolled onto her side and looked at him. "I know you are *the one,* because you can understand what I say," she said. "Only someone of Garde heritage could do that. Plus, Durgot told me who you were. But I would have known anyway, because I have finely honed skills of perception."

"Ah, yeah, okay," Kayden said. He was uncertain how to proceed with this strange little creature. "Um, so can you tell me what you heard and where you were at the time?"

"Ooh, of course I can!" she squeaked, appearing delighted to be asked. She scrambled to her feet, clasped her paws behind her back, stuck her tiny pink nose in the air, and began speaking very fast. "I was scavenging for food in Respiele's old fortress, in the Araleesh Mountains, because the Resistance, or those of them that stay to guard King Ludwig Larkender, asked if it would be possible for me to sneak in and see if I could find out what Malahd is doing, since I told them earlier I was only too happy to do that very important work, due to my aforementioned skills of perception, innate sense of direction, and ability to sneak into rooms undetected."

She stopped to take a breath.

"Hang on!" Kayden said, taking advantage of the lull in the torrential rain of her report. He held up a hand in protest and thought of Mrs. Muskego, a teacher from grade school who always admonished kids for run-on sentences. "Could you try to speak slower and throw in a few pauses? I can't follow you, and I don't want to miss anything."

Durgot nodded approvingly as he sliced bread at the counter.

"Alrighty-roo," Millinworth said, undaunted. Flinging her head back and shutting her eyes, she started again, albeit a trifle slower. "Anyway, I was in the great dining hall of Respiele's fortress when Malahd and Snurler—that's the captain of his defense—came into the room to talk. Well, I guess to be strictly accurate, Snurler *was* the captain. But he isn't any more because he's dead." Opening one eye, she looked at Kayden. "Is that slow enough?"

"Yes."

She closed her eye and began once more, faster. "I could tell you every detail, because my mind is just *that* good. But if you only want the highlights, I can tell you that Malahd plans to kill King Larkender before the waning of the next full moon. How he plans to accomplish this I do not know, because he did not say, but I have no doubt he means to fulfill his threat."

She finished as though expelling this information had been part of winning some strange race. Somehow, Kayden had managed to catch it.

"Was anything else said?"

"No," she answered promptly. Then, with a little

screech, she leapt into the air and screamed, "Yes! They talked about you."

"Me?"

"Yes. Malahd wants to kill the king, so he can get the sceptre and take over Erinbourne. But Snurler reminded him about the heir, which is clearly you." She pointed a dramatic paw at Kayden. "Malahd wants to kill you too, except he thinks you went back to your own kin through the portal and he doesn't have to worry about you."

She took a deep breath. "…That is all."

With that, she lay down upon the table, curled up into a little ball, and fell fast asleep.

"What. Was. That?" Kayden lifted his hands as Durgot turned to face him holding two steaming bowls and a plate of sliced bread.

"Well, I did *not* say she was easy to understand," Durgot said dryly. "But the Resistance did ask her to spy on Malahd, and she is adept at surveillance."

He clunked the dishes onto the table and turned around for more. "We must formulate a plan of action this evening."

"Can I help with the food?" Kayden asked, getting to his feet and following Durgot.

"Yes. Please fetch the olive oil from the cupboard next to the window and two spoons from that drawer."

Durgot set a bowl of ripe yellow fruit, two cups, and a jug of red juice on the table. "There now," he said, once Kayden had added the required items. "We may partake."

They ate together in companionable silence. Kayden, lost in thought, couldn't help but wonder what his mother would think of serving a meal beside a snoring rodent, but he pushed that aside.

Durgot's meal was delicious. The soup was creamy and

rich green in colour, while the brown loaf was freshly baked and soft. He watched what Durgot did first, then imitated him by picking up the olive oil, pouring a stream of the rich gold liquid liberally over the bread, and topping it with sliced tomatoes. He took a big bite before looking at Durgot. The little man chewed thoughtfully.

"What do I do with the information? And how can I reach King Ludwig in time?" Kayden asked, at length. It felt strange to know that a sorcerer was actively trying to kill both him and the king. But he was here in Erinbourne, packed and able to leave immediately to help save his great-uncle.

"Millinworth did not tell me that last part," Durgot said, then took a sip of juice. "I confess to a feeling of trepidation. That is to say...I feel concern for your safety."

"Yes, I knew what you meant, Durgot. That worries me too, but I'm also wondering why Millinworth would come here instead of getting this message straight to the king? I mean, she didn't know I'd be here. No one knew. And you don't leave your post so..."

"I expect it was because she caught a ride and had to go where they went," Durgot said. His forehead wrinkled. "Yes, I'm sure that was it. Most often Talbot is here and could have taken the message for her, so it was reasonable she should come to me."

"What do you mean she had a ride?"

"She rode here on a goose." Durgot began to gather up the dishes as though it were quite common for rodents to ride about the countryside on the backs of geese.

Kayden shook his head as if to clear a nasty fog that had slipped inside when he wasn't paying attention.

"She rode—on a goose. Yeah, that's normal," he said with a sarcastic drawl. What did he expect though? That maybe she'd caught a bus? He sighed and picked up their used glasses before carrying them to the sink.

He might as well get used to this sort of thing. After all, he was in Erinbourne. He was back into the thick of trouble too, with Malahd plotting to kill the king that Kayden had risked his life to save on his previous visit. Not to mention the sorcerer's desire to kill him too.

After helping to tidy up after their meal, Kayden sat with Durgot at the table beside the slumbering mouse.

"I believe it is best you take my boat as far as possible toward Larkender Castle," Durgot said, ignoring Millinworth. "It will be the fastest mode of travel, as the river flows in the direction you need to go. I shall equip you with oars and if you keep the shore in sight at all times, you should be fine."

"I *should* be fine?" Kayden asked. "I've been to Norbern, but doesn't the river join an ocean at that point?"

"It flows into the Kalainian Sea, yes," Durgot said.

He stood up from his chair, bustled over to a drawer, and rummaged in its depths.

"Ah, here it is," he said, lifting a long scroll. He walked to the table, unfurling the hand-drawn map, and laid it in front of Kayden. "As you know, I can let you through the gate to the northern side of this mountain where you will find the same boat as before. Then, ride the Enchanted River to where it exits the mountain and allow the stream to carry you to Rin Lake."

"I've been through there before, although I didn't know what the lake was called. Talbot and I met Camden and Edna at the far northwest end." With a finger, Kayden followed a further arm of the lake that headed slightly northeast. "So, you want me to head straight up this tributary until it empties into the sea just south of

Norbern, and then continue along the coastline? How far?"

"There is a natural harbour, here." Durgot jabbed a stubby finger at the map. "And the town that grew up around it is called Tunish. The King keeps a fleet of sailing boats docked there and much fishing takes place in the surrounding waters. If you can land the boat in Tunish, you can locate the road leading to the castle. It is not far from there. Anyone should be able to tell you which road leads to Larkender Castle."

Kayden considered what had been said. His eyes fastened on the staff leaning against the wall beneath his coat.

"Why can't I use my runestaff?" Kayden asked.

"What do you mean?"

"I mean, why can't I ask the runes on my staff for something that could just carry me there—like the falcon?"

Durgot's face relaxed with understanding. "You may call upon the runestaff for short periods of time. In a battle, to escape danger, or for protection, but not to make a journey that would take hours at a time. It is not possible, lad. The staff could not maintain the transformation and it would revert back unto its true self."

"Oh, I see. Glad I asked then. In any case, I can get there by using the boat," he said. He leaned back in his chair only to sit bolt upright with a sudden, frightening thought. "What will Millinworth do now? She won't want to go with me, will she?"

The mouse gave a tiny snore and turned over to her other side.

Durgot glanced at her. "No, Millinworth will ride out from the mountain in the boat with you, but she has informed me that she has other business to attend to. I suppose I shall leave her here for the night. He motioned to the door leading upstairs. "I suggest you get some rest, young man. The bed is made up in the room you had before. I shall call you before sunrise. This message must be taken to the king as soon as possible."

Kayden tiptoed to where he'd thrown his backpack against the wall.

"Goodnight," he said, turning to see Durgot gently place a small cloth over the mouse.

Durgot straightened and waved Kayden on to bed. Yet his face was grave and Kayden knew the situation was dire. He only hoped he could reach King Larkender in time.

Chapter Five

After a hurried breakfast, Kayden and Millinworth, who peeked out his shirt pocket, were let through the north gate by Durgot, and made their way down to stand beside the Enchanted River. It was an easy matter for Kayden to retrieve the boat from its hiding place in the stone wall now that he had Durgot's boussole.

Carefully, Kayden lowered the boat into the water, laid his runestaff and two oars along the far edge, and sat inside. He moved slowly and carefully, afraid of a splash from the treacherous waters. Once he was settled Kayden let go of the rocky verge, used his runestaff to push off, and nodding a farewell to Durgot, who watched with much hand wringing from above, they floated away. Since the boat barely fit beneath the rock where the mountain met the river, Kayden flattened himself as much as possible, on the bottom of the vessel, careful not to crush Millinworth who squirmed in his pocket.

They slipped beneath the rock face. The only sound was

the water gurgling and licking at the sides of their craft as it propelled them along.

"Now what? Can we go faster? Faster, faster!" Millinworth crawled onto Kayden's chest and crouched there. The darkness was so complete that Kayden could only feel what she was doing. He raised a tentative hand to trail his fingers along the rock just over his face.

"We stay low and wait until we come out from under the rock. It'll take an hour or two so you might as well just rest. I can't make the boat go any quicker than it already is." Kayden hoped she didn't want to strike up a conversation with him. He was sure, if she started, her incessant chatter would wear him out before they broke free of the mountain. He counted himself lucky when she subsided into silence.

Kayden's own thoughts turned to what lay ahead. Navigating this boat as far as Norbern didn't worry him at all. He'd done it in the past. He was most concerned about hitting the open sea. Nevertheless, it was vital that he reach King Ludwig before the man could be harmed.

And Rosalyn. How was she? Would she have forgotten him? Or be happy to see him return? Durgot had said she was part of the Resistance who lived at the castle and protected King Ludwig.

Kayden thought of Rosalyn and the adventures they'd had every day since he'd left. Sighing, he shifted uncomfortably on the hard bottomed boat. He would find the answers to his questions soon enough.

"I see light ahead, light, light…light ahead," Millinworth squeaked. She ran circles on Kayden's chest in her excitement.

Kayden lifted a tentative arm to feel for the ceiling, but only empty air met his hand. Water sounds echoed in the cavern, and he raised his head to look. It was true. A thin beam of sunlight had slipped under the rock, providing enough light to see that they had floated into a rocky chamber. Kayden knew that he had to be ready to prevent them from making another endless loop on the Enchanted River.

"Millinworth," he said, "I have to get up now so I can use my staff. Can you climb off me and get to the back of the boat, please?"

Obediently, she slid down and pattered off behind his head.

He manoeuvered onto his knees and crawled forward, retrieving his runestaff as he went. Kayden squinted into the gloom. Grasping the staff with both hands, he laid it across the bow, ready for action. He knew that once the narrow channel appeared, the river they were on would turn sharply to the right. He'd have to act fast in order to fight their way out of the current. To accomplish this, he'd use the staff to push them in the right direction, since it was longer than the oars.

There it was! The narrow channel, hewn from rock that led to the world beyond the Ildune Mountain. Kayden thrust his runestaff down into the black rushing waters until it met with the stone below and then he pushed hard. It sent the boat across the current, but the nose of their vessel was caught again, and they turned back to the right. Lifting his staff, he repeated the process again and again, each time lifting it carefully from the flood lest even a drop of the magical waters should touch him. At last they were free. The boat floated down a channel that was barely wide enough for it to slip through.

Sunlight streamed in from the round opening at the end, illuminating the dark passage. With each moment, Kayden's excitement grew. He was on his way. They burst into the green shadows of low hanging shrubs and trees; no doubt planted to obscure the entry. He battled branches that slapped him in the face and scratched his arms. Kayden placed his runestaff on the bottom of the boat and looked eagerly at the world unfolding before him.

Groves of the trees he had found so unusual during his first visit, dotted the hillsides in either direction. They were tall trees, with branches uniform in length and exactly perpendicular to the trunk. The scent of new-mown hay reached his nostrils. On one side, a field of long grass had been cut and was curing in the hot sun. A line of graceful willows dipped their toes into the water beside them and their rich green fronds hung over the waterway.

The mountain was behind them now, and the channel cut its way through rich brown earth. All around him fields of grain were beginning to head out and flower, looking like a thick green carpet that rolled up and over the nearby hills.

Kayden grinned and stretched out his legs. Despite the dire circumstance, which he hadn't been expecting, he was still glad to be back.

"Excuse me!" Millinworth said. "Your enormous body is in my way, which is becoming most bothersome. I have no possible wish or deep desire to be crushed or meet my end just yet. Plus, I will need to leave soon and must watch for my friends, if that is quite alright with you? May I come up to the front without fear of being squished beyond all repair, or is that space reserved exclusively for the likes of you and your kind?"

She sniffed to punctuate her statement.

Kayden wheeled around to apologize. "I'm so sorry, Millinworth!"

With utmost care, he moved out of her way and watched in amused fascination as she paraded to the bow of the boat on her hind legs with her head held high and her forearms crossed.

"I was so caught up in the beauty of Erinbourne that I forgot you were there," he added. "Forgive me."

"Well," she said primly, "I can't say I appreciate being utterly forgotten, but...I forgive you." Reaching Kayden's backpack, she scrabbled up the side and seated herself on top, so she had a better view of her surroundings. "Now, when we reach Rin Lake, I shall ask you to stop on the left, as that is where my friends were told to await me."

She gave him a sideways look and stretched her lips over a set of miniscule teeth in a not quite believable smile. Kayden smiled back at her. He wasn't about to ask for details. It was one of her shorter declarations and Kayden felt grateful.

He sat down cross-legged and turned his attention to the countryside. The channel was still too narrow to use a paddle here, but fortunately the water moved quickly and the blue expanse of a lake shimmered in the sun ahead. To his left, the hayfield had ended with a sturdy pole fence which divided it from a field of corn. The thick green leaves rustled together in a slight breeze from the northwest. In the distance, at the end of the cornfield, several white buildings nestled together, their red roofs partially hidden by trees. *Was it a farm?*

It must be close to noon since the sun was nearly overhead and getting hot. Out of habit, he glanced at his watch, but it was pointless. As far as he could tell, it had stopped working the moment he'd stepped through the portal.

He gripped the sides of the little boat as it skimmed the water and looked ahead. They were coming close to the mouth of Rin Lake. Kayden picked up one of the oars and got onto his knees, ready to paddle. The last thing he wanted was for Millinworth to miss her friends on the left bank.

Kayden and Millinworth gushed from the narrow channel into the lake and the boat slowed significantly. Kayden applied his oars and moved them toward the shoreline. Several large birds bobbed on the surface of the water, and he aimed for them.

"Those are your friends?" he asked, nodding toward the waterfowl.

Millinworth began to jump up and down delightedly, her good humour restored.

"Yes, yes, yes," she cried, clapping her tiny paws together. "Margaret—Gretchen—Hilda!" she called.

However, her voice was only loud enough to be heard by him, and the sound of her little shrieks were like a series of tacks being rammed into his head. He rowed faster.

As they drew close to the birds, Kayden beheld the largest, blackest geese he'd ever seen. Actually, they looked more like an unusual breed of swan, until they began to flap their wings threateningly. The trio glared with beady, reddish eyes, and hissed a warning, but as soon as they recognized Millinworth, they opened their beaks and began to honk, making a horrible racket.

"Halt!" Millinworth screeched, holding up a paw to Kayden.

He jumped and pulled in his oars abruptly. Then Millinworth danced across his backpack as she faced him.

"Thank you so very, very, very much for bringing me to meet my dear and much beloved friends," she said, the words tumbling from her mouth like a waterfall. "I am simply so pleased to be away from Durgot's dreadful dungeon, to breathe the fresh air, and see my oh-so-lovely friends. You have been most kind—apart from forgetting my very existence, nearly trampling me to death, and mashing my person with your enormous, lumpish body. Yet I can forgive such things and wish you well on your journey. Although, I'm not quite sure where you're going since I fell asleep on the table, but that's alright. I know you'll take care of whatever it is you have to do, and you will look after the king since he seems quite incapable of looking after himself."

She took a deep breath. Kayden's back was pressed into the rear of the boat and his mouth hung open.

He clapped it shut.

"You're welcome," he managed to say.

As Millinworth had been speaking, one of the geese had paddled up to the side of the boat. It eyed Kayden with round vacant eyes, waiting until Millinworth hopped from the backpack onto her broad back. The mouse grabbed a feather in each paw, just behind the bird's arched neck, and pulled herself upright.

"This is Gretchen," she said. "Perhaps we shall meet again one day, Kayden. Although I doubt it, since it's clear we travel in different circles, but I would appreciate it greatly if you would remember me to the king, unless he's dead already. And if he is, would you, as future king, kindly keep in mind all that I have done for you and the people of this land, because I feel it would only be fair that I be compensated in some way or other."

Kayden could only focus on her imminent departure, and how happy he'd be to never think of the little mouse again, but he nodded dutifully and said, "Yes, of course."

"Farewell," Millinworth squeaked.

With a rush of squawking, flapping wings, and a few lost feathers that floated on the water around the boat, the three black geese took flight and were soon lost to view in the clear blue sky.

"Why the heck didn't they just fly that silly mouse to see the king herself?" Kayden said.

However, he had no time to waste in idle thought. He lifted the second oar, fitted each of them into small brackets that were built into the sides of the boat, and began to row for the far north end of the lake. Every stroke brought him closer to Rosalyn, the king, and his destiny.

Chapter Six

Kayden only paused in his rowing to get a drink of water and eat something from his bag. He felt a sense of urgency such as he had never felt before. The closer he got to his destination, the more he had a sense of impending doom, and he renewed his effort to reach the other side of the enormous lake before dusk.

He had thought to aim for the lodge belonging to Camden and Edna, the beavers who had helped him and Talbot last time. However, he'd decided it would be too far out of his way to the west, since the mouth of the river leading to the Kalainian Sea was in the eastern corner. Nonetheless, his body wasn't used to rowing for hours at a time, and he was tired.

He leaned against his backpack. Moving it from the front to the back of the boat had allowed him something to rest on when he took a break. He gazed around. There wasn't much to see as he hadn't followed the shoreline, but had struck out across the middle of the lake. To the east there was nothing but water, but to the west a blue shadow of land rose into a mountainous ridge. There were so many mountains in this land. It was crazy.

A movement on the horizon caught his eye. It was a strange bank of clouds that grew closer at a dizzying pace. He sat up, studying it. The shifting mass reminded him of something he couldn't quite place and then, as the black storm grew closer, he remembered. The cloud looked like the birds that had passed over him and Rosalyn as they climbed toward the Honistel Pass. He would never forget that huge flock of starlings, sent by Malahd to search for the Emerald. In their dreadful wake, the fowl had drawn the deceiving purple mist Malahd had used to sicken people's minds and track Kayden's progress toward the king. What could these creatures want now? He sat as if turned to stone, craning his neck to watch them come and clutching the sides of his craft, his knuckles white.

The thought came to Kayden that he should hide himself from them, and fast. But where? He was in the middle of a huge expanse of deep water! His fingers flew to untie the laces of his boots and frantically he kicked them from his feet before plunging over the side of his boat. Clinging to the opposite side of the birds' arrival, he watched as they assaulted the western sky. There were thousands upon thousands of them.

Just before they reached him, Kayden took a deep breath, submerged himself, and moved under the boat, hoping his form would be harder to detect from above. He clung to the bottom, fingernails digging into the wood, and watched the shadow of the birds reflected on the surface of the lake. Wheeling and curling through the air, they converged above him in concentric circles.

Long moments passed. Kayden closed his eyes, his lungs already screaming for air. He wasn't sure how much longer he could hang on. He lifted the boat off the water and stole a quick breath, but it tipped ominously. He was afraid of losing all that he had inside, mostly his precious runestaff. He let the boat drop and a shadow darkened the water.

Then, suddenly, his body was jolted, and he lost his tentative finger-hold on the hull, as the starlings hammered themselves on the boat. It rocked wildly, but he found purchase once again. Kayden imagined machine gun fire would sound like this. Yet, it was tiny beaks and bodies pounding against the flat wooden stern that made the noise. The boat was made of strong stuff and withstood the bizarre onslaught. There was a short break, and then the world darkened once more as the flock dipped down across the water, martyring themselves in a fresh assault against the sturdy hull. Kayden felt himself growing dizzy. His knees bumped the underside. He needed air, and badly. He couldn't wait any longer.

Just as the swarming flock had appeared, so also they left. The cloud lifted and winged their way to the north.

Kayden gave a feeble kick and managed to lift his face to break above the lake water. His body heaving in protest, he took several shuddering breaths and coughed. Reaching up, he grasped the edge of his vessel and hung there with eyes closed, drawing air into his lungs. He waited until he'd recovered enough to pull himself back in the boat. Gentle waves lapped at him, pushing dead birds against his neck and shoulders.

His eyes flew open in shock. Quickly, he crawled over the hull to lay on the bottom of the boat—thankful to be alive, marvelling at the wonder of breath.

Finally, he got to his hands and knees to survey the craft for damage. He crawled to the stern and looked over the edge. Several hundred starlings floated nearby, their lifeless bodies drifting across the water on waves stirred up by the evening wind. He tore his horrified gaze away and made himself examine the wooden boat. It had been chipped away and battered, but there were no holes that Kayden could see.

He sat back on his haunches. Dodged another bullet, he thought. He knew the birds were significant to what was happening with Malahd, and he was sorry he hadn't stayed closer to shore. At least then he would have had a chance to hide and not allow Malahd to know he had returned to Erinbourne. Kayden snatched up the oars and began to row even harder. Sweat trickled down his face and, frowning, he brushed it away with a sleeve. His feet braced against the sides of the boat, and his body tensed as he lifted the oars to plunge them into the water only to lift them and repeat the process again—over and over. The little boat scudded across the glittering water and then Kayden saw the northern shore.

Trees crowded the hillsides ahead and to each side, while willows and rushes ornamented the ragged shoreline. He glimpsed a few buildings set back within the rolling hills to the east. They appeared to be brightly painted houses, glowing in the sinking sun. *Must be a small village.*

He focused on directing the boat to the mouth of the river. The current caught him, and he and the boat were swept along with little effort from him. The waterway narrowed to the width of a two-lane highway, and the current moved fast.

He lifted the oars and sniffed the briny breeze that had shifted to float over the lake from the north. He was close to the sea now, although he couldn't see it yet. A silvery fish leapt out of the water beside him and he jumped, shocked to see any form of life after the starlings.

He began to think of stopping somewhere and pitching his tent for the night. It wouldn't be wise to allow sleep to take him unawares. Not when he was so close to the open waters of the sea where he would need his wits to keep the western shore in sight at all times.

Coming up on his right, a sandy beach rose onto a low mound. It would be easy enough to bring the boat to shore. Also, there was a stand of thick trees at the top of the slope where he could collect a little wood, if he chose to light a fire. He rowed for it at a brisk pace, hoping to get the prow of the boat onto the sand high enough that he wouldn't have to drag the boat through deep water.

Kayden was rewarded with a scraping sound beneath him. His small craft nosed onto the sandy bottom but there was still an expanse of shallow water to navigate. Bending, he untied the laces of his boots and rolled up his pants. He tucked the oars away and hopped out, dragging the boat clear of the river. Dry land! It felt good under his bare feet and he curled his toes into the cool sand.

He stretched and walked up the rise to where the sand ended, and the trees began. Scanning the area, Kayden spotted a small clearing right at the edge of the ridge. Perfect. He hurried back to the boat, grabbed his runestaff, bow, his boots, and backpack, and lugged them over to his chosen campsite.

Flopping down on the crest, he rubbed the sand from his feet. Putting his boots back on made him feel better and he began to make camp.

Setting up his tiny tent was easy, and Kayden leaned inside it to roll out his sleeping bag. Then he foraged through the bushes, gathering kindling and an armload of wood. It was almost like one of the camping trips he'd taken with his dad back home—except for the worry that gnawed at his insides.

The sun was a glowing rim across the western horizon when he finished his preparations. His socks, jeans, and shirt had been draped over sticks he'd shoved deep into the sand with hopes they'd dry by the heat of the fire.

Kayden dropped down by the crackling flames feeling ravenous. He set out an orange, a mangled peanut butter sandwich, and a zip-lock bag of crumbs that used to be Oreos. It wasn't much, but he was grateful.

He finished his meal, took off his boots, and leaned back to warm his feet in front of the fire. A strange sound startled him. He sat up and grasped his runestaff from its position at his side. It sounded like a low flying plane was coming straight toward him from the west. Impossible.

He squinted into the darkness, as if by doing so he could see whatever it was that made the unearthly noise, but the sun had long since disappeared. It wasn't the sound of rushing wings he'd heard earlier. It was more like the hissing roar of some huge object, propelled by an engine—or at least nothing that was living.

A path of red sparks appeared high in the sky like a fiery jet trail. The ruby-coloured embers blazed and hung thick in the air before they fell like fireworks, fizzling out long before reaching the earth. On and on they cut a path through the night sky, and with them, the roaring increased in volume until it was deafening.

Kayden covered his ears, but couldn't tear his eyes away from the extraordinary sight.

The stream of sparks didn't come near him. They burned up long before reaching where he sat in the sand and blazed a trail into the north, following, Kayden assumed, the shoreline of the Kalainian Sea. Then, they exploded in a river of red flame that spilled all the way down to the surface of the sea. Blinding, even at a distance.

"What in the world…?" he said aloud.

His eyes, still riveted to the spot where the thing had disappeared, blinked, but the red lights remained, burnt into his retinas. The night returned to silence, as though nothing had ever happened at all.

Kayden blinked again. The breeze rustled through leaves behind him, and water gurgled a few meters away. The noises seemed at complete odds with the bizarre scene he had just witnessed.

Slowly, Kayden packed up the remains of his meal and kicked sand over his fire to put it out before crawling into his sleeping bag. What a day it had been. He puzzled over the bizarre trail of red sparks and the starlings' attack, knowing they both had something to do with the plan to kill King Ludwig. Somehow, he had to stop Malahd. But he was too tired to stay awake now. Tomorrow would bring its own set of problems.

Chapter Seven

"Wake up," a voice said by Kayden's ear.

Something prodded him in the shoulder and, half asleep, he winced. Then his eyes flew open and with a shout he reared up in his sleeping bag, grabbing his runestaff as he scrambled to his knees in the dim light of morning.

"Relax," said a familiar voice, with a sarcastic drawl. "It is only me, Talbot."

"Talbot?" Kayden said in disbelief. "You're kidding me!"

He rubbed his eyes. Although the sun was only just rising, he could see the hedgehog crouched on top of his sleeping bag.

"I never...kid," Talbot said dryly.

"No, I guess you don't," Kayden admitted with a grin. "It's great to see you. But how did you find me?"

Kayden laid the staff on his rumpled bedding and began looking for the clean socks he'd laid out the night before.

"A bright orange tent, glowing in the morning sun not

twenty paces from the waterway where I was told I could find you, does not make for a difficult search." Talbot stood up and placed a paw on either side of his waist. "But I must say it is good to see you as well, young Kayden. It has been a long time."

"Durgot told you where I was?" Kayden shoved his feet into his boots and hurriedly laced them.

"Yes. He also revealed the importance of your mission."

"But…how did you get here so fast?" He looked over at the tiny animal and a sudden image of Millinworth came to mind. "Please don't tell me you rode a goose, or caught a passing swan, or hired several sparrows to carry you in a sling."

"Would that be so bad?" Talbot asked with a laugh. "As it happens, I can cover a lot of ground when necessary, as you may recall if you thought about it hard enough. And I travelled through the night."

"Right, I hadn't considered your other form," Kayden said. "If you wouldn't mind stepping outside, I'll roll up my bed and take the tent down. Then we can go."

Talbot nodded and turned to leave.

"Talbot?" Kayden called.

The hedgehog stopped and spun about to face him.

"I really am very glad you came."

Talbot flashed him a tiny smile in the growing light of dawn and scurried outside.

Kayden stowed everything into his pack, slung his bow and Runestaff into the boat, and began to drag the vessel down to the water.

"I'm ready to go," he called to Talbot. While he waited, Kayden ate a granola bar and the orange he'd brought, then washed them down with the last of the water from his thermos.

The hedgehog stood on the ridge where Kayden had pitched the tent, staring into the northeast and sniffing the air. Kayden buried the peels from his fruit in the sand, stuffed the wrapper into his coat pocket, and shivered, waiting for Talbot in the shade of the riverbank. The morning was cool and crisp, but the sun was now fully awake. Hopefully it would warm up soon. He rubbed his arms briskly.

Dropping to all fours, Talbot finally scampered down to the boat and Kayden stooped to lift him inside. Then, he pushed the boat out into the current and leapt aboard. The swirling speed of the waters caught them and they raced down the widening river toward the sea.

"Do you have any idea how or when Malahd will attack?" Kayden asked Talbot once he retrieved the oars and started to row. "And have you seen Rosalyn lately? The king too, of course," he added, avoiding the hedgehog's eyes.

Talbot perched on Kayden's backpack at the front of the boat, both paws braced against the prow, leaning into the wind.

"Until I saw Durgot late yesterday, I had no idea such a thing was planned," Talbot said. Giving up his surveillance, he sat down on the backpack to talk. "We knew, ever since Malahd disappeared, that the sorcerer would be back one day with revenge and domination on his mind. That is why a group of the Resistance stays with King Larkender at all times, to protect him. But until Millinworth was asked to spy on Malahd, nothing conclusive was known. It still isn't known, apart from you and me." Talbot stiffened, his spines standing on end. With a sigh, he continued.

"Rosalyn is well. She resides at the castle and is very

close with the king and queen, accompanying the king on all of his excursions abroad."

"That's great to hear," Kayden muttered, looking down at his oars. "I mean about Rosalyn. Not so great about Malahd."

Remembering the events of the previous night, he looked up and said, "I saw a trail of weird red lights crossing the sky last night. They came from the west and turned north just about there."

He pointed with his index finger.

Talbot jumped to his feet and resumed his observation of the landscape ahead of them.

"That would likely be just above Norbern," Talbot said. "Anything else?"

"Yeah, it eventually made a loud noise and then seemed to explode over the sea, northeast of where we are now."

"We must hurry," Talbot said, his voice low and tense. "This is ominous news indeed. You should have told me sooner. Malahd is moving into position. It would appear we are running out of time to alert the king."

Fortunately, the current was strong, and with Kayden rowing, they soon saw the mouth of the river where it emptied into Norbern harbour. Beyond and to the right, the sparkling blue of the Kalainian Sea yawned before them.

To the left, the peaceful town of Norbern rose from a long wooden dock and up a gently rolling hillside. The village looked sleepy, much like it had on Kayden's previous visit, apart from the scuffle that had taken place at the docks during that time. The houses, made of rough, cream-coloured stone, were each topped with bright red rooves and separated by fleecy, pale green trees. A bell in a church tower, high on the hill at the center of town, chimed five times, but no movement was seen. Kayden supposed it was a little early for much activity.

Their boat sped from the river into the harbour where Kayden knew another river from the west, the Spye River, joined it. Bending into the oars harder than ever, he steered them around a rocky point at the far north end of the waterfront, and out to sea. He was feeling trepidation—to quote Durgot. A small rowboat wasn't much of a match for some of the waves that crashed against the shoreline ahead.

He was puffing from exertion by the time they rounded the point. Somehow, he set them on a course far enough out to sea they avoided the breaking waves, but not so far away they lost sight of the shore.

Now the real work begins.

"How—far—is—Tunish?" he asked between strokes. Rowing this hard was testing his strength to its limits. He couldn't imagine keeping the same pace all day long.

"We will not reach it today," Talbot said. "But neither shall you strive by yourself."

They were well past Norbern now, and the beach to their left stretched lonely and barren into the distance where farmland began once more. Talbot stood tall on Kayden's pack and peered around them as though ensuring they were quite alone, then dropped to the bottom of the boat.

"Please take your pack and move it behind you for a moment," he said. As Kayden rested the oars and reached for his bag, Talbot's eyes glinted with mischief. "Prepare yourself, young man."

With that, the hedgehog ducked his head, rolling himself into a ball on the bottom of the boat, as one might coil a tightly wound spring. Then, with a bound, he flew straight up into the air over Kayden's head, revolving, expanding and enlarging, upward and outward until he became a huge grey blur. As his torso thickened and grew muscular, long, lethal spines sprang from his back. The wind whined through them as he spun. Kayden flung himself away, still holding the oars, but bringing them up to shield his face from the deadly spikes. Talbot's arms and legs grew until they were as long as Kayden's own, before he landed with a resounding thump on the bottom of the craft.

Although Kayden had known what to expect, he was always struck dumb with amazement at Talbot's transformation. He wondered with concern, if the weight of the mighty warrior would be too much for the little boat. Though, as before with the attack of the birds, it appeared to be made of a strong construction.

"Now," Talbot said in a deeper voice, "give me your oars and allow me to help you."

White teeth gleamed beneath his pointed dark nose and his black eyes glittered with mirth.

"There is not much to laugh about today," he said, "but the look on your face is at least worth a chuckle."

Kayden handed him the oars without a word. Talbot seated himself on one of the two narrow slats of wood that served as seats and began to row with powerful strokes. They moved through the water so swiftly, there was a wake behind them. This was going to get them somewhere and fast!

Thankfully, it was a calm day with not much breeze and the waves were manageable. The western shore wasn't close, but green fields pushed up to the rocky edge of the sea and an occasional farm could be seen far in the distance. There was nothing but water to the east and Kayden turned away from it. He wasn't afraid of water, being a decent enough swimmer, but travelling across a sea in a tiny little rowboat, without a lifejacket, seemed risky. He wondered what sort of lifeforms lived beneath the crystal clear waves—sharks, fish, sea urchins; maybe porpoise like those that existed in the world he knew. But this *wasn't* the world he knew. He'd seen some pretty strange beasts when he was in Erinbourne before, and it stood to reason there might be strange beings beneath their largest body of water too.

He picked up his runestaff and studied the symbols etched in the wood, searching for sea creatures. There was one, he guessed. He tipped the staff so he could get a closer look at the bottom where there seemed to be the image of a shark or a whale or something. Nothing that looked too formidable though. Kayden laid his runestaff carefully alongside him down the boat's length and stayed quiet. It was challenging to keep working against the endless tide that tried to push them ashore. There was no time for idle chit-chat.

In an hour, Talbot passed the oars back to Kayden and in this way they took turns, making slow progress along the edge of the Kalainian Sea. Kayden was beginning to think they'd do better to just put the boat on shore and walk, when Talbot spoke, interrupting his thoughts.

"We should get as far as Dalal today," he said, in the deep, throaty voice he had when in this form. "It is about halfway to Tunish Bay. Did Durgot show you a chart?" He spoke in short sentences, puffing between each pause.

Kayden leaned his chin on his hand, trying to remember the map and where they might be now. "Yeah, I think so. But we won't stop at the town, right? We'll camp somewhere along the way."

"Correct."

The waves were getting choppier, and Talbot strained to keep the boat on a steady course. It was well into the afternoon and Kayden's stomach growled so loudly that Talbot heard it.

"Eat something." Talbot inclined his huge head toward the backpack. "There are a few more hours to go before we stop."

"But what about you? I can share, but I don't think I have anything you'd want." Kayden rummaged through his backpack, coming up with a bag of dried fruit and his last, squashed bar. He held them up in silent question.

"Do not trouble yourself." Talbot shook his head. "There are not enough insects to fill me at this size, and that looks positively revolting. I will find something when we stop for the night."

Kayden unwrapped the crunchy snack and ate without enjoyment, gazing across the sparkling blue of the ocean.

"How far away is the home of the Silpeth?" he asked between bites.

Talbot took a breath and hauled on the oars. A brisk wind had picked up, and the water was getting rougher.

"Two, maybe three days. Straight east across the sea to the Mareele Islands," he said.

Talbot leaned forward, bending into his work. Kayden nodded, wanting to ask questions about the great winged horses who lived there, but knowing it was too much for Talbot to both row and talk. He put the remains of his lunch away and was just preparing to take over the oars when something white glimmered in the sun on the horizon.

"When you hand me the oars, take a look out there." Kayden pointed into the northeast. "Almost looks like the top of a sail."

Talbot laid the oars in Kayden's hands and twisted his body to look.

"You are correct," he said, after a moment of contemplation. "And now there are three of them. I only know of one fleet of sailboats such as this and it belongs to King Larkender. He often takes them out for an excursion."

He shaded his eyes against the glare of sun on water. "We must change direction and head toward the sailboats with haste."

"You think he's in danger out here?"

Talbot swivelled around to pierce Kayden with his jet-black eyes. "I think it was no coincidence you saw, and heard, something explode over the sea last night. We need to get to those boats. Row as hard as you are able for fifteen minutes and then I will take a turn."

Kayden bowed his head and threw everything he had into pulling the little boat through the surf. They were driving against the tide. As they hit each new wave, water splashed up and over the prow, soaking them both before their little boat plunged through to the other side. Kayden shook his head to clear wet hair from his eyes and plowed on.

When Talbot took over, Kayden glanced at the shoreline behind them. They weren't making much headway, but the boats ahead were getting closer, nonetheless. The billowed sails of three tall sailing boats could easily be seen cutting through the sparkling sea, headed on a course that would soon cross in front of him and Talbot.

"It would appear they are headed for Norbern," Talbot said between puffs of air, as he handed the oars to Kayden after his turn. The hedgehog stood up rather precariously on his hind legs, waving long arms to flag down the sailboats.

One after the other, the schooners sliced through the dancing sea until finally the first was close enough that Kayden could see tiny figures moving about on the deck.

Each boat had multiple sails that were bleached stark white in the sun. The boats were beautiful. Kayden took a moment to catch his breath and squint at the people on board. Was one of them Rosalyn? Or King Ludwig Larkender? They were too far away to tell.

No one on board appeared to notice their tiny boat bobbing up and down nearby, and the first sailboat swished past with a spray of water. Granted, it was still some distance away from their small craft. He and Talbot were awfully small in the vastness of the turbulent sea. Kayden added his voice to that of Talbot's and the two of them hollered at the occupants of the second sailboat that came skimming through the water. It was a little closer.

Several figures moved on the deck of the ship. But one moved to the nearest side, leaned on the railing to peer at them, and lifted an arm in greeting.

Kayden dropped the oars, threw both arms in the air and, forgetting where he was, and leapt to his feet screaming, "Stop your boats!"

Talbot sat down abruptly and gripped the sides of their boat in an effort to steady it as it swayed and almost capsized. Kayden lost his footing. He lurched along with the boat as it listed to one side, taking on water. With a shout, he toppled over the side. Like lightning, Talbot stretched out an arm and grabbed hold of his jacket to haul him back.

"Thanks," Kayden said breathlessly from the bottom of the boat.

He and Talbot watched as people on the sailboat grasped one of the huge sails and swung it to the side, slowing the schooner. The third boat, further behind and to the east, must have been watching, because it did the same at a distance. The person who had waved turned away to help bring the boat around and slow it, in order that

Kayden and Talbot might row closer. As the sailboat nosed through the waves, closing the gap between them, Kayden could make out a few faces of the sailors. There were none he recognized until the same person again moved to look over the rails.

It was Rosalyn. At least he thought it was. Three years of his time had changed her somewhat.

"Kayden! Talbot! Is that truly you?" she cried. A long braid fell over one shoulder as she leaned toward them. It took everything Kayden possessed not to leap to his feet again, but he steadied himself.

"Rosalyn! It's so good to see you!" he shouted. Like a grinning fool, he had forgotten the reason they were there in the first place. Talbot had not.

"Young miss," Talbot yelled, "is the king on board? We must take him to safety immediately. An attack is imminent."

"No! He is in the schooner ahead of us." Even at this distance, Kayden could see her face fill with fear.

They all turned to look at the first ship that had passed. It skimmed across the turquoise waters well ahead, unaware of the danger it was in. Rosalyn turned to the others on her boat and spoke. They jumped to attention and moved the sail back into position where it caught the wind and billowed forth, sending them cruising after the king.

The third sailboat followed in its wake, a few members of the crew saluting Talbot and Kayden as they passed, too far away to communicate. It would be up to Rosalyn to stop the king now, Kayden thought, keeping an eye trained on her ship.

Talbot reached for the oars and plunged them into the water to hold their position and wait. Rowing wouldn't help them catch anyone at this point. The first boat was quite far away already.

Without warning, the sea heaved beneath them. It was a great rolling surge that moved opposite to the waves they had been fighting against. The surf lifted their boat high into the air as though some great creature had sliced through the waters beneath them. Their craft slid backward down the other side as the being passed. Kayden clutched the sides of the little boat and stared over first one side and then the other, frantically trying to see what had lifted them. A huge grey shape, almost like a barely submerged submarine, shimmered like a shadow a few meters below and then was gone. The swelling wave moved past them swiftly, on a collision course with Rosalyn and the king.

Chapter Eight

"What the heck was that?" Kayden hollered.

But he didn't need Talbot's answer. He knew deep inside that nothing natural had passed below them. It was the magic of Malahd. Kayden watched in horror as the undulating wave disturbed the usual flow of the waters. Whatever it was, the creature's trajectory lay in direct line with the first boat of the fleet. Talbot had turned their tiny craft and was rowing with all his might, but it was useless.

"We have to do something!" Kayden yelled. But what could they do? Kayden fumbled for his bow and arrows, but he knew they would be of no use against this mighty unseen foe.

And then his fingers came in contact with the runestaff. Grasping it, he felt the polished wood quiver in response to his need for help. He held the staff in front of his eyes, unsure what to even ask from it.

I have to calm down and think. Right now, I need to get to the king.

He set the Runestaff down, his mind swirling.

"Talbot, if you were small, I could get us both over there," he said. Not waiting for a response, he grasped his quiver of arrows, slung them over his back, and followed them with his bow. Then, he snatched up his runestaff and wheeled around for Talbot.

From the floor of their boat, the small, bristled hedgehog looked back at him with flashing black eyes. Bending, Kayden picked him up and placed him on his shoulder so that Talbot could easily leap off and transform himself if necessary. Talbot gripped Kayden's coat with his sharp claws.

"Go," Talbot said.

Holding his runestaff in front of him, Kayden closed his eyes, concentrating on the image of a falcon that held a prominent place on the slender wood. The Runestaff shivered and became warm to the touch. It leapt from Kayden's grasp, contorting itself high in the air as it grew, first sprouting the huge head of the falcon. Then the body and feathers erupted, and long, outspread wings slowly flapped to hold the massive bird stationary. Legs lengthened into talons, curled back for flight.

Kayden sprang onto the bird's back, digging his hands into the strong feathers around its neck. He gripped the falcon's sides with his knees as they careened into the sky with a piercing cry from the great hooked beak.

Up, up they soared, then levelled out and flew, the falcon's powerful wings beating against its body, catching the wind and propelling them forward. High above the sailing ships, Kayden and Talbot passed the third boat in their race against time, but it was not the one in danger. Below them, like a shadowy arrow, the shape of Malahd's weapon, whatever it was, pulled alongside the second craft where Rosalyn, unaware, stood at the helm. In a heaving gush of water, the thing breached only a few meters from Rosalyn's sailboat, and Kayden had his first glimpse of the creature.

It was easily much longer than the sailboat, a steely grey in colour, and cylindrical in shape. As he watched, the thing raised a torpedo-like head, just above the screening waters of the sea. At the base of the head, bulbous eyes swivelled to and fro as the creature swayed, assessing its surroundings before plunging beneath the swell once more. It was as it dove under water again that Kayden saw, with horror, long tentacles slithering through the water behind it.

With a waving, almost gentle motion, they opened, spreading each appendage wide apart. When they squeezed together again the movement expelled water behind and thrust the creature forward. It rushed past Rosalyn toward the first boat in the procession. The creature was searching. Kayden knew, without a doubt, the monster hunted the king and the sceptre that was never far from the monarch's hand.

Kayden's thoughts turned back to the need for urgency, and the falcon responded to his request. Stretching out its neck, the bird uttered a piercing cry. People on the ship below stared up and shouted in surprise. Rosalyn, standing at the wheel, did not flinch. She kept the ship on course. So intent were these people on reaching the boat that bore the king, they hadn't even noticed the sea creature.

"Drop me onto the deck," Talbot yelled into the wind.

Kayden nodded. He knew Talbot would transform as he fell and land on the deck to do everything in his power to defend King Ludwig Larkender. Talbot dug his claws in harder.

Kayden directed the great falcon to swoop as low as possible over the schooner. Then, he concentrated on locating the menacing creature that lurked where none could see. But the sea monster was gone. There was no indication whatsoever that he had seen the thing at all. It must have driven itself deep into the shadows where sunlight couldn't reach.

Kayden pressed the falcon to greater speeds. The king's sailboat, unaware of its impending doom, skimmed across the azure water.

Without warning, the creature struck. The thing reared into the sky above the sailboat, water streaming from its slick grey sides. A massive, bulbous head, too large to be supported by the tentacles, rose above the sails and wobbled there with glassy, bulging eyes, searching the deck for its prey. It looked like a mammoth squid, Kayden thought with horror.

The monstrous thing swung several undulating tentacles over top of the boat, and they crashed across the main deck, stopping the sailboat dead. Then, the creature used slimy limbs to haul its body on board and drive its bulk down upon the masts, crushing the rigging and sending the white-washed sails into a tangled heap of ropes and broken poles.

Each long appendage was lined with huge translucent suction cups that opened and closed with a grim slurping sound. The monster used them to draw itself onto the boat, nearly capsizing the vessel in the process.

The sailboat tipped dangerously to one side, taking on huge amounts of water, and the people onboard slid, shouting, and tumbling over the deck. Well-dressed men and ladies in long dresses clung to the rails, before they fell screaming across the upended boat. Others plunged head-long into the churning sea. Yet there were a few men and women that, despite all odds, lifted their weapons.

The falcon swooped low over the stern. Talbot leapt from Kayden's shoulder and flung himself down to the flailing boat, becoming nothing more than a revolving black blur as he descended.

Out and over the water, the falcon banked hard and corrected itself in order to glide back over the sinking ship. Kayden whisked his bow from his back, pulled an arrow from its sheath, and fitted it into place.

Frantically scanning the scene, he spotted King Larkender. He clung to the wooden edge of the ship with one hand as he fought to maintain his balance, and lifted a sword of battle in the other to hack at the grasping tentacle closest to him. He would not go down without a fight. The king was a warrior. *But where was the sceptre? Was it safe?*

Kayden focused on the monster's eyes, each one protruding like a greasy globe. They were large, easy targets, one on either side of the flopping, gelatinous head. Kayden took aim. Yet, he couldn't get a clear line of sight, because the many appendages of the squid-like brute were complicating matters. They seemed to be everywhere all at once. Waving in the air, sucking and seeking who or what they could, then latching on to curl and crush each victim or chunk of the ship. The squid was systematically tearing the schooner apart in its search for the king and his sceptre.

Kayden's falcon swerved and flew back for another pass. From the corner of his eye, Kayden saw Rosalyn's boat arrive and align itself beside the one under attack. Sword in hand, she leapt aboard, balancing as she skidded across the sinking ship to aid the king. Away from the squid, sailors from Rosalyn's boat helped haul people from the water to safety and others, still clinging to what was left of the king's sailboat, transfered over.

Talbot, in his warrior form, poised beside the king, hackles raised and sword in hand, fending off the huge arms of the sea monster as they sought to grasp Ludwig Larkender.

Silently, Kayden communicated with the falcon, directing him how to manoeuver. Down they flew, swooping under a tentacle that reeled back from a wound it had sustained at Rosalyn's hand, and up in front of the monster's head. Kayden shot once, twice, three times in quick succession. His arrows pierced the flesh of the monster just short of one eye and the watery black orb swivelled in his direction.

A gummy slime oozed from each of the wounds and the creature writhed in pain. It flung up two front arms and flipped its enormous head backward to reveal a cavernous mouth that emitted a high-pitched scream. An arm swung up and swiped across the drowning boat, dragging Rosalyn, King Larkender, and Talbot along with it. Snapping the tentacle up, the creature hurled its prey into the churning waters.

Kayden's instinct was to rush to their rescue, but he knew the monstrous beast must first be dealt with before anyone could be saved.

The falcon banked on the opposite side and soared back across the boat. Kayden was armed and steady. This time he took care to aim. He drew back the tightly strung cord and waited. At just the right moment, he released the arrow. It flew straight and true, piercing the round dish of an eye that darted back and forth over the remains of the boat. Kayden's next arrow found its mark deep inside the beak-like mouth of the monster.

The squid shrieked in agony and thrashed its arms. The head flopped back, and the cavernous mouth opened to reveal two fangs and a tongue that lashed out like a whip, spewing venom in Kayden's wake. But the falcon was too fast, and soared beyond the monster's fury.

Wheeling about in the sky, Kayden made ready for another attack. He banked sharply. His eyes flickered along the trajectory of the venom the monster continued to spew. Ruby red in colour, it was not hard to see against the deep blue of the water, and he watched with growing horror as the poison arced toward his friends. Talbot had left the king and Rosalyn. He struggled back onto the sinking vessel, but Rosalyn swam with King Ludwig to her own waiting schooner.

Rosalyn looked up at the toxic substance flying toward her and plunged beneath the waves, pulling the king with her, but it was too late. Venom splashed onto their heads and into the water around them. The sea hissed. Its waters rose to bubble around the pair like a boiling vat of blood. An enflamed steam filled the air and when it cleared, both Rosalyn and the king lay face down, floating motionlessly.

"No!" Kayden's fear lent urgency to the falcon.

The bird folded its wings and dove like a bullet from the sky. Kayden rammed his bow over his head and laid himself flat against the bird's neck, his fingers fastened like wires round its feathers. As they plummeted to the sea, Kayden's concentration changed. Rather than focusing on the falcon from the surface of his runestaff, he envisioned the image of the sea creature.

As they plummeted downward, the bird changed. Its feathers sucked back into itself and in their place a smooth, hard hide grew under Kayden's hands. His legs were pushed wider to accommodate the killer whale he now rode. Yet he had no trouble staying aboard as it plowed into the water beside Rosalyn and the king.

Above him, the monster thrashed. Tentacles churned

the waters around them as it sank from view with the remains of the schooner. Kayden paid it no heed as he caught the arms of his friends and dragged them across the broad back of the killer whale. Willing the orca to take them to Rosalyn's boat and out of harm's way, he checked them both for a pulse. Weak, but steady. A movement caught his eye, and he looked up.

Talbot had found the sceptre!

The huge hedgehog had ventured back to the sinking vessel and was standing on the last scrap of boat that was above water—holding the short golden staff. With a mighty leap, the hedgehog lunged for the sanctuary of Kayden's whale.

The sea monster came up beneath Talbot as he sprang, sweeping him into the air and catching his body with several of its rippling suckers. Its tentacles closed around Talbot and squeezed. With a muffled shout, Talbot went limp before both he and the sceptre dropped into the swirling waters of the Kalainian Sea.

The monster dove after the sceptre. Kayden went rigid with shock. He knew what it meant for the gemstones to fall into the wrong hands, but he couldn't risk the lives of those he cared about. He swallowed his desire to follow the squid and save the gems.

"Hurry!" he said to his runestaff.

The orca shot through the sea to the spot that Talbot had disappeared, then stopped as Kayden took a long breath and slipped from its back into the murky depths. Taking a breath, he dove beneath the churning waves. It took a moment for his eyes to adjust, but he spotted his friend and swam toward him. Kayden grasped Talbot's long bristly arms and thought how thankful he was they were in water where Talbot's weight was lessened. He tugged the hefty body toward the light above, pushing him to air. Quickly they surfaced.

The whale had moved closer as per Kayden's instructions, and he dragged Talbot across its broad back. Breathing heavily, Kayden sent him to the safety of the two sailing ships where people awaited his three unconscious friends with open arms. Kayden dove again and again for the sceptre, but came up spluttering each time. It was not to be found.

Treading water and breathing heavily, he watched with horror as one lone tentacle broke the surface of the sea. It coiled and twisted, waving its narrow tip high into the blue above them, before rocketing downward and winding itself about the king's ankle. Kayden made a strangled sound and screamed a warning, but there was no one able to heed it. Like the cracking of a whip, the arm snapped backward, flipping King Larkender high into the air. The king's body dangled against a backdrop of blue sky before the tentacle slithered down to vanish into the foamy deep.

Kayden prepared to leap into the water after the king, his heart in his throat, but the water before him began to swirl counterclockwise. Faster and faster, it spun, forming a widening vortex. The spiraling sides, built of the turquoise sea, rose up, creating a deepening cavern below.

Kayden ordered the whale to swim away lest they be caught up in the maelstrom and sucked beneath the waves to their deaths. Then he, and the people on the boats, watched in despair as the vortex slowly rose into the air, forming a violent waterspout. It sucked at Kayden's killer whale, pulling them into the powerful whirling water. So great was its velocity, that the other two sailboats anchored some distance away, were also drawn inexorably toward it.

Just as Kayden thought everyone would be lost, the fearsome wind howled with the wild laughter of Malahd. The storm slowed. A dark shadow was drawn from beneath the waves, into the base of the vortex and passed through the eye of the storm.

The shade reached the pinnacle of the swirling mass and paused, revolving too fast to be clearly seen. Then, Malahd slowly rose above the twisting water and stood on the very crest of the tumult. *The giant squid must have been Malahd himself.*

Malahd's black robes were caught in the furor, and spun out from him like the wings of an enormous bat. And, above his head, although his one good hand was shredded from Rosalyn's sword, Malahd held the most prized possession in all of Erinbourne—the king's sceptre.

Shock and revulsion ripped at Kayden's insides. He could clearly see the bleeding lacerations his arrows had made in the sorcerer's forehead, and the pulpy remains of his hollow, oozing eye. But the Emerald gemstone of healing flashed as it revolved in the ornate crown of the sceptre and before Kayden's eyes, Malahd's wounds were made whole.

With a perverse howl of triumph, Malahd and the twister lifted off the face of the water and became airborne, bearing the sorcerer into the clouds and away with the sceptre raised in victory.

Chapter Nine

Kayden plunged into the sea. His thoughts directed the whale to take Rosalyn and Talbot to the safety of the two remaining schooners without him. He dove time and time again, searching the water for any sign of King Ludwig Larkender. Yet, he knew in his heart there would be none. Malahd had achieved his goal—to steal Erinbourne's Gemstones of Power and kill their beloved king. Treading water, Kayden scanned the distant waves, unable to give up just yet.

"Young man!" an unfamiliar voice called. "Please, come aboard. Your efforts are fruitless."

Tears mingled with the briny water that dripped down his face, yet Kayden knew the voice was right. He struck out for the boat, waves splashing into his face. He was exhausted. Hands reached down to haul him over the side of the boat and stand him up. Wearily, he leaned against a railing and looked for his companions.

Rosalyn and Talbot lay on the opposite side of the deck. He rushed to them and knelt.

Looking up, he saw five or six faces clustered around. "Does anyone know what to do? Can we help them?"

A woman crouched beside Kayden and pulled a long strand of wet hair away from Rosalyn's face.

"Give it time," she said. "This poison is something we have not encountered before. We can only hope her youth and health will prevail. Talbot, I believe, is merely unconscious."

She straightened and offered Kayden her hand. "I am Honore, captain of this fleet of schooners. May I ask who you are and how you come to wield such a powerful ally as a runestaff?"

He jumped to his feet. "My runestaff!"

His mind had been too preoccupied with the fate of his friends to have called for its return.

"Sorry," he said, "but I have to get it back first."

He stepped through a group of concerned people, many of whom had been saved from the king's sinking ship, calling to the staff as he went. The runestaff responded, transforming back into the humble shape of a walking stick and appearing over the side of the boat. It snapped into his outstretched hand, dripping wet.

Kayden returned to his friends. Blankets had arrived and Honore, a petite woman dressed all in black, and a tall, blond man were carefully laying Rosalyn onto them and wrapping her up. She looked pale and lifeless. Kayden's brow furrowed.

"Alran, please see that Rosalyn is helped out of her wet clothes in the cabin and kept warm," Honore said to another woman who stood nearby.

With a nod, the woman moved to take the other end of the blanket. Between her and the man, they lifted Rosalyn and shuffled to a small door leading into a cabin at the far end of the sailboat.

"I'm not sure what can be done for Talbot," Honore said. She stared at his deadly-looking spines. "In any case, he seems to be waking."

The huge hedgehog stirred and Kayden let out a sigh of relief. He caught Honore's eye.

"Thank you," he said. "My name is Kayden Bramley. I was travelling with Talbot in hopes of reaching the king to warn him of attack."

Sighing heavily, he added, "Clearly, I failed."

"I see." Honore looked out over the water that now was strangely calm. "What is *clear* to me is that you did your best. No one could have done more. I watched your every move and know you would have given your life for any one of them."

She looked down at Talbot who was raising himself up to one elbow. "Excuse me." Honore left them to speak in private.

"Is it lost?" Talbot croaked, peering up at Kayden. He clasped his arms around his torso and winced with pain at the effort of speaking. "I may have a few crushed ribs."

"The sceptre is gone. Malahd took it, but I'll get it back," Kayden replied, with more confidence than he felt. He bent to place a comforting hand on Talbot's shoulder. "Get some rest, my friend. Can you transform or would that be too painful?"

"I think I shall just lie here for now and see how I feel when we get back to port." Talbot sank back with a groan and closed his eyes.

Kayden straightened and looked for Honore. She was busy checking the other survivors for injuries, of which there were a few, and organizing basic treatment.

"We did not set sail with provisions for a situation such as this," she said, lifting her hands.

Her eyes filled and spilled onto her lined cheeks.

"The king is lost to us." She shook her head in disbelief. "What will I tell his queen?"

Her shoulders shook as she moved away to stand alone at the railing opposite to where Talbot lay.

Kayden followed, tears of his own threatening to overflow. "I understand. King Larkender was a great man. If only I could have reached…but there is no sense in going over that again. I'm truly sorry, Honore, but I know he would want us to go after the sceptre. His heart was always on taking care of his people. How soon can we get back to a port?

Honore shrugged. "It depends on the wind, of course, but perhaps in three hours we could be in Dalal."

"And is there a doctor there for Rosalyn? Or anyone who might be able to help her?"

"There is a healer there, yes. If her trouble was a broken bone or some other natural illness, he could help. This, I believe, will be beyond his expertise. I shall ask Alran. She may know of someone."

"Thank you," Kayden said. "Is your crew able to set sail immediately? I can help, but you would have to show me what to do."

"You do not need to help us. I will assemble them. And thank you—Kayden Bramley." She brushed the tears away with the back of her hand and straightened. "That is exactly what our dear king would wish."

Giving her a faint smile, he nodded and strode to the other side, calling out to the other boat.

"Set sail," he shouted to the crew who gathered at the

side to listen for direction. "We're heading for the port at Dalal immediately."

He had only one last task before removing himself to a corner in order to let the crew move the rigging back in place. He needed to speak to Alran, the woman who watched over Rosalyn. He tapped at the cabin door and waited for her to open it a crack.

"My name is Kayden," he said. "Get word to me immediately if there is any change in Rosalyn's condition. Will you do that, please?"

She nodded gravely.

Carrying his most prized possession in one hand, he moved away from the sails where the crew worked, and went to stand near Talbot. The runestaff had saved him and others in many dangerous situations thus far. Though despite having the runestaff's as a powerful ally, he hadn't been any match for Malahd today.

Kayden looked out over the Kalainian Sea, willing the wind to be in their favour. He laid his runestaff down and went to shove his hands into the pockets of his jeans, realizing too late they were glued shut. He was soaking wet. But it didn't matter. Nothing would matter if he lost both his great-uncle Ludwig, *and* Rosalyn.

Kayden sat up with a start as the boat bumped against the pier in Dalal's harbour. The two schooners docked while the last rays of the sun set the hazy blue of the western mountain range in sharp relief. Kayden had dropped to sleep on the deck beside Talbot soon after they set sail. Now awake, he looked for the hedgehog.

Talbot was gone. Scrambling to his feet, Kayden scanned the occupants of the boat fearing some further trouble, but all was well. Each crew member was occupied with his or her own task in settling the boat. Although the people were upset after the afternoon's events, nothing more seemed amiss.

On the raised helm of the ship, stood the tiny version of Talbot, his black nose twitching as he sniffed the air. He caught sight of Kayden, and with a glad cry, he leapt to the deck and scampered across the deck.

"Before you ask, yes, I feel much improved," he said, standing on his back legs and holding up a paw to prevent further questions. "Not quite myself yet, but getting there."

"Has there been any word of Rosalyn?" Kayden blurted.

Talbot's eyes shifted away. "No, not yet. But Alran has been with her and there will be help in the town. A doctor of sorts, I'm told…someone skilled in the healing arts."

"That sounds hopeful." Kayden's voice was low. "I'm ready to go as soon as we can disembark."

He rubbed some of the stiffness from his now dried jeans and took a step toward the cabin door where Rosalyn lay.

"The sooner we get her off this boat and take her for treatment, the better."

"I was told about King Larkender," Talbot said, his voice sad. He dropped to all fours. "We were too late to warn him, but it was a valiant effort. Your quick actions saved my life, and Rosalyn's as well. You would have saved all three of us if it weren't for Malahd's final blow."

Kayden stopped and closed his eyes, images of the horrible afternoon running through his mind.

"I have to focus on Rosalyn now," he said finally. "But then, I'll go find Malahd and take back what belongs rightfully to the King of Erinbourne." He ended on a forceful note, banging a fist into his palm.

"You mean what belongs to you?" Talbot asked quietly.

Kayden whipped around to stare at him. "It doesn't belong to me! Why would you even say that?"

"Because you are Ludwig Larkender's great nephew and his only living relative. Much as we do not want to accept it —King Larkender is dead," Talbot said flatly. "You now will take his place on the throne."

Kayden's mind spun. He felt the blood draining from his face as he considered what Talbot just said. Logically it was true, since even his grandmother had told him one day it would happen. But that was supposed to be in the distant future, and as such, a situation that would never actually take place. Certainly not now! He was no king. He was an eighteen-year-old kid that had struggled to get through high school—not the ruler of an alternate universe.

"Okay—I can't cope with this right now," Kayden said, after a long moment. He shook his head to rid himself of the unwanted images. "All I care about is getting Rosalyn to a doctor. I'll deal with the sceptre and Malahd after that."

Grabbing his bow and quiver of arrows from the deck where he had slept, he slid them over his head. He strode away from Talbot, picking up his runestaff as he went.

The sailboat was secured to the wharf, fully docked. Honore and her crew were helping people to climb the few steps and make their way down the wooden pier.

Kayden paused at the cabin door and took a moment to tie the runestaff into the quiver strap that held his arrows, so his hands were freed. He rapped loudly and the knock was answered quickly, as though the person had been waiting for him. It swung wide and Alran beckoned him to enter.

Ducking, he stepped within, his eyes adjusting to the dim light. Rosalyn lay on a cot along one side. He rushed to her and knelt, taking one of her hands in his own. It was like ice. Her face was pale, the colour of chalk. It appeared hollow and shadowed, like a marble statue. Even her usually red lips were pale, and she barely breathed. Her dark hair in its loosely woven braid was flung across the pillow, and she was wrapped in several thick blankets.

Standing, Kayden slipped his arms beneath Rosalyn's head and legs, and lifted. He nestled her close to him and turned to Alran.

"You know where this doctor can be found, right?"

"Yes," the woman answered simply. She picked up a thick yellow candle for light, and shading it with her hand, she looked at him.

"Lead the way." Stooping, he eased Rosalyn carefully through the doorway and marched after the woman who bustled in front of him in long brown skirts. "Coming?" he called back to Talbot, but the hedgehog was already there, running beside him.

Their footsteps were hollow on the wooden pier as they hurried past fishing boats and sailing vessels of all sizes, and trudged up a steep, cobblestone slope where a few shops selling fish and a weather-beaten tavern squatted. It was almost dark, and Kayden stumbled over the uneven ground.

The buildings were not quaint to look at, like they were in Norbern. They slouched in jumbled disorder near the waterfront—signs hanging from squeaky hinges, and white-wash faded and peeling away. It appeared to be a rough sort of place.

Without a word, Kayden stayed close to Alran, following her closely as she turned left down a narrow side street that wound past a string of dingy houses. A pack of scrawny dogs slunk out of a black alley and followed them, while suspicious faces, caught in the flickering light of the passing candle, peered from grimy windows. Thankfully, Alran seemed to know exactly where she was going and soon stopped in front of a particularly shabby dwelling.

She glanced back at Kayden and reached up to pull on a rusty bell that hung from a hook by the door. Kayden gazed at Rosalyn, her head lolling over his arm.

He hadn't been in time to save the king, but would he be in time for Rosalyn? And could this so-called doctor even help her? Rosalyn slipped further away from him with every passing minute.

The door was yanked open, and a wizened old woman stood silhouetted in the entrance of a filthy, cluttered room. It was drab, dark, and dank inside. A foul stench flooded through the door and drifted around Kayden in waves so thick he could almost see them. The stink was like boiling cabbages and old socks, mingled with the odour of rotting fish.

Kayden wrinkled his nose with distaste. *This* was the doctor?

Alran whispered hoarsely, "Magda, a girl desperately needs your help. May they enter?"

The old woman looked from Rosalyn to Kayden, her eyes lingering on his face, and then she flung the door wide. Alran stepped back into the shadows and disappeared. Magda waved impatiently for them to enter.

"I shall keep watch here, for now," Talbot said from the ground. "I had no idea the doctor they spoke of was Magda. All will be well."

Kayden stepped through the entrance and, as the door was slammed behind him, he entered another world. The smell disappeared, replaced by the fragrance of roses.

Magda, who barely came up to Kayden's waist, bolted and latched the door at his back. With the final snap of the lock, the lights came on and the darkness fled.

Sunlight streamed in from apertures built into the roof, flooding the room with light and sunshine. From where this sunshine came, Kayden couldn't say; the sun had long since sunk behind the mountains. A few chairs and an old sofa covered with brightly coloured afghans occupied one side of the room, presumably for people to await their appointments, but he gazed at the most remarkable aspect of the space—the walls. Each of the four sides was lined with shelves that ran top to bottom, close together and filled with glistening, glass jars of colourful, glowing pebbles. Kayden squinted in the dazzling brilliance of them. Hope sprang in his heart.

Every colour of the rainbow was represented starting near the door with lemon yellow and running around the base of the room growing a shade darker with each jar. Almost imperceptibly the yellow morphed into green, then into orange, red and so on, graduating to the next colour, and the next. It continued all the way up to the roof where they ended with the deepest navy blue of a starlit night. Some jars were filled with round smooth nuggets and others with square or triangular ones. All were mesmerising and sparkled with intense colour. He gazed at them in wonder.

"In here," Magda said peevishly from another doorway. She held up a curtain of lime green beads that clattered together as she yanked them aside. "Hurry!"

"Her name is Rosalyn." Kayden tore his gaze away from the room to rush after the lady. He entered a long hallway, with periodic doorways leading into other rooms. The doors were almost unnoticeable due to rows and rows of plants that lined the walls. Short leafy plants that left a pungent tang in the air, ones with long trailing fronds, tall leggy plants, and ones with sweet-smelling flowers waved their leaves at him as he passed with Rosalyn in his arms. It was as though the foliage was aware of them and acknowledged their presence with a bow. There were hundreds— no, thousands—of plants. And each one basked in the cheerful warmth of sunlight pouring in from above.

"Are you coming?" Magda called from somewhere ahead, and out of sight in the vegetation. "I do wish you would hurry."

He broke into a jog to catch up and rounded a corner to see the little woman, in her long, creamsicle-coloured dress, flit into a room whose doorway was hung with long, twining vines of purple wisteria. Rosalyn bounced in his arms. Entering the space, he gazed around with renewed astonishment.

In the center of the room was a raised bed and Magda stood at the head of it, motioning for him to place Rosalyn on the mauve coverlets. A faint scent of lilacs rose to meet him as he did so, and he breathed deeply, then noticed with surprise that Rosalyn had done the same.

Kayden stepped back. The squat little woman paid him no further notice. Her hands flitted over Rosalyn's body, never touching, only fluttering delicately like the wings of a butterfly overtop, and all the while, the woman hummed. It was such a soothing sound that Kayden himself felt cheered as he observed the ritual.

As Magda swayed her way around the table, Kayden noticed that a faint aura surrounded her, changing colour and becoming more intense in the space between the little healer's hands and Rosalyn's body. It glowed a pale, cornflower blue as the woman twinkled her fingers over Rosalyn's right leg then changed to a perfect shade of rose over her feet. As the woman came up the other side, it turned to a deep purple, almost like the periwinkles that grew along Gran's garden path, and then shades of fuchsia appeared as her fingers flickered over Rosalyn's torso. Around the girl's face a pale green, like the first leaves of spring, appeared, but then, as Magda moved to the top of Rosalyn's head, an angry, flaming red emerged.

Magda drew back sharply, and her humming stopped. She muttered something unintelligible and hastened to a long workbench under a window covered with lacy lavender curtains, where she selected two metal pots from the shelves above. She flipped the lids off with nimble fingers and reached for a mortar and pestle with which to grind her ingredients. Adding lavish amounts of the two compounds together, the woman mashed at them vigorously. A cloud rose into the air and the scent of it drifted across the table to Kayden. He had images of a wheat field freshly harvested and of a grove of black poplars on a warm summer's day before his daydreams were interrupted. Magda spoke not to him but to herself.

"No, that is not right," she said, and stood tapping an absent toe upon the flagstone floor. "Got it!"

Snatching up a stool, she stepped several paces over, plunked it down, and climbed on top. Precariously, she stretched for a jar that was almost out of reach. Somehow, she secured it safely and clambered down to add a pinch of whatever it contained to her mixture. She stirred briskly. This time, Kayden smelled rain falling on a parched and thirsty land. He gave his head a shake.

That's crazy. How can I be smelling and thinking that?

Wheeling around, the old woman smiled and dragged her stool over to the bed. Picking up her skirts, she clambered on top of the stool to position herself directly above

Rosalyn's forehead and began her humming once more. Then, she reached into a pocket of her voluminous dress and drew forth a set of tiny silver tongs. She lowered them into the mixture, scooped up a little of the medicine, and sifted it, a few sunflower-yellow grains at a time, over Rosalyn's brow. There was a sizzling sound. As the crystals fell, they popped, crackled, and transformed into a shower of miniscule sparks like a halo of blood orange around Rosalyn's face.

Magda kept sprinkling, humming, and swaying to and fro on her stool. Her eyelids drifted shut and she seemed oblivious to all that was taking place beneath her medicinal touch. The world was a peaceful place.

Rosalyn's eyes flew open and her body went rigid. Her hands gripped either side of the table on which she lay. She moaned and rolled her head from side to side as though in pain.

Still, Magda did not waver in her attention to the crystals. She continued the application as though nothing at all had happened until Rosalyn relaxed. Her lashes fluttered closed, and a smile of contentment curled the corners of her mouth. The normal pink hue had returned to Rosalyn's face and Kayden felt himself sag with relief.

In a very businesslike manner, Magda hopped off the stool, returned her tools to the bench, and washed her hands in a small basin of water. Rubbing them dry on a small yellow towel, she looked across at Kayden.

"Rosalyn will recover. It is well you brought her to me, or she would not have lived through the night." Through gold, triangular spectacles, her yellow, birdlike eyes captured Kayden's own, and the woman's face creased into a wealth of smiles reaching back to her ears. "Be you hungry, lad? Only yesterday the raspberries allowed me to make a most excellent compote of their fruit, and I know they would be most pleased if I cordially entreated you to join me in a spot of supper."

She bustled to the foot of Rosalyn's bed and drew a lavender sheet over her. "The girl needs to rest. Come."

Wordlessly, Kayden followed Magda through the doorway and down her extraordinary hall. After this display, it followed that the kitchen would be something splendid to behold.

But there was a nagging feeling he couldn't shake. Kayden knew this woman from somewhere. But how? And from where?

Chapter Ten

Magda's skirts swished as she preceded Kayden to the end of the hallway and back to the entry. Once there, she stopped and turned to face him.

"You are anxious to ask your friend, the hedgehog, to join us, I am sure," she said. "Just ensure you bolt and latch the door once he is inside. Then, when you have removed your weaponry and runestaff, of which I approve heartily by the way, you may both join me in the kitchen. Through here."

She gestured to the first of two closed doors.

"I keep the scullery free of contamination," she said. "Not that you are a contaminate." The lady giggled behind her hand like a schoolgirl and then continued. "It is my laboratory you see, and must be kept pristine."

She gave him a broad grin before pushing the door open and disappearing inside.

The answer he'd been pondering flashed into Kayden's mind. She was very much like Durgot! She talked like him, was about the same size, and just seemed...well, Durgot-ish.

Was she too one of the Garde, the ancient race of people inhabiting the inner sanctums of the mountains?

He crossed the foyer, slid back the many bolts and locks she used to bar her door, and yanked it open.

He stuck his head into the darkness outside. It was foggy and oppressive after enjoying the brightness and colour of Magda's house.

"Talbot?" he whispered.

There was an answering rustle from the rotting wooden step below, and he held the door open just a crack to allow the hedgehog entry.

"How is Rosalyn?" Talbot asked, as Kayden locked the door. The hedgehog watched as Kayden peeled off his bow and damp overcoat.

Carefully, Kayden set his runestaff by the door. "Magda says she'll recover, but that it was lucky we got her here when we did." He felt almost buoyant as he relayed this piece of good news. He motioned for Talbot to follow him to the kitchen door and continued in a low voice. "It was quite an amazing treatment, but effective. I wouldn't have missed it for the world."

He reached for a glass knob that first glowed blue then melted into purple as if reflecting the colours housed in the room behind it. He turned it with a soft click. The door opened smoothly of its own accord, and they were greeted with welcoming sights and smells.

The kitchen was huge. Windows faced them, forming the whole south wall and reaching from floor to ceiling, but outside was dark. Nothing could be seen. A red brick fireplace took up the far west side of this space and a fire burned brightly, adding warmth and cheer to the room. Over the flames hung several pots that steamed and gurgled with the promise of a fine meal. Candles spluttered and wavered in the gust of their entrance, from sconces placed along the walls, and from a large square table set in the center of the room.

On the table was laid three each of plates, tiny porcelain cups decorated with yellow roses, and tall glass flutes. Down both the right and left wall, on either side of where they stood, were counters and cupboards above and below with closed doors. Some fronts were painted a soft rose petal pink, some a bright yellow, and others were the pale blue of a wintery sky. Haphazard as this sounded; it worked. Kayden looked around with appreciation.

The floor was set with squares of coloured stones, but these formed designs that became a little mesmerizing if stared at too long. Kayden tore his eyes away to look for the owner of this strange, but appealing house. Without warning, a small door opened from among the cupboards, close to the floor on their left, and Magda's head appeared by Kayden's feet.

He took a step back in alarm. Magda appeared to be climbing steps from somewhere far below. The woman pulled herself through the door with one hand, and clutched a rather dusty, long-neck bottle in the other.

"Cellar," she explained. Puffing a little as she hurried to the table, cleaning the bottle on the material of her dress. Tenderly, she set it on the table. "Some of my best elder-flower wine," she announced proudly. "They were quite pleased with it too."

"Who was pleased?" Kayden asked, raising his eyebrows. Hesitantly, he moved further into the room with Talbot close beside him.

"Why, the elderflowers, of course," she said, as though this fact could have been concluded without a silly question. "Now, we haven't been properly introduced."

Kayden made a mental note not to ask any more stupid questions. You never knew what sort of answer you'd get in Erinbourne. Not that he doubted what she said. He could just imagine a row of elderflowers all smiling their approval as Magda popped the cork.

She marched toward them with arms extended. "I am Magda Roudel, keeper of vivacity and life, and healer to all those who still believe in the ancient arts."

Now that the crisis had passed, Kayden had a moment to look properly at Magda. She had grey hair knotted in a bun on top of her head, woven all around with flowers that, as Kayden stepped forward to clasp her hands, appeared to move on their own. He could have sworn they nodded their colourful little heads to him in greeting. Magda's spectacles perched on the end of her nose. She peered up at him, and into his very soul. Further proof she was Garde.

The tiny lady gave him a wink, as though pleased with what she saw, and bent over double to speak with the hedgehog.

"And I am Talbot, of the Ildune Mountains, close companion of Durgot Flandish," he said. "You know of him, I presume?"

"Yes! Oh, of course I know Durgot," she exclaimed. "Does he keep well?"

"He does, madam," Talbot answered gravely.

She clapped her hands together. "I am so glad to hear it!"

With a flouncing of her creamsicle-coloured skirts, she stood and said, "Pray, seat yourselves at my humble table. Our evening meal is ready."

Then she scurried away to fill their plates from pots bubbling over the fire.

They wasted no time talking, but set to work on the

scrumptious food right away. Kayden wasn't sure what everything was, apart from the raspberry sauce served over a creamy frozen sorbet for dessert, but it was all good. There were light, flakey scones and vegetables cooked into a meatless, tomato-based stew, served on what he thought might be polenta.

"Thank you so much for this wonderful meal," Kayden said. Pushing back his chair, he unfolded his legs from under the table and began collecting their dishes. "Can I help you wash up?"

"No, no, we shall simply pile it on the counter," Magda said, vigorously shaking her head. "There isn't much. I would prefer to know the reason you are in Dalal. And, perhaps you have a few questions for me as well."

Jumping up, she and Kayden cleared away the food and set the dishes in a basin near a small hand pump mounted on the counter. Then, they seated themselves where Talbot, replete and happy, lounged on the table near a bright purple saltshaker. Magda poured them each a small glass of her elderflower wine.

Kayden, fairly bursting to ask, couldn't wait any longer. "Are you one of the Garde?"

"Why, yes, I am," she answered, clearly taken aback at his first query. "I come from the western mountain range of Araleesh, but circumstances being what they were, I was forced to leave. Why do you ask?"

It was clear to Kayden this lady was trustworthy, and he decided to tell her more than he otherwise might have.

"I come from another land," he said slowly. "Beyond the borders of your world. Durgot opened the Southern Portal, because I carried something precious from my world to the king. Because of my heritage, I sort of belong here too."

Magda wiggled to sit straighter in her chair and leaned forward to listen intently.

"My grandmother is half Garde," Kayden continued. "She was also from the Araleesh Mountains. Her name was Alainea Illstyne and her father…" Kayden looked fully into the lady's eyes to gauge her reaction. "Her father was Respiele Larkender."

Magda gasped. She placed a hand on the table to steady herself and hurriedly took a sip of her wine.

"You are the boy—now a young man," she corrected, "who carried the Emerald to King Larkender during the war."

It was a statement more than a question. Kayden nodded. She set down her glass, flopped back in her chair, and used the top portion of her multi-layered dress to fan her face.

"Then I am most pleased to have met you! I knew your grandmother once upon a time." Magda lowered her dress and leaned forward again, her eyes bright. "Now I understand why you carry a runestaff. And the girl, Rosalyn you called her, she is part of the Resistance that guards the king, yes?"

"Yes," Talbot said, smoothly interjecting himself into the conversation. He rose onto his hind feet to speak. "But today, out on the sea, our beloved king was maliciously killed by the hand of Malahd, sorcerer of the late Respiele Larkender. Kayden rescued Rosalyn and me, but not before the girl was poisoned. Bless you, good woman, for saving her."

"Oh, la la…" Magda fanned herself again and the flowers on her head visibly drooped. "These are terrible tidings indeed. The king…dead."

A tear escaped her eye and slipped down her rosy cheek. She mopped it up with her dress and took a deep breath.

"What of the king's sceptre?" she asked. Sitting up, she waited breathlessly for the answer.

"Stolen," Talbot said.

"You will be going after it?"

"Yes." Kayden drummed his fingers on the table.

"I shall provide you with food and whatever else may aid you in this journey," Magda said, smacking her hand on an orange clad knee. Her lips tightened. "This cannot be allowed. The fortress where Malahd lives is not well known to me, as I left when I was only young. However, I can direct you to passages within that mountain that have been used by the Garde since time began."

"Thank you," Kayden said.

"How will you travel?" she asked, looking back and forth between them. "Do you think Malahd will expect you to follow him?"

"We haven't sorted any of that out yet," Kayden said. "Everything just happened today, and we were concerned about Rosalyn first."

"Well, you cannot count on the runestaff to take the three of you that far," she said, tapping a finger on her chin. "It is impossible. You *are* all going, correct?"

She fixed them with a look. Talbot and Kayden nodded.

"Then I may know how to arrange transportation," she said briskly. "And word must be sent to the Silpeth, the Stiyaha, and what is left of the Resistance. They must be informed immediately. The fields and the grasses will do much of this for us."

Kayden sat up a little straighter.

"You're going to ask a *field* of *grass* to carry messages?"

he asked, already forgetting his mental note not to question such statements.

"Yes," she said, considering. "Brome and Timothy are the best, although the occasional fescue can be trusted."

The flowers on her head perked up to listen.

"As well, there are many oat varieties that are fine fellows and naturally wheat can always be counted on. I shall speak with them directly. Barley can be a bit persnickety, and I've often found quack grass to be a wholly untrustworthy lot. But all the rest will help—even what you people consider weeds are good folk." She smiled brightly, and the flowers in her hair nodded as if in complete agreement.

Kayden's mouth hung open. His brain was struggling to take it all in. He'd accepted this alternate world and had learned that being part Garde meant he could speak to animals—which was pretty crazy too. Heck, it had even become commonplace that gemstones and an old walking stick of his grandmother's held magical, transformative powers. But this? Using a bunch of grass as a messenger service? Wow.

Talbot clapped his tiny paws together to snap Kayden out of his reverie.

"Magda is a very special woman," the hedgehog explained, once he had Kayden's attention. "She does not speak only with animals, as you do. As she told us in her introduction, she communicates with and cares for all living things, particularly plants, and is responsible for their colour, vivacity, and verve. Very few are allowed an audience with her. We are honoured to be in your presence, Magda," he finished.

Turning to the little lady, he bowed low.

"Oh fiddlesticks," she said, flushing even rosier than she

was before. She hopped off her chair. "Thank you, Talbot. It is true not many are invited into my home, but I could discern what motive lay in your hearts at once. Now, I think it best you both sleep here. This town is not the safest place to be at night and I believe I am correct in assuming you will have no money to pay for an inn, or clothes, or supplies to take on this journey."

This was half statement and half question.

Kayden inclined his head in agreement. "Everything I brought with me was left in a small boat, floating somewhere at sea," he said. "I have nothing but what I brought to your door."

"Fine," Magda said. "I shall take care of it. All will be arranged in the morning. Now I must check on my patient and you must get some rest. Yes?"

She looked questioningly at them.

"Yes," both answered at once.

She led them back down the hallway of plants, which made more sense now that Kayden knew who Magda was, and into a room not far from where Rosalyn lay.

"Could I see Rosalyn?" Kayden asked, as the lady used her candle to light several others around the room.

"Not tonight, I'm afraid," she said. "That girl absorbed a deadly poison I have not encountered before. It took a great toll on her. Let her rest now and in the morning we will see."

With a rustle of skirts, Magda hurried out the door, closed it softly behind her, and was gone.

Talbot shrugged. Taking a running leap, he hopped onto one of the two beds in the room.

"Rosalyn is in capable hands," he assured Kayden. "As long as she is well enough to travel, we will make plans to leave in the morning. Good night."

Leaning over, he blew out the candle next to his bed, curled up in a ball, and went to sleep.

It wasn't that easy for Kayden. Sleep was elusive. He laid for a long time staring at the ceiling, a lone candle flickering on the nightstand beside him. This bedroom was strangely empty, considering the other rooms in this house. He rolled onto his side and his thoughts drifted back to his first sight of Rosalyn on the boat. She had changed, but only for the better. She was a beautiful young woman. He smiled, feeling grateful for Magda and her healing arts.

Kayden's thoughts went dark. His hands gripped the edges of the bed beside him as he recalled the first ripples as the monster appeared in the water beneath him. An image of the huge beast crashing down onto the king's ship flashed through his mind and the horror of it spewing poison.

Argh. He had to stop replaying the scene and try to sleep. There was a mission to plan in the morning, a journey to take, and a sorcerer to face at the end of it all. Besides, if Malahd had created that creature, *before* he had the sceptre, how strong would he be now? Malahd was in possession of the most powerful object in this universe. It was going to be a monumental, if not impossible, task to defeat him and get the sceptre back.

Would any of them survive?

Chapter Eleven

Kayden pushed open Magda's kitchen door and entered. In the sunshine, green plants and trees heavy with fruit grew in profusion outside the wall-to-wall windows before him. He yawned and scratched his back where his shirt had bunched as he slept. Then, his eyes focused.

Rosalyn stood up from the table and strode toward him. Her hair was loose and fell to her waist in long dark curls. She wore a simple green skirt and cream coloured tunic given to her on the sailboat, when her own clothes were wet, but despite the drab colours, she was lovely. Colour and vitality had returned to her face, and her red lips curved into a cry of delight.

"You're awake!" Kayden rushed forward to greet her. He swept her into his arms and lifted her off her feet to swing around the room, his face buried in her neck.

"Kayden," she said, laughing. "I cannot believe you are here."

He set her down and she drew away smiling, but he retained her hands.

"You're feeling better?" he asked, bending to search her face with a frown of concern. "Should you be up?"

Her laugh tinkled again. "Yes, I'm perfectly alright. Thanks to Magda."

She looked across the room at the little woman who was crouched before her fireplace, coaxing a flame to life. Talbot sat on the table examining a map that was held open on one end by the sugar bowl and the other with the purple salt cellar.

Kayden released her hands and Rosalyn linked her arm with his as they walked to the table together. A shadow of sadness crossed her face.

"Talbot told me of King Ludwig. He was more than my king—he was good, and kind...he was my friend." Her voice broke. "Queen Mirabelle will be grief-stricken. Thankfully, there are people at the castle who will care for her."

"Yes, yesterday still seems like a nightmare." He pulled out a chair for her to sit. "Have you been well, all these years?"

"I have," she said. Shyly she looked down at her lap and fiddled with the laces that fastened her belt. "I spent them at the castle mostly. A group of us were always at the king's side. It seems unbelievable to think, despite our best efforts, that he is gone."

She glanced up at Kayden, her eyes bright.

He reached for her hand again and squeezed.

"We'll properly grieve when the sceptre has been recovered," he said with resolve, but his tone softened as he saw her pain. "I'm so sorry I wasn't able to do more."

She sniffled and squeezed his hand back before letting go. "I know. You are not responsible for what happened.

You saved Talbot and me, and tried valiantly to save the king. You could not have done more."

She turned her attention to the map, or what could be seen of it as Talbot scampered to and fro, muttering about the direction of predominant winds, land formations, rivers, and the various towns along the route he had chosen for their expedition.

"So, we are back in the thick of trouble." Rosalyn looked at Kayden with unshed tears. "And once again we must leave on an adventure into the unknown."

"To call it an adventure sounds pleasurable," Talbot said. He paused in his calculations with a frown and placed paws on hips. "There will be nothing enjoyable about this journey."

"I fear this is true." Magda came up behind them and clunked a pot of tea, a steaming saucepan of oatmeal, and some toast onto the table. "Talbot and I have deliberated, and we believe Malahd's next target will be you, Kayden. You are Ludwig Larkender's successor and have already proven yourself to be a threat to Malahd and to his plans for the domination of Erinbourne."

Crimson roses hung from a leafy vine that was tucked into her hair and she wore a gown of pastel green, lightly patterned with daisies. The odd thing was, Kayden thought as he looked at it closely, the flowers on her dress looked as alive as the ones in her hair. He could smell the spicy perfume of the roses in her hair, but there was also the fresh fragrance of new mown hay as she came near to deliver fruit, jam, and dishes. The daisies bobbed up and down on the silken carpet of her dress as the little woman walked.

Kayden tore his gaze away. What a remarkable woman Magda was.

"Put the map away, please," Magda said crisply. "You must fortify yourselves for what is ahead. Then we talk."

No one needed to be told twice. There were no bugs for him to enjoy, but Talbot ate toast, and far more than would normally be recommended for a hedgehog his size. They all relaxed. As Kayden and Rosalyn cleared the table and washed up, Magda hopped on a chair to help Talbot lay the map out once more.

"Do you have a boussole?" Magda called to Kayden as he dried the dishes.

"Yes, in my pocket, although it must have gotten pretty waterlogged yesterday," he said. He put away the last bowl, folded the towel neatly, and joined Rosalyn in hurrying back to the discussion.

"A boussole is indestructible." Magda waved a dismissive hand in the air. Looking at Talbot she said, "The coordinates must be set for Respiele's old fortress. I shall provide you with these and describe what I remember of the interior, although it has been a long time since I darkened those halls. Kayden must be able to find the fortress and the entrance without help, should the need arise. Yes?"

"Yes," answered Talbot. He looked meaningfully at Kayden who pulled the silver object from his pocket and gave it to the hedgehog. Talbot flipped it open, and Magda gave Talbot directions as he busied himself with the dials.

Magda went on. "I have procured clothing for you, Kayden, so you will not draw unnecessary attention to yourself. I do hope the items fit." She eyed his long legs uncertainly. "Also, I have packed a bedroll and provisions that should take you quite far. Much ground must be covered before you reach the Mountains of Araleesh."

She took a deep breath.

"As for your transport..." Magda hesitated, as if unsure

of how to break this plan to them. "I am certain you will not have heard of these creatures, Kayden, but I imagine Rosalyn has." She looked down at her skirt and fussed with a few of the flowers who hastily moved out reach. "I know that Talbot will have, although perhaps he will not be keen on riding them," she concluded quietly.

She was so vague and nervous; Kayden began to worry. He had been thinking they would saddle up horses for the trek, not clamber atop some strange creature no one had ever heard of.

Talbot snapped the boussole shut and narrowed his eyes. "What are you trying to tell us, Magda?"

"Well..." Magda wrung her hands together and stared at the ceiling. "They are a rather unpredictable creature, a nuisance really...heaven only knows I myself have despised them for what they have done to my herbaceous borders. But they are very fast, not afraid of the danger ahead—mainly because they are too silly to understand it—and..." She drew a breath. "This one has agreed to carry you as far as you require."

She spoke quickly as though needing to get everything said before someone raised an objection.

Talbot sniffed with displeasure. "That is all well and good, and I daresay we appreciate all you have done, but you have *not* told us what *they* are."

Barely above a whisper, Magda said, "I speak of the whinsomey giants."

"What!" Talbot leapt to his feet in alarm and paced back and forth across the table. "You cannot be serious?"

"What's wrong with them?" Kayden said, trying to ease the tension and reassure the woman who had helped them so much. "I trust Magda's judgement."

He directed this last statement to Talbot. Rosalyn remained silent.

Secretly, Kayden's imagination ran amuck. What the heck was coming now? He imagined his group lumbering across the plains on the shoulders of trolls, or maybe sliming through bushes on the backs of gigantic slugs. However, he suppressed these wild thoughts. Magda knew what she was doing. He was sure of it.

"What is wrong," Talbot answered irritably, "is that the ridiculous Whinsomey Giants obey no one. They are unpredictable, goofy, hulking oafs that would step on you as soon as look at you."

Talbot made an exasperated sound, rolled up the map, and handed it to Kayden before jumping off the table. "However, we have no time to dilly dally."

He scampered to where Magda sat twisting one of the vines in her hair. The daisies on her dress were all leaning one toward the other and whispering behind their leaves.

"I could perhaps have done better if I had more time," she said worriedly. "But you must retrieve the sceptre quickly, before Malahd does further harm, and a whinsomey will get you there faster than any horse. If a Silpeth was here, it would be different, but…"

Her voice trailed away, and Kayden thought of the great winged horses of Silpeth, feeling sad when he remembered the great Thatus. He wished they were coming instead.

Talbot bowed, acknowledging her kindness. "Thank you, dear Magda, for all of your wisdom and aid. We would have been lost without you. I am sure you do know best, as Kayden says, and we will ride the whinsomey giant with gratitude. I cannot help but have my doubts, but, regardless of them, I think we should be going. Can you take us to the giant?"

"Yes, of course," Magda said.

She hopped from her chair without another word and led them to her front entry where they had left their things the night before. She had prepared parcels of food and flasks of water in tightly woven bags that tied over their backs.

As they readied themselves, she said, "The whinsomey has been called and warned to obey." She thrust her chin into the air as though daring them to disagree. "His name is Steve."

Kayden barely suppressed a laugh. This monstrous, unknown creature was called Steve? It seemed a bit anti-climactic. He grasped his runestaff, shrugged on his coat, and slipped his bow and arrows over his shoulder. Rosalyn busily strapped on a similar bag followed by a sword that leaned in a far corner of the room.

"I went down to the ship this morning and got it," she explained as he looked at her questioningly. "I cannot be without a sword."

Kayden flicked her a smile and then bent to pick up Talbot and place him in his jacket pocket. Magda hovered in her beaded hallway door. With a wave, she bade them follow her.

"The whinsomeys do not come into town for fear of reprisal," she said. "They are not well-liked as they tend to destroy anything in their path. We shall meet Steve beyond the outskirts of Dalal, on the other side of my garden."

"Of all the creatures we could have…" Talbot grumbled, but only loud enough for Kayden to hear.

Magda took them back through the kitchen and out a small glass door, only big enough for her, built into a corner of her windowed wall. Rosalyn ducked to follow the lady but Kayden was almost forced to crawl in order to wedge himself through. Once on the other side, they stood looking in wonder at vegetation that covered every morsel of space. Trees, twice the size of any Kayden had ever seen, rose into the morning sunlight while shrubs and plants, reaching a height far over Kayden's head, filled the grounds.

How would they fight their way through it?

As Magda moved forward, the rustling plants parted, stretching themselves upright to reveal a narrow path. Magda passed through like a queen. She held her daisy skirt with both hands and nodded regally to either side as she floated past, humming. In turn, each plant or tree bowed to the little lady before snapping to attention.

About fifty meters to either side, a tall board fence ran along the perimeter. Kayden estimated it was three or four times his height and nothing of the neighbouring houses or town could be seen or heard. A fence that tall must be necessary, since the flora it protected was like a wilderness.

Kayden looked up at a group of daffodils with stems like the trunks of young saplings. Rosalyn paused to sniff blue-bells she could have plucked and worn as a hat.

Eventually, they reached the south line of fence that marked the end of Magda's property. They stopped at a large wooden door.

Magda fitted a key into an ancient padlock and turned it with a complaining screech. She looked back at them once, seeming to reassure herself they were still there, then pushed the door wide. They filed through and Magda locked it behind them. Kayden and Rosalyn looked for the strange creature that was to carry them.

Off to their left, the Kalainian Sea sparkled in the early morning sunlight. In front and to the right of them nothing could be seen but a wide expanse of closely cropped pasture, dotted with sheep.

Magda, in her colourful dress, tipped her face to the sky, put two fingers into her mouth, and whistled three notes. They were piercing and high-pitched, yet melodic.

The earth began to thump rhythmically, like the beating of a drum.

"Here we go." Talbot disappeared down into Kayden's pocket.

"He is coming," Magda said unnecessarily. Glancing down at their feet, she added, "You might want to watch yourselves. Whinsomeys often have trouble understanding personal space."

Rosalyn and Kayden stared at one another.

"Will it accept us?" Rosalyn asked in a worried voice.

"Oh, yes. He owes me a debt that I have asked him to repay in this manner. You, yourself, are part Garde are you not, Rosalyn?" Magda asked. When Rosalyn nodded, Magda continued. "Then, you should all be able to speak to him. Keep your instructions simple and clear. Yes?"

Magda looked steadily at Kayden.

"Yes," he said.

A muffled snort of ill humour rose from Kayden's pocket.

Directly south of where they stood, a set of what looked like curved poles, rose over a hill. Protruding from the end of each one was a round knob that flew back and forth with the creature's movements. The poles grew in length as each thump of the ground could be felt, until they towered in the air, high over the knoll. *Whatever this thing was, it seemed to be jumping.* Kayden was curious, though in a moment, it became obvious.

The poles were actually long antennae that waggled

back and forth with each leap. A large, flat, dark orange head bounded into view and then, with another lunge, an enormous cylindrical-shaped body appeared. It was fitted with a pair of long hind legs on either side of the body that bent double as the creature leaned back and gathered itself, and then straightened as the whinsomey pushed himself to rocket forward. He used all four hind legs to thrust and balanced on two shorter legs at the front of his body.

Steve propelled himself forward, each time, in a leap that must have equalled the length of a football field.

"Look out!" Kayden shouted.

Magda bounded one way, while he and Rosalyn threw themselves the other in order to avoid Steve as he vaulted through the air toward them. Talbot went flying out of Kayden's pocket, rolling over and over in the short grass before coming up to splutter angrily. Lucky thing they'd moved too, as the beast stood looking at them with wide, glassy eyes from the exact spot they had stood upon only seconds ago.

The whinsomey giant towered above them. Antennae sprouted from the center of a head that was long and pointed. Its mouth was a thin slit, curving up the side of its head. His eyes were black, expressionless discs, and he gave no sign of greeting, nor did he acknowledge that they were there at all. His body was segmented into two parts. Tucked up flat alongside and overtop of the two smaller front legs, were wings of a shimmering bronze.

However, the most remarkable thing about the whinsomey were the armour-like plates of burnished orange that covered it entirely and rattled when it moved.

"What did I tell you?" Talbot asked Kayden. The hedgehog picked himself up and dusted off his spines. "They are blundering fools!"

The whinsomey tucked its legs underneath its body and dropped, settling itself much like a cat, and laid its pointy chin on the grass. Magda trotted around its head and came to stand beside Rosalyn, Talbot, and Kayden.

"As I said, you must watch yourselves around him since the whinsomey giants do not get along with humankind very well. However, he will obey you, Kayden, because I have asked him to." Turning, she addressed the whinsomey using short loud words. "Steve, this is Kayden. You will take him and his companions to the Araleesh Mountains. You remember—yes?"

The giant whinsomey flicked one antenna in agreement, at least that appeared to be how Magda took it. She rounded on Kayden and smiled.

"I have done all I can, except for one last thing." Magda reached into a voluminous pocket of her flowery dress and pulled from it a tiny glass jar. Its contents glowed with an incandescent green light. "This is potent. Please use it sparingly, if at all. It is my own special concoction."

She held it lovingly to the light and studied the sparkling contents. "I call it Eluvia. The granules form a vine stronger than any rope made by human hands. Do not touch it until it is formed. Just sprinkle a little, very lightly in the direction you wish it to grow. Depending on how much you use, it can reach to the highest heights or sink to the lowest depths that you may need to climb or descend."

She pressed the jar into Kayden's hand and reached for his other to clasp them both together.

"It has been an honour to meet you, my future king." Her eyes twinkled up at him before she moved to Rosalyn. "And you, my dear."

Avoiding the sword strapped to Rosalyn's back, she drew the girl down into her arms for a hug.

Magda squatted down to speak to the hedgehog. "Farewell, Talbot. Guard them well. Good fortune to you all," she said, straightening. "And may you be successful in this worthy quest. Word has been sent to your allies, but remember, the fields and hedgerows also know your names. There are friends everywhere." She cast her arms wide.

"Some are not ones you expect or are you familiar with, yet. But if you open your eyes and call, they are ready to stand at your side and fight. Goodbye." She stepped away as Kayden placed Talbot back into his pocket.

"Thank you for all you have done, Magda," Kayden said. He moved hesitantly toward the whinsomey's face to address the monstrous creature.

"Hello," he said, in a strident voice. "I am Kayden. Thank you for carrying us."

Then, the enormity of this proposition hit him.

Whipping around to face Magda, he whispered, "How are we supposed to get on or stay up there when he jumps?"

In answer, Steve, the whinsomey, said nothing, but rolled onto his side. He offered up his broad back and raised a few of the armoured plates that sheathed his body. Despite almost pinning them to the ground in the process, Kayden could see Steve was trying very hard to be helpful. Walking forward, Kayden helped Rosalyn to get tucked in behind a plate further along the whinsomey's neck. Then he wedged himself behind her and adjusted his runestaff and bow so they were not poking the creature. To Kayden's amazement, the armour that lay across his thighs was light, but felt as strong as steel. He felt quite secure as Steve rose to his full height, angled himself in the right direction, and leaned back ready to spring.

Lifting a hand in salute to Magda, Kayden held on tight with the other. He could feel tension building in the creature as it bent its powerful legs back and then catapulted forward. Wind whistled past Kayden's face and his hair lifted off his head as they careened high in the air. His body lifted with the force of their takeoff too, but he was tightly wedged beneath the shields of the whinsomey's body. It was strangely like riding an enormous rocking horse. And so, they began the long trek to hunt Malahd and take back Erinbourne's Gemstones of Power.

What fate would meet them there?

Chapter Twelve

Clouds, gilded with setting shades of pink and gold from the westering sun, adorned the sky before Steve, the whinsomey giant, ceased his passage cross the land. He seemed tireless, covering ground rapidly. He didn't spread his wings however, and Kayden wondered what good they were, since all Steve ever did was jump.

It had been a long day. The creature had not stopped once and Kayden had not asked him to. The quicker they got to their destination, the better. Along the way, he and Rosalyn had been able to access their bags enough to grab all three of them a quick snack, but they were cramped and sore from travel. Everyone was grateful when Steve stopped. The whinsomey laid down beside a stream that flowed from high above in the Honistel Mountain range, Kayden's old nemesis. The whinsomey waited for them to disembark.

Feeling stiff from sitting in one position all day, Kayden lifted the flaps of armour that bound him, eased out from under, and slid to the ground. Stepping out of the way, he waited for Rosalyn to land lightly beside him, before lifting

Talbot from his pocket and setting him down. The whin-somey giant shuffled off to drink and to nibble at shrubs growing near the water.

Talbot had been sleeping and stretched with a yawn. Then, he began to snuffle in the long grass for bugs.

On the opposite side of the stream, the land, although wooded, rose steeply to the sheer rock face of the nearest mountain. A waterfall splashed down its side, ending in a foaming pool to their right, ringed with trees. Rosalyn and Kayden walked to the brook, only a few paces away, and knelt to sluice their faces in the icy liquid.

Thankfully, the trip thus far had been uneventful. Apart from a few flabbergasted farmers, who gaped at the sight of the seldom, or never seen, whinsomey giant, they had met no one. From Dalal they crossed a road, only once, and then struck out southwest. It was the main road leading to Norbern, and it had been silent and empty. A few farmyards and villages had been spotted in the distance, but Steve seemed to understand that they were to be avoided. Kayden didn't relish trying to answer any questions that might be posed from passers-by. Or come up with unpleasant expla-nations if Steve accidently crushed their houses or laid on a cow.

"Do you think it's safe to light a fire?" Kayden asked, looking first at Rosalyn, and then Talbot. "Or would it draw the wrong attention?"

"I believe it is best not to for two reasons," Talbot said. "One, the whinsomey might be frightened by flames and run, and two, a fire will attract interest. We want neither."

"I agree," Rosalyn said.

Pulling the bag off her back, she opened it and removed the bedroll Magda had thoughtfully provided. Spreading it out, she sat down on the flowery mauve bedding and rummaged for food.

"Better get set up for sleeping now," she said. "The sun is almost gone."

Kayden, who had been staring off toward the deepening blue of the Araleesh Mountains in the west, bent with a sigh and picked up his bag. He only then noticed that Steve was gone. He looked around worriedly, but the creature had only hopped some distance away. Where the whinsomey had lain to let them off, the grass had been chewed right to its roots, and at present, Steve appeared to be feasting on a lush hedge. This was likely the reason Magda wasn't overly fond of whinsomeys.

"Do you really think Magda can talk to grass?" he asked, looking around at the tall green fronds.

Rosalyn's mouth was full of a fruit whose juice ran down her chin. She flicked it away with her fingers.

"Of course," she said, after swallowing. "If Magda says it, I believe it."

Kayden pulled a bottle from his bag and tossed it to Talbot who had just joined them after scouting around the area. "Here's dinner."

Talbot sat down and opened the bottle with a pleased smile on his face. Digging a small fist inside, he pulled out a worm and bit into it with relish.

"That—is revolting," Kayden told him laughing. His tone became serious. "Rosalyn, how is your father?" he asked. "I haven't had a chance to ask you much about what has happened since I've been gone."

"He is well. Thank you for enquiring. He still tends his farm, and I visit him whenever I can." Rosalyn brushed her hands along her skirt and fastened the top of her carrying bag. "How is your family and your life in—what is the place you come from called again—Cando?"

"It's Canada, and they were all good when I left." He grinned at her. He had that same feeling of unreality the last time he was here, when thinking of his family back home. It was bizarre to know that only yesterday he had bridged the gap between two worlds.

In the time it had taken to eat and put away some of the food Magda had packed, the sun sank beneath the western horizon and was gone. Kayden could see nothing, not even a hand in front of his face. He felt for the boussole that served as both compass and a faint source of light in times of need. Its wavering beam cut through the darkness as he flipped the boussole open, and everyone turned to watch as Steve lumbered across the field toward them. Thankfully, the whinsomey had decided to walk rather than jump, a decision which probably saved their lives.

"We should get some sleep." Rosalyn tossed her thick braid over a shoulder and straightened her bedroll before lying down and pulling the blanket over top. "We do not know when the whinsomey will want to leave. Have either of you talked to him?"

She stifled a yawn.

"To be honest, I haven't tried," Kayden said. "Have you, Talbot?"

"No, I prefer to keep my interactions with whinsomeys to a bare minimum. That problem aside, I think one of us should keep watch tonight. There is a strange scent on the wind, and it concerns me. I shall take the first shift. Get some sleep." Rising, Talbot handed the jar of wriggly bugs back to Kayden for safekeeping and melted into the gloom.

Kayden sat rather nervously on his bedroll until he saw, by the boussole's light, that Steve had settled himself for the night some distance away. He wasn't keen on being trampled. It'd be hard to explain when he got back home. He could see it all now…

"Hey Kayden," his friends would ask. "How'd you lose that arm?"

"Oh that," he'd reply, all casual-like. "I was riding this monster creature, see, and late one night, after gorging on a hedge, it jumped on my legs. I barely made it out alive…"

Chuckling to himself, Kayden closed his boussole and slid it back into his pocket. Darkness enveloped him as he laid down. Unlike the night before, Kayden dropped off to sleep right away.

———————

A sharp breeze swirled down the mountain and washed over where they lay sleeping. Shivering, Kayden reached for Magda's warm coverlet, but in doing so, his hand brushed over the long grass at his side. He sat up in alarm. It was almost as though an electric shock had passed from the tall waving fronds and into his fingertips, sending a warning coursing up his arm and through his body.

Something was wrong.

Reaching for the runestaff that was always at his side, he came up into a crouch, listening intently. Nothing. Yet the hair on his neck stood on end. Barely making a sound, he crawled to where Rosalyn was lying, leaned down to locate her ear, and whispered into it.

"Rosalyn. Wake up. We're in danger."

She awoke and grasped for her sword. Then, they stood together, back to back, their ears attuned to the smallest of noises.

Though he could see nothing, Kayden sensed they

weren't alone. He shuddered, his eyes scanning the darkness for he knew not what. Finally, from the shadows, three figures emerged, the outline of their cowled forms framed in a thin line of red light. They carried no weapons that Kayden could see, yet the menace that radiated from them was terrifying.

He'd met these beings before. Long ago, on a hill near Norbern, they had surrounded him, but the cowled figures had ridden on strange beasts then. They had attacked him just before dawn, operating best in darkness.

Now, they were alone, and closed the space between him and Rosalyn slowly, advancing almost as though they hovered over the ground. Kayden knew beneath their flowing robes they were nothing more than shadows of what had been, their blackened skin stretched and withered against their bones.

They were men of a bygone age, without life or substance, their only animation provided by the dark magic of Malahd and amplified by the power of the sceptre. Kayden knew why the beings were here. They had been sent by Malahd to kill him. Desperately, he tried to think how he, Rosalyn, Talbot, and the whinsomey could escape.

Unfortunately, if Rosalyn felt any of what he was experiencing, Kayden knew she couldn't move a muscle. He was paralyzed by an unseen force. The power of these unearthly beings had increased since last Kayden had dealt with them, and he found himself unable to summon even the might of his runestaff. It felt heavy and leaden in his hand, when it should have been warm and alive in the face of evil.

Even if he or Rosalyn could have used their weapons, these apparitions could not be struck down with steel or arrows. These spectres were beyond the human state of either life or death, and moved forward to surround and destroy their prey.

Extending skeletal arms, they began to chant in a strange tongue, their voices thin and shrill as they drifted closer. Without haste, appearing sure of their kill, the beings closed in around Kayden and Rosalyn, shutting off their escape and filling Kayden's mind with dread.

He could clearly see the dull red glow that fringed each one of his enemies now. It was much like the aura that had surrounded Magda. Only in this case its presence was threatening, not calming. As they drew nearer, the intensity of colour deepened and expanded its cloud of angry red light to reach out and pluck at him with icy fingers.

Kayden willed himself to move, to break free of the stupor with which his body was ensnared, but he could not. His very breath was in the dark spirits' control. One moved close and the talons of this enemy passed like ghostly weapons through Kayden's flesh and curled around his lungs. He gasped, but it was cut short as the claws tightened. He wheezed, his mind churning, eyes closing as he succumbed to the greater will. His knees buckled and he began to fall into darkness.

Yet, in the haze of his own demise, Kayden felt something swish and curl around his ankles. What was this fresh horror? With a monumental effort, he dragged his eyes open a crack. In the reddish hue that surrounded the dark trio who held him, Kayden caught sight of what had caused the sensation at his feet.

Trailing grasses, growing high in the moisture-laden soil beside the stream, began to twist, twirl, and wind themselves around the dark beings. They wove in, out, and through the otherworldly fabric of the spectres' flowing cloaks. At first, the sinuous stalks of grass had little effect on the apparitions. They grew thicker, piling upon themselves row upon row and braiding themselves one upon another, they began to overtake the movements of the dark assassins and slow them down. The beings clawed at the braids that threatened them, trying to rip them away. More braids replaced what had been torn.

Yet, the creatures slogged on until all three were close enough to Kayden that he could feel their hollow bodies touching him. Kayden's tortured lungs strained for air. Despite the encroaching grasses, the first apparition curled its claws, its internal grip squeezing the very life from Kayden's body.

Kayden collapsed. Still, he did not lose consciousness, nor feel his body slam to earth. Instead, his fall was cushioned by a gentle swath of meadow grass and his eyes beheld a strange sight. Anchoring the three dark spirits to the solidness of the good green earth, the grasses continued their winding attack. Layer upon layer they crawled over the three entities, pushing them back, and covering their dark intentions with the smell of new-mown hay and yellow clover. Then with a snap, the grasses broke the spectres' hold over Kayden. Their evil faltered.

Kayden felt his staff come alive.

One word flooded his mind—sunlight. Bringing his runestaff up, Kayden grasped it with both hands and the grassy swath rose to stand him upright again. He leaned on the wood and felt for the likeness of a golden sun. Drawing on every ounce of strength he had, Kayden swiveled the image toward the spectres and focused.

His chest was in agony, his brain torn between darkness and hope, but he brought the image into his mind and concentrated harder than he'd ever done before. Furrowing his brow, he poured everything he had into calling the sun to shine with a radiance so blinding, it would banish the shadows of darkness. A groan burst from his lips as the energy required brought Kayden to his knees, but slowly, the sun around his fingertips grew bright.

The spirits struggled against the sinewy strength of the grass. They hissed and their chanting grew louder as they tore savagely at the plants that wound themselves in, around, and through the robes that swirled over their skeletal frames. The inflamed aura around them had ebbed, but once again it surged with power, and the winding webs of grass fell aside, burnt and blackened.

Golden beams of sunlight streamed from the runestaff. Like gilded spears they gored at the darkness. The spirits screamed, drawing their cowls across the hollow pits that served as eyes in hatred of the dazzling brilliance, and slithered backward, losing control.

"Rosalyn!" Kayden shouted. "Get to Steve. Find Talbot."

His instructions were short and terse. The strain of holding these nightmares at bay created a sweat that ran in rivulets down his face and stung his eyes. His arms shook with the pressure exerted upon him to hold the runestaff steady.

"Talbot is here," Rosalyn said. She sounded half-asleep from the paralysis they had suffered.

Kayden heard her footsteps, first walking and then running away from him. He stood firm as the dazzling light from his runestaff hurt even his own eyes. Sunlight flooded the space between Kayden and the spectres, pushing them back further. They writhed and hissed against the light, their grotesque shapes withering as they shrank to half their former size. There was no aura about them now, and Kayden held fast to the sun that banished them. Aloud, not trusting himself to keep his concentration if he used his thoughts to reach out, he could manage only a whisper to call the whinsomey giant.

"Steve?" Hoping against hope, he waited for a response, his hands upon the runestaff remaining resolute.

Why hadn't he tried talking to the creature before this? Seconds passed. Kayden felt himself weakening.

"Yes—governor. You—want—me?" The whinsomey spoke as though drugged.

A sob of relief rose in Kayden's throat, but he swallowed and addressed the giant. "We are in danger. Get ready to take passengers, and then to run as fast as you can." He felt, rather than heard, the whinsomey's acquiescence. Kayden carefully began to back away. His heel came in contact with something hard and bending. With one hand, he picked up his bow and arrows, and slung them over his head. Yet, his gaze and the encircling light never left the spirits. Next, he reached for his bag and moved away further still.

Kayden heard the shuffling sound made by the whinsomey when on the move, but it wasn't jumping, and realized Steve was trying to come for him. Yet, Kayden couldn't risk turning to see where the giant was or aiming the staff anywhere but at their adversaries.

Then, he felt something like a thick, rubbery cord, wrap around his waist and hoist him into the air. The light from his staff illuminated one of the giant's antennae. In one fluid movement, Steve swung him up and deposited him into the familiar seat between his scales, and with a bound they were airborne.

The whinsomey giant unfurled its raspy wings. There were three layers of them, all paper thin and crinkling like parchment as they worked in conjunction with his powerful legs to thrust them forward and fly. They flew far beyond the distance Steve had previously jumped.

"Put out your light!" Talbot murmured from behind Kayden, probably from the folds of Rosalyn's cloak. "You are providing them with a beacon to follow."

Kayden extinguished the light of the rune and silently blessed his staff. He would have been dead long ago without it.

The whinsomey giant ate up the kilometers with his enormous lunging strides and the careful angle of his wings. It was wonderful.

Kayden took a few minutes to recover his breath. He massaged his aching torso and checked for puncture wounds.

"Did you feel that?" he asked Rosalyn. "Like those—things, were crushing you from the inside out?"

"No. But they were not trying to kill me. That was their plan for you. I would have died along with you though."

Kayden digested this. "So, you're alright? And Talbot?"

"Yes, we are fine. I am sorry I was unable to do anything to stop them. By the time I got back to our camp, you were regaining control." Talbot patted Kayden's back with a tiny paw. "I am proud of you, young man."

"It wasn't me. I'd be dead by now if it weren't for Magda and her plants..." Kayden tried taking a deeper breath, found he could do so, and continued. "Who would have ever thought I'd be indebted to a patch of grass?"

But he was, and he sent a silent thanks to the fields and hedgerows that Magda had mentioned before they left her. He closed his eyes, trying to banish all memory of the skeletal hand that had thrust itself into his chest to snatch away his life, but knew the image would be with him for life.

Sleep was not altogether safe, given their precarious position atop the giant whinsomey, although Kayden and Rosalyn did doze a little. They covered a lot of ground during the midnight hours. It turned out the whinsomey had excellent night vision and was able to avoid any major pitfalls, such as leaping on a church or trampling herds of sheep.

By the time Kayden opened his drooping eyes, they had passed the Honistel Mountain range and were looking at a vast sweep of green pastureland in the rosy light of dawn. It was a magical hour of day, flooding the land with a warm glow. As the sun arrived, it revealed a rolling landscape stretching as far as the eye could see toward the deep blue peaks of their destination. Dense bluffs of cottony-looking trees followed the line of the valleys, seeking out moisture. *It's a beautiful area, much like home*, Kayden thought with a pang.

He knew that back on the ranch, very little time would have elapsed since his departure. The divide between the two worlds was distinct. Although life here was something like stepping back into the Middle Ages, the land itself was not so different. There were some foreign-looking plants and trees, but most of the animals were the same. He braced himself for another lunge and clutched the whinsomey's armour for support.

What was he thinking? There were all kinds of strange beasts, creatures, and types of people here. He couldn't recall ever hearing of an evil sorcerer using the undead to try taking over Canada.

"Are you awake?" Rosalyn asked from behind Kayden. "I wonder if we should stop for a while and give Steve a rest."

"I agree." Leaning forward, Kayden looked across the

expanse of scaly neck to where the tall antennas wagged back and forth as the giant jumped. "Steve?"

The giant appeared not to have heard him, so he tried again.

"Steve, please stop for a break." Kayden closed his eyes, reaching out to the whinsomey in his mind. "And thank you for your fast action during the night."

The giant skidded to a stop; his antennae aimed back at Kayden as though listening. The whinsomey laid down on the ground and they piled off. All three of them walked around to ease their stiff joints while Steve shuffled off to find himself food.

After consulting the map that Magda had sent along, they ate a few dry, but tasty biscuits in grim silence and lay on a hill in the sunshine to nap. The next leg of their journey would be the most dangerous. Kayden had valiant friends who would fight alongside him, and a runestaff to call upon for help, but the three spectres had immobilized them all. The life had almost been squeezed from his body and none of them could have stopped it happening without help from Magda and her ability to communicate with plants.

How would he ever face down a sorcerer who held the most powerful weapon in the world?

Chapter Thirteen

Judging by the sun, it was around noon. Kayden roused himself and sat up to look for the others. Rosalyn and Steve still slept nearby, but Talbot was gone. Kayden hoped the hedgehog didn't sense something evil in the wind again. That last episode had almost been the end of them. However, as Kayden stood and began to gather his things, Talbot appeared, his small black nose twitching.

"We should move along," he said. Scuttling over to where Rosalyn lay curled up in the warm afternoon sun, Talbot tapped her arm, then jumped out of the way as she came up on her feet, sword in hand and ready for battle. "My goodness! Your reflexes are excellent."

Rosalyn sheathed her sword and smoothed her rumpled skirt. She eyed them both. "Have you two been awake for long? Why didn't you call me?"

"I just opened my eyes a few minutes ago, but Talbot's been scouting the area for a while it seems. Anything out there we should worry about?" Kayden asked.

"Nothing is amiss thus far," Talbot replied. He waved a

paw toward Steve. "Who is going to tell him we should prepare to leave? Doubtless those spectres will be searching for us tonight and we may not be so fortunate again."

"I'll call him. You have to admit, the whinsomey giant has been very helpful." Kayden threw Talbot a mischievous grin. "He hasn't done any of those things you said he would, although I understand why he isn't Magda's favorite creature. He must eat a ton of plants every day."

"True," Talbot said grudgingly. "I admit we would not have done so well without him."

He opened Kayden's bag and crawled inside to rummage for his bottle of grubs. Pulling it out, he popped a few into his mouth and crunched, closing his eyes with a rapturous expression. Rosalyn plunked down beside him and opened her bag to eat as well. Clearly the sight of a hedgehog gobbling bugs didn't affect her appetite.

Kayden averted his eyes and hurried toward the giant bulk that was Steve. The creature was at least twice the size of an elephant. Who would have believed he'd be riding such a thing? The whinsomey's huge head extended across the ground before him. His glassy, black eyes were closed and both antennae drooped in slumber.

"Steve," Kayden whispered, trying to wake the giant with care. The last thing he wanted was to startle the creature and have him lunge to his feet. He would crush everything in his path. But, the whinsomey merely lifted his head a little and half-opened an enquiring eye.

"Yes—governor," he said, dragging out his words in the monotone voice he had used before. Kayden concluded this was how the creature normally communicated, and thought, *for as fast as Steve could move, he certainly spoke with slow deliberation.*

"Good morning, Steve. Did you get enough sleep?"

There was a long pause before the whinsomey replied. "Yes."

"That's great!" Kayden answered with forced enthusiasm. It was difficult to be enthusiastic when Steve was so deadpan. "Anyway, if you could carry us again, we'd appreciate it."

Slowly, Steve nodded an antenna.

"Thank you. We should leave soon, so you might want to get something to eat."

"I—ate—when—you—were—sleeping." Steve lumbered to his feet and lifted a huge hind leg to scratch his stomach, the claws of his foot making a squealing noise against the armour. The sound was almost deafening at such close range.

"Okay," Kayden yelled above the din. "We'll get ready. Don't come to us—we'll come to you."

Wheeling about, he hurried back to Talbot and Rosalyn.

"Here." Rosalyn tossed Kayden something from her bag. "You should eat. Who knows when we shall stop again?"

"Thanks." The fruit he caught smelled somewhat spicy and resembled a peach in shape, but was a rich purple in colour. He sank his teeth into the firm flesh. It was unlike anything he'd ever had. And it was delicious. There was brown bread, a soft cheese, and squares of a flat sweetened cookie that he enjoyed too. Kayden had figured out long ago that the Garde never ate meat. Every animal was a friend.

After their hasty meal, the trio walked toward the whinsomey. It had been decided that today they would aim to reach the mountains just north of Respiele's old fortress, where Malahd now ruled. It was the only route that afforded them cover. They couldn't just ask Steve to hop up to the front gates of the castle. Malahd would have guards on high alert who would kill them all before they ever even saw the sorcerer, let alone engage him in battle and rise victorious. Malahd knew Kayden was coming, and why. Their attack would need to be planned with care.

All three of them had listened as Magda had told them how to enter an ancient gate, long disused, that led into the inner sanctum of the mountain. Kayden's runestaff was the key. From that point, there were tunnels through the mountain leading up and out a stone door within the fortification. This was their only hope to gain entrance without alerting Malahd to their presence.

Talbot peered out of Kayden's pocket as they climbed aboard and settled themselves safely within the whinsomey's armour. Then, with a bound, they were off.

And people say riding a camel is weird, thought Kayden. He clutched the armoured plate of the giant with one hand, and his runestaff with the other. He wasn't fastening it behind him today. He might need it at a moment's notice.

The Araleesh Mountains were much closer, their dark peaks rising like spikes from a bed of nails. They looked sinister and foreboding. Kayden felt Rosalyn shiver behind him as she too looked out in the clear light of morning and beheld their goal.

Down they went into a shady glen, lined with the odd trees whose branches ran perpendicular to the trunk. The same ones that Kayden had liked on his first trip to Erinbourne. Without smashing too many of them, or trampling an excessive amount of underbrush, Steve was able to follow the valley as it wound along the lower plains before the mountains. In this way, they hoped their coming would not be detected as easily by any of Malahd's lookouts. In perhaps two or three hours, according to Magda's map, they would see the small town of Maldone which they would skirt to the north. It was important to remain hidden.

Rosalyn leaned forward to grab one of Kayden's shoulders and pull his ear closer. "How long will you stay in Erinbourne this time, Kayden? I missed you."

Kayden's heart flooded with joy. She had missed him. "I guess a couple of weeks. Maybe a bit more, but I don't want my parents to worry back home."

Ah," she said, her voice sounding downcast.

Talbot scrabbled about in Kayden's pocket and poked his head out the top. He'd been catching up on the sleep he'd missed while standing guard.

"You must make arrangements to be here now," he said. "If not all the time, then at least for most of it. Henceforth, your duty lies in Erinbourne, so you might as well accustom yourself to the fact."

Rosalyn gasped. "I was not thinking! Of course—when King Larkender died, you became next in line to the throne. No wonder Malahd wants you dead." Rosalyn patted his back. "You have no choice but to stay here, my liege."

Kayden frowned. "I'm not a king whether some distant blood relation dictates it or not. I can't just drop my life in Canada, move to an alternate universe, and plunk a crown on my head. It doesn't work that way."

"What way does *it* work?" Talbot asked. "No one is born into this world knowing what path life will take them down. Consider what you have accomplished already. Is that not more than you ever thought possible?"

Kayden lapsed into silence, thinking about what Talbot said. "I suppose you're right."

"Naturally, I am right."

"But what about my parents, my sister, my grandmother,

and the friends I've made?" Kayden's voice rose in agitation. "I was planning on going to university in the fall. What about all that?"

"What is a university?" Rosalyn interjected.

"It's a really big school where you learn a profession." Kayden wiped a hand across his brow.

"In answer to your questions," Talbot continued, "you would visit your family and friends, just the same as you would visit if you moved far from home in your own world. It might not be often and explaining your absence to those in your homeland might be hard, but it is not insurmountable."

"Your grandmother did it, did she not?" Rosalyn asked.

"In reverse, yes." Kayden sighed, thinking about Gran. "But I don't think she ever came back here for a visit."

Of course, because she was from Erinbourne herself, she would understand the situation and could ease the confusion his parents might feel at hearing such an outlandish tale. But maybe the truth would make a complete mess of things. If Gran was forced to tell them she was from an alternate universe to their own, it could upset a lot of people in his family.

Then there was his best friend Matt. They were planning to attend the same university. How could Kayden explain why he'd suddenly changed his mind, and disappeared off the face of the earth, so to speak. If he couldn't at least text or email someone, it would be considered pretty weird, and people would be suspicious.

Fortunately for Kayden, the spire of a tall building appeared over the trees on their left and they fell silent. Getting past a town needed to be done quickly, as the thunderous sound of Steve's landings would be enough to scare people and bring them out to search for the cause.

In two huge leaps, they were past the few whitewashed buildings that nestled together to form the village. They hadn't seen a soul. Kayden realized he'd been holding his breath and let it out in a whoosh just as they rounded a corner.

The valley they were in grew narrower, and looking ahead, Kayden realized he'd relaxed too soon. Six riders waited, spanning the valley on horseback.

Okay, Kayden thought, not so unusual. People did travel, work, and ride horses here. It didn't mean they were searching for *him* or were sent by Malahd. And whinsomey giants were occasionally seen in this land, so it shouldn't be a problem. But as they advanced upon the riders, Kayden despaired. Moving to strategic points along the side of the ravine, the riders fitted arrows into their bows and drew them back, waiting for a clear shot.

"Steve!" Kayden yelled. "Look ahead and be careful. We're about to be attacked!"

Rosalyn and Talbot came alive. The hedgehog flung himself from Kayden's pocket, arching through the air and transforming into his warrior self as he hurtled to the earth below. Rosalyn shuffled away from Kayden along the whinsomey's back. Her sword clanged as it was unsheathed.

Kayden knew there was no point in evasive tactics, although he'd never been trained in warfare. They might outrun the riders for a time, but these six enemies would separate and alert others to their presence. There would be no way to sneak into Malahd's fortress if that happened. No. They must win this battle now and there must be no survivors.

One more leap and the whinsomey giant would be upon the riders. Kayden lifted his bow and steadied himself. As they lunged, a volley of arrows whined through the air toward them.

"Get down!" he hollered at Rosalyn, but there was no need. The whinsomey screamed in fury and raised the armoured plates on its body until each one stood up on end. The enemy arrows clattered uselessly against them.

And then the whinsomey landed. In a flash, Rosalyn disengaged herself from Steve's protective shields and slid to the ground, landing lightly on her feet. Kayden was right behind her. He turned, bow still raised, and shot. His arrow went wide. He wasn't used to shooting at a moving target and the rider had wheeled away to attack from another angle.

Grabbing another arrow Kayden set the arrow into the string while diving behind the trunk of a large tree for cover. An arrow whined past his right shoulder. He looked across at Rosalyn. She moved like greased lightning. With a cry, she bounded onto the back of a horse as the rider wheeled his mount to face her and thrust her blade into his chest. He slumped in the saddle. She shoved him off with her foot and sliding into his place, she urged the horse to follow a rider who was escaping up the side of the gorge toward town. Her horse lunged into a gallop, and they streaked up the hillside in pursuit.

Kayden stepped out into view again, braced himself, and calculated the trajectory this time before loosing his arrow. He hesitated. He'd never even killed a gopher, let alone a human being. *Could he do it?* It was either him or the other guy. The string sprang back with a twang. The rider galloping to meet Kayden with sword upheld caught the arrowhead full in the chest. He dropped to the ground, rolled to a stop, and lay still.

Reaching for another arrow, Kayden turned to see

Talbot take down two more of the riders. Malahd's emissaries were not expecting a whirlwind of deadly spikes to leap at them from the branches of a tree.

There was only one of Malahd's assassins left. The cowled figure kicked his horse viciously and lashed at it with his reins, forcing it to labour up the opposite side of the ravine. It was too far to send an arrow and, since the rider was on horseback, Talbot would not reach him in time either.

Kayden closed his eyes. Reaching out in his mind, he called to the horse beneath Malahd's messenger of death. It was only a poor beast of burden forced to serve a cruel master. He reached out with soothing words and asked only one thing of the animal. Then, knowing he could do no more, Kayden opened his eyes.

Somehow, the horse responded. At the edge of the summit, the animal reared, endangering himself as he thrust his front legs high in the air, unseating his rider. Malahd's assassin flew backward. The horse, pawing frantically with his front hooves and bunching its powerful hindquarters beneath him, leapt up and over the brink.

The rider was not so fortunate. Tumbling over and over down the steep side of the ravine, he came to a stop not far from the silent whinsomey giant. Steve had stood quietly with head lowered since the fighting erupted. Now, he moved his head only slightly to look with flat, disinterested eyes at Malahd's agent, and rising, the whinsomey plodded over as the man struggled to stand. For a moment, Steve stood impassive, and then the whinsomey giant laid down on top of the cowled figure, squishing him flat.

"Well!" Talbot walked up to stand beside Kayden. "I did not think I would ever say it, but that whinsomey is a remarkable ally."

Kayden lowered his bow and grinned. "Do you see Rosalyn?"

He twisted to look in the direction she had gone, shading his eyes against the glare of sunlight that had risen high in the sky. A crashing of trees announced her arrival from behind them as her horse loped down the hill. The horse slid to a halt at the bottom and Rosalyn swung her leg over the saddle to drop to the ground. Then, swiftly removing the rigging, she tossed it into the bushes before patting the bay horse fondly. It trotted away.

"What fun activities has Malahd planned for us next?" she joked, flipping her braid over her shoulder. "I dealt with the one I followed. No problem."

Kayden smiled at her, feeling much relieved. Talbot nodded approvingly.

"I think, grisly as it may be for you, Kayden, as you are not used to this sort of thing, that you should collect your arrows and clean them as best you can. Then, we need to continue on our way. These will not be the only adversaries sent to stop us."

Talbot resumed his smaller shape. Kayden did what he asked, and then they were atop the whinsomey once more. They held tight to Steve as he leapt down the ravine.

"Thank you for your help," Kayden said to the giant as they lunged along.

Steve waggled both antennae back at him.

"We—Whinsomey—Giants—want—to—see—the—sorcerer—defeated—too," he said.

It was the longest sentence he had ever uttered, and Kayden patted the neck in front of him, unsure if Steve would even feel it through his armoured plates.

"I appreciate that." Kayden settled into his familiar spot and prepared for a long journey.

"What did he say?" Rosalyn whispered. "Try as I might, I have trouble understanding him."

"He told me that all of the whinsomey giants want to see Malahd defeated. How many of them do you think there are in Erinbourne?"

"Not many, I don't think," she replied.

"There are precisely seven," Talbot said in a muffled voice from the bottom of Kayden's coat pocket. "And... while I might once have said that was seven too many, I since have changed my mind."

———

It was late afternoon when they stopped again. The valley they had travelled ended at the edge of the River Spye. It was at that point they had turned north, to avoid getting too close to the fortress. They continued to the beginnings of the River Spye found at the foot of a waterfall that began in a glacier high above the fortress.

There was little cover here. The land was made up of rolling hills leading to the foot of the Araleesh Mountains. They tried to stay as low as possible, but it took them much longer to work their way around the hills as opposed to going over them. Nonetheless, they soon came to the rocky edges of the mountain and realized Steve could take them no further.

"I—shall—stand—watch—and—do—what—I—can—here," the whinsomey said.

Rosalyn disentangled herself from his scales one last time and slid to the ground. "Thank you Steve." She rested a hand on his front leg.

Kayden jumped down as well, then walked around to face Steve.

"Your help has been invaluable," he said, trying to decide which eye to look into since he couldn't do both. "This trip could not have been accomplished without you and we are all grateful."

Kayden swept his arm to encompass Rosalyn and then Talbot who stood on his hind legs in the rocks nearby.

"Even—the—hedgehog?" Steve asked. This was the most interest he'd shown since the beginning of their adventure.

"Yes," Talbot said wearily. "Even the hedgehog."

Steve turned and lumbered off without a backward glance. Kayden bent to pick Talbot up and put him in his pocket. He, Rosalyn, and Talbot turned their faces toward the mountain and began to climb, knowing each step took them closer to doom.

Chapter Fourteen

There wasn't much time before all light would be gone, and the three focused their efforts on finding a safe spot to spend the night. Once the sun disappeared behind the mountains, shadows fell rapidly.

Some distance apart, Rosalyn and Kayden climbed the craggy boulders from a long ago rockslide, watching for possible places to both hide and keep a watchful eye on the plains below.

"I think I've got something," Rosalyn called.

Kayden stopped just as he was about to jump from one rock to another and traced his way to her. She stood on a narrow platform backed up against a sheer wall of stone that reared straight up about thirty-five meters, before disappearing over a ledge. On either side, the platform was framed by fallen rock. This created natural barriers well over their heads, probably nine or ten meters high, but out front there was only a low ridge of stone. It was perfect. Kayden scaled the wall of loose rocks and dropped inside.

Carefully, he lifted Talbot from his pocket and sat him down.

Kayden sagged against the wall behind him.

"This is a great spot, Rosalyn. But what a day." He bowed his head, and his next words were almost inaudible. "I've never used my bow to kill *anything* before, let alone a man."

Rosalyn dropped her bag with a crunch into the gravel at her feet and took two steps to reach him. She wrapped her arms around his neck and laid her head on his shoulder. Kayden gathered her close.

"It had to be done," she said at length, pulling away. "Those men made their choice long ago and it had nothing to do with us. They chose to follow evil for its own reward."

"There are times when hard decisions must be made," Talbot added from where he stood on a rock, surveying the landscape. "It was either them, or us, and we did what was necessary."

"I know you're right." Kayden ran a hand through his hair, causing it to stand out at right angles. "Yet, I can't help but feel I'm justifying the slaughter of six people, evil or not."

"Well, you had best get over it fast, because I see more of them out there," Talbot said. "And they do not have those same qualms."

Both Kayden and Rosalyn rushed to the ledge and peered in the direction Talbot pointed. Lengthening shadows made the enemy hard to detect at first, but soon Kayden saw movement in a copse of trees not far from where they had left Steve.

"There are five of them," Talbot said in a low voice. "I just watched them canter into that bluff on horseback, and it would appear they are surveying the mountain from the treeline."

"There is no light for them to search for us now," Rosalyn said, lifting her gaze to watch a flock of lazy crows flap past, squawking madly. She dropped down to sit cross-legged on the rocks below the ledge. "We must keep a watch tonight, without fail, and move before dawn."

"I agree," Talbot said. "As usual, since I am nocturnal, I will take the first and longest shift. Let us eat and then you must sleep."

Somewhere in the night, Kayden was startled into wakefulness by the sound of a scream, so piercing it echoed off the mountains and rattled the very rocks around his head. He and Rosalyn scrambled to their feet. All thoughts of sleep forgotten, they stared unseeing into the inky night.

"It sounded like Steve," Kayden whispered, his voice raspy and fearful. "But whether it was a scream of anger or —pain, I couldn't tell."

Rosalyn reached for Kayden's hand and held it tight. "It sounded more like anger to me, but we cannot risk going down there to check. He did his best to get us this far. We cannot jeopardize that now."

The first glow of a rising sun lightened a faint crack of the eastern sky before them.

"Talbot did not waken us for a shift. Where is he?" Kayden's throat constricted. Darkness still obscured the mountainside, but within moments the sun would lift over the edge of the world, and they would be revealed.

"Come," she said. "I am concerned about him too, but we cannot linger. If we wait for him here, we will be seen and captured. Malahd's men do not want him, they want you. Talbot is a formidable opponent and skilled at tracking. He will find us himself."

Rosalyn stooped to grab the bag she had rested her head upon. Gripping Kayden's arm, she shook it to rouse him from his reflection.

"There is no time for sentimentality. Move. Now!"

With barely a glimmer of light to see, Rosalyn edged her way up the side of their rocky enclosure with Kayden close behind. But the footing was unstable. As Kayden reached the top left side of their hiding spot and took a step, loose stones slid out from beneath his weight and skittered down the mountainside gathering speed and sound as they went. He fell heavily, the air knocked from his body, and slid a few meters, gasping for air.

From below came more noise, though this didn't sound like a rockslide. It sounded more like the passage of feet, hurrying toward them.

Rosalyn leapt lightly down beside him and tugged at Kayden's arm.

"Get up!" she said. "I see three pursuers, not far away."

Kayden got to his hands and knees, panting for air, but these small efforts only caused him to slide a little further. He grasped for a handhold in the slithering rocks, unable to control his passage. Movement caught his eye to the left. He squinted against the gloom and could make out a figure climbing steadily toward them. Cranking his head to the right, he scanned the rocks for more. There was another. In minutes, Malahd's men would be upon them and here he was lying flat on his stomach in a pile of rubble. It was no way to enter a battle.

Kayden tried to move forward again, but this time he only succeeded in slithering into the protected ledge where they had spent the night. He tumbled to the gravelly floor with a thud. Above him, Rosalyn also lost her footing. With a huff of expelled air, she too fell onto the smooth shale that surrounded them and slid down beside Kayden.

"We are trapped," she moaned. She scrabbled to her feet, standing on tiptoe to look over the ledge toward the swiftly rising sun. Drawing her sword, she braced herself, ready to face the killers who scaled the mountain after them.

"Not yet!" Feverishly, Kayden ripped open the bag Magda had given him and dug through the contents inside. "A-ha."

He pulled out the small glass bottle filled with a swirling incandescent green light.

Eluvia!

With some effort, he pulled off the thick cloth cover, noting that inside the neck of the bottle was a stopper with several holes punched into it. That's great, he thought, I don't want to use too much of this stuff. With a light hand, he bent low and then swooped the bottle up as high as he could reach along the sheer face of the cliff behind them.

Fine granules of a sparkling iridescent green powder sifted from the bottle and then took shape. Each tiny particle latched onto the other, climbing until they formed a thin, lime-coloured rope that sprouted tiny golden leaves as it went on, growing onto itself and mounting up and up, higher and higher, until it disappeared over the edge of the precipice above them.

Kayden reached out, took hold of the vine, and tugged. It held fast. The sound of boots hurrying over the rocks and a few shouts grew closer. He and Rosalyn only had a couple of minutes. Although he'd never been too great at climbing ropes in gym class, now was not the time to fail. As he tucked the glass vial away, he urged Rosalyn to grab the vine and climb. But the plant had other ideas.

The fragile leaves, glowing with a pale translucent gold, rustled as they extended on long twining stems toward first Rosalyn, and then Kayden. Twisting round and round, from their ankles to their torsos, the leaves enveloped them, curling and weaving until both were securely bound. Then, they were raised off their feet and became airborne. Kayden and Rosalyn exchanged long looks as they were slowly lifted away from the men who hunted them. They grinned with delight.

"Thank you, Magda, wherever you are," Rosalyn said softly.

Howling sounds of rage erupted beneath them as the men converged upon the cleft in the rock that had been Kayden, Rosalyn, and Talbot's sanctuary. Arrows whistled past them, most clanging uselessly against the cliff, but a few hitting their bodies with thuds. Yet neither of them was harmed. The vine and the leaves deflected the attack. Kayden bent his head, with some difficulty as he was so tightly bound, and looked below.

Where was Talbot? The hedgehog was nowhere to be seen although it would be hard to pick out such a small animal in the rubble at the base of the cliff.

"I'm worried about Talbot," Kayden finally put his fear into words.

"I know you are, but remember he is a skilled combatant," Rosalyn replied. "The good news is that Steve appears to have dealt with two of our pursuers."

As Kayden watched, the men abandoned their attempt to shoot him and Rosalyn with arrows and began instead to climb. They fanned out to avoid the problematic shale.

Kayden turned his attention up, seeing that he and

Rosalyn had almost topped the ledge. This vine was amazing. With a bump and a tug, they were up and over, laying at the top of the cliff. The vine loosened its grasp, unwinding from them quickly and flipping its gilded leaves back onto the broad expanse of rock.

Kayden and Rosalyn got to their feet and looked in wonder at the shriveling vine until all that was left of the lush green plant, and its golden leaves, was a little shimmering dust that floated away on the breeze.

"That was incredible!" Rosalyn said, pressing her hands to her cheeks. She bent to shake out her skirt and straighten the bindings that held her sword.

Kayden also felt a little cramped. His bow, and the runestaff, had been pressed against his back so hard that he could feel grooves in his shoulder blades. But he wasn't complaining.

"We have to keep moving. They won't be far behind us." Kayden unhooked his runestaff, deciding he needed to keep it close.

As they jogged across the flat plateau, Kayden scanned the rock for Talbot, despite knowing the hedgehog was much more capable of taking care of himself than he was. It was just that, in his tiny form, as a hedgehog, Talbot seemed so vulnerable. Kayden felt a rush of concern for his friend, even though Talbot was formidable and could defeat far greater adversaries than the three men who followed them.

Kayden knew they would have to find the door that Magda had spoken of, if they were to get inside the mountain and have any hope of reaching Malahd. With cutthroats close behind them, trying hard to end their lives, or worse, take them to Malahd, Kayden wondered how it would even be possible.

As if reading his thoughts, Rosalyn spoke. "I do not think we can lose those men who were after us, and it is not safe to leave them free to sound an alarm. What do you think we should do?"

"Capture them and tie them up?" Kayden raised his eyebrows. "I'd rather not do any more killing if possible."

"I understand. Yet, my rope is gone."

"I think Eluvia should do it," Kayden said as they strode along.

They were on a flat slab of rock, with boulders reaching high on either side of them. The climb to find the door at the mountains edge would soon begin. "Magda's map said to look for a distinctive ring of standing stones, hidden in a cleft just beneath that peak ahead of us, right?"

"Yes. But if they," Rosalyn said and jerked a thumb toward the men who hunted them, "follow us and find the gate, there is no hope in a surprise attack on Malahd. All would be lost."

"I get it." Kayden rubbed the back of his neck with one hand and drove his runestaff into the midst of a dead bush with the other. Then he looked at the staff and the germ of an idea began to form. "I wonder if Magda's vines would work as a net as well as a rope."

"Perhaps they would, at least for a time." Rosalyn flashed him a smile.

"I think so too." Kayden pointed. "See that narrow corridor, between the rocks ahead?"

She nodded.

"If I appear beyond it, as the bait to lure them in, you could climb up there, on that side above the pass, and drop a net over them. Then we bind them up and *voila*, no more trouble." His eyes brightened before he thought a little more and frowned. "Of course, there's always more trouble in

Erinbourne, but we'll figure that out later. What do you think?"

"It could work," she said.

They dashed to the spot where the plateau narrowed. Boulders had fallen down the craggy sides, forming a natural gateway beneath a large flat rock. This was where Rosalyn climbed while Kayden fished the small glass vial from his pouch again to see if his idea would work. Magda had told them it would create a rope to climb with; she'd said nothing about forming it into a net.

He held the vial up in the early morning light and gazed at the twinkling green particles within. Sure hope this works, he thought, mentally crossing his fingers. There was not a second to lose. Kayden sprinkled the smallest amount possible in a crisscross pattern on the rock in roughly a two-meter circle, and then stepped back to see what would happen.

The granules danced in the air. Then, they came together, forming narrow bands of green and gold that intersected and fused together. He lifted the makeshift net, and it draped gracefully over his hands and spilled around him on the rock like the most intricate of lace cloths. He tugged at it. The crystals formed a latticework light to the touch but impossible to break.

"I think it worked," he said. He was shocked. Nothing was ever this easy, especially in Erinbourne.

"Throw it to me," Rosalyn hissed from over his head. "Hurry!"

Placing the lace net on the end of his runestaff, he tossed it up to Rosalyn who then hid herself strategically.

"Get ready. They will arrive any minute," she said.

Kayden jogged beneath the overhang and ran a good distance away to wait on the other side. He needed to act as a decoy yet still maintain enough distance to avoid being impaled by a dozen arrows.

The first of the men reached the summit on the far-right side and dragged himself over the top to lay on the flat rock. The man crouched to wait, as the other two men hauled themselves up further along to the left. Moving warily, bows stretched at the ready, heads swivelling back and forth, they hunted their prey. Motioning to one another, they made moves to split up.

Kayden had reckoned on this. He had to attract their attention as fast as possible, in order to have them all move forward at once, so he jumped out from behind a boulder and fell to the ground with a yell.

"Ow!" He clutched his ankle in full view before flopping back to the stone.

That should get 'em, he thought grimly. He was a sitting duck, yet almost impossible to shoot. He flattened himself and rolled around as though in agony, turning his head so he could get a better view of the men's next move.

The group appeared startled to be presented with such an easy solution. Of course, they must have seen that Kayden had at least one companion. One man darted to the left, another to the right, and the last fellow came straight for him, trading out his bow for a sword and holding a shield before him.

"Great," Kayden muttered. "Why are there always curveballs?"

In order to keep attention on himself, Kayden kept up a steady stream of whining and moaning, hoping it would cause the men to be a little less vigilant. As the man with the sword got closer, Kayden feigned fear and struggled to pull himself away, dragging one leg behind him. He didn't want the one guy to get too close, after all.

Whimpering quite realistically, Kayden dragged himself across the cold stone, keeping a close eye on the man who was pursuing him. The other two had disappeared into the rocks on either side of the passage. Kayden's only visible pursuer broke into an eager jog, no doubt hoping to have the joy of telling Malahd that he alone had slain Erinbourne's future king. However, the man did have the presence of mind to glance up and around the overhang before passing beneath it. But even Kayden couldn't spot Rosalyn, so how could the warrior?

Malahd's agent passed beneath the stone, came out the other side, and bore down on Kayden's prostrate form. The dull metal of the man's shield and his upheld sword gleamed, while the sound of the man's huffing breath and flapping cloak at his side seemed loud.

Where was Rosalyn?

She leapt. Springing from a spot that was unexpected to both the man and to Kayden, she enveloped him with the lacy green net and twisted as she fell so it wrapped around him completely. The lace tightened of its own accord, tucking their attacker up into a neat package, almost as though it had known Rosalyn's intention all along. The man was not smothered, but he was held immobile, apparently it even extended to his mouth, since he made no sound at all.

Rosalyn leapt to her feet, drawing her sword in one smooth movement. "Well, that did *not* go according to plan, did it?"

Without sparing even a glance for Kayden, Rosalyn watched, with narrowed eyes, for the other men to attack.

Kayden clambered to his feet and looked down at the man they had captured. He glared through the web of living vines.

"You should be grateful," Kayden said, hauling the

man's body to one side and propping him against a dead tree. "We could have killed you."

Joining Rosalyn, Kayden lifted the bow from his back and loosely fitted an arrow. They moved cautiously down the passageway, each watching a side.

A pebble bounced toward them from somewhere on the left. They both snapped to attention. Rosalyn squared her stance and lifted her blade. Kayden drew back on the bowstring.

To the south of them, up the side of the fallen boulders, several other rocks were dislodged and rattled portentously as both men leapt from hiding. Across the rocks they came, brandishing their swords. It seemed clear to Kayden that he and Rosalyn were meant to be taken to Malahd as prisoners rather than corpses, as their pursuers had not taken the clear shots they must have had. Kayden braced himself for the onslaught.

Kayden's only defence was his bow. He fired twice in quick succession, but the men, leaping from stone to stone, moved too quickly for him to aim. His arrows shattered against the rock. And then the attackers were too close for him to raise his bow again. Kayden threw it down and lifted his runestaff, jumping aside as one of the men lunged at him, slashing his heavy sword.

Beside him, Rosalyn met her assailant head on, their swords clanging as she parried his blow and dealt one of her own that left the man reeling. She stepped forward and thrust. The man regained his balance and met her blade with his. They hung there, steel grinding against steel, continuing the battle as they broke away.

Kayden raised his runestaff in both hands to protect himself as the man's sword sliced the air again. Each time, however, Kayden was able to block his opponent's blow with the runestaff. An actual oaken staff would have been hacked to bits by now. Yet the runestaff did not suffer the slightest harm.

The man's cruel smile broadened as, with repeated attacks, he pushed Kayden across the open space until his heels hit the rocks behind him. Then the man pressed his advantage, and stepped forward, striking the runestaff over and over as he sought to overpower Kayden.

What am I doing?

Kayden realized how foolish this all was. He could hear the harsh, clanking blows of swords nearby, and the grunts of strain as Rosalyn and the other attacker battled. From the corner of his eye, he could see she was fighting an aggressive adversary, and his mind clenched with panic for her safety. But she was a warrior and he needed to block fear from his mind. His focus was now upon the many runes that ran down the full length of his staff, and he chose to project every thought upon a carving he had often longed to bring to life.

The man before him paused, breathing hard, his eyes flicking over Kayden.

Kayden knew Malahd's warrior only needed Kayden to make one wrong move and the staff would be flipped out of his hands. Kayden would have no recourse but to run, and the man could easily take him down with a well-placed arrow.

Yet that would never happen for the warrior now, because the staff was shifting. The warrior drew back with a gasp of surprise and unhappy realization, as the head of a cougar burst from the top of Kayden's runestaff. Its ears were laid flat against the broad head and the great, gaping mouth snarled, revealing its gleaming canine teeth. The runestaff became a sleek, powerful body twisting in the light of daybreak, shaking itself as it came to life and dropped to earth on huge, padded feet.

Kayden's attacker screamed. Holding his sword in front of him in feeble defense, he backed away, shouting for the other man to take notice. Then, his nerve broke and his sword clattered to the rocks as he turned and ran. It was to no avail. Muscles rippling, the tawny body was lithe and strong. The massive cougar coiled itself and sprang, pinning the man beneath razor sharp claws. The man's screams were muffled as the cat's two front paws spanned his chest, driving the air from his lungs. Kayden raced to him, his glistening bottle of Eluvia ready.

Red-faced and puffing, Rosalyn's attacker was backed up against a boulder. Kayden glanced at them. He had seen Rosalyn fight, and no one yet had come close to matching her abilities. Still, as Kayden bent to entwine the constricting magical vines about the hands of his assailant, he sent his thoughts toward the cougar who waited for instruction. He asked the runestaff to put a swift end to Rosalyn's battle.

With her back to him, Kayden knew Rosalyn had not noticed the events of the last few minutes. Not even the cougar's snarl had intruded on her focus. Her strength was aimed solely upon the man who had tackled her; a man well-trained in the art of combat, from what Kayden could see, but one that was losing, nonetheless.

Kayden stood up from securing the vines in time to see Rosalyn flinch as the powerful body of the animal brushed past her arm. Then the cougar leapt, growling, lips drawn back over its teeth. The man's eyes widened in terror. He screamed, lifting his sword with both hands and bending backwards over a boulder. He thrust it up at the beast, penetrating its breast as the cougar's body came down upon the man and crushed him to the rock.

With a stab of fear for his runestaff, Kayden ran to them. But the only blood that ran red was that of Rosalyn's adversary. The man slid down the rock, a gash on the back of his head leaving a long streak behind him, while Kayden's cougar, once pierced, had merely transmuted back into the familiar staff. It lay waiting for him beside the dead warrior.

Rosalyn staggered back to lean against the side of the passage, breathing heavily.

"Well, that was a fight," she said, sliding down to squat.

Kayden crouched down to check for signs of life from the dead man. Rosalyn sheathed her sword and stood as Kayden straightened and walked toward her.

"His death could not have been helped," she said quietly. "What now? Is it not a cruel way to leave the others?"

Kayden took her arm and led her away so that no one could hear. "I believe that once we have found the gate and passed through it, my influence over the vines will be broken and the vines will disintegrate as they did before." He shrugged. "Of course, I don't know that for sure, but something tells me it will work that way. In any case, we have no choice. I can't kill them in cold blood."

"I understand." Rosalyn pushed her damp hair away from her face. "We should go then."

She stepped off along the narrowing corridor, but since there was only room for one to pass at this point, Kayden followed closely behind.

Nothing else seemed amiss, although they kept sharp eyes on the rocks above lest more attackers appear.

A rock dislodged and fell. Then something small and

grey bounced from above and bowled along the path before them. They came to an abrupt standstill, peering up to either side, and readied their weapons once again. All was silent. Yet, stones didn't just fall on their own. The tiny rock came to a stop and Kayden eyed it suspiciously.

"Hello!" the rock said brightly, unfurling itself into a mouse.

"Millinworth?" Kayden's mouth hung open and his eyes bulged. "It—it can't be!"

He lowered his bow and shook his head in disbelief.

"You know this vermin?" Rosalyn looked incredulous. She pointed the tip of her sword at the little grey body, awaiting further information.

Kayden knelt down to speak to the mouse.

"Tell your friend to cease and desist!" Millinworth squeaked, running to cower behind Kayden's knee. "I simply came to aid you in your worthy quest after returning here with my friends, which was quite a journey I can assure you. But well worth the trouble in that I am sure you were able to warn the king. Although word has it, he died, so perhaps you were not in time after all. Yet I can hardly be blamed as I did my—"

"Enough," Kayden said sternly, scanning the rocks around them for signs of more trouble. He looked up at Rosalyn. "Yes. I know her. Millinworth is a spy for the Resistance. She came to Durgot just before I arrived with word that Malahd intended to kill the king."

"I see," Rosalyn said, without enthusiasm. "Yes, I too have heard the name of Millinworth, but have not had the opportunity to meet her in person."

She turned to focus on the rocks around them as though she wasn't too interested in taking advantage of the opportunity now either.

"Look, Millinworth," Kayden said. "We're in a bit of danger at the moment, so could I just put you in my pocket to keep you safe and we can talk later?"

"Certainly," she squeaked.

Kayden opened his hand and laid it, knuckles down on the ground for Millinworth to scamper onto his palm. Lifting her, Kayden released the mouse into his voluminous pocket.

"We must not stay here," Rosalyn said tersely. "Keep going."

"You certainly ought to!" said an emphatic Millinworth, creeping up the side of Kayden's pocket to peep her head out the top. "Although I could not see what happened, as I hid quite carefully from the sight of those awful men. I am not ashamed to say that the whole skirmish gave me quite a fright." She took a tiny breath. "May be permitted to speak my mind?"

Millinworth paused as though asking a question—but continued because of course, she was not. "I am thrilled to hear that you finally intend to look for the ancient door into the mountain, and make your way secretively to Malahd's chambers, where I am sure you shall take him unawares. Such a diabolical sorcerer as he can seldom be taken by surprise, but perhaps if you are very stealthy you may do it, with my help and expertise and crafty abilities, not to mention my winning personality. Although—"

"Yes, thank you for your insight, Millinworth," Kayden interjected. "And though I'm not sure what good a winning personality will do for us; I do appreciate your offer."

He looked up, hoping to share an eye roll with Rosalyn, but she gave no indication she was even listening to the incessant chatter of the mouse. She kept her back to them both and marched sturdily on.

"Are you saying you know where the old entrance into the passages of the Garde may be?" Kayden directed his question back to Millinworth.

She wiggled with glee at being asked a question of such importance. Craning his neck, he looked down at her. The mouse gripped the top of his pocket with tiny claws, her small black eyes watching the path in front of them.

"Yes, yes, yes, of course I do," she said, her back claws scrabbling for a foothold in the coarse cloth of his coat. "I would be only too happy to aid you and your—girl companion, to whom you have not yet given me the courtesy of an introduction. I must say, it is rather bad manners, young man. I mean, we are associates of the highest order, sent forth to deliver the king or at the very least to take back what was his and restore order and peace to the land, despite the fact we are only a boy, a girl, and a mouse. Granted I am a mouse of very high standing among such important people of the land as I cannot even begin to tell you. Although I could tell you if you wish to hear of my many exploits and dealings with influential—"

"Do *not*, I beg of you!" Rosalyn stopped short, turned on her heel, and addressed the mouse in a voice threaded with steel. "Please do not trouble yourself to regale us with tales of your stature among the hierarchy of this land. I am sure we are not worthy of such knowledge, nor do I, for one, wish to hear about it at all. My name is Rosalyn. If you are able to point us in the direction we should go, or help us once we are within the mountain, I would be obliged to you. Apart from that, I would appreciate travelling in *silence*."

She emphasised her last word with such vigor that Millinworth let go of her grip on Kayden's coat and toppled down to hunker at the bottom of his pocket.

"Well! I have never been treated with such disdain," she

grumbled. "Who does that girl think she is, I ask you? Someone told me once that she was close to the king, which seems quite difficult to believe since he would not allow such rudeness from his subjects, I am positive. I could no more…"

Kayden tuned out the mouse and hurried to catch up to Rosalyn who strode along faster than before. The path had broadened again, making it possible to walk side by side, but it was quite steep as they climbed in search of the standing stones.

"I do not think we need help to find the door," Rosalyn said over her shoulder. "I see the tips of the standing stones just as Magda described them to us."

She pointed to where several pointed rocks poked over the slight rise in the flat expanse of rock leading up to the face of the mountain.

"Perhaps Millinworth will help us once we're inside," Kayden said. "Magda did say it was a maze inside the mountain. Many of the Garde used to live here, before Respiele took it over."

"Perhaps," Rosalyn said absently. She gazed up into the rocks on either side of them. "I have now joined you in your concern for Talbot. Malahd will have sent many other search parties to find us. The hedgehog could well have been captured."

"Did I hear that girl say that Talbot was travelling with you?" Millinworth asked in a muffled voice.

"Yes," Kayden said in an aside to the mouse. To Rosalyn, he answered, "That's my fear too."

Millinworth shuffled uneasily in Kayden's pocket. "This is not good news at all. I had thought you to be alone with the girl." She became still and then added a bit louder, "I wish he were here. We shall need all the help we can get once reaching Malahd's fortress."

Coming over the final swell of rock, they reached the first of the standing stones, surprising a crow, who had been sitting on the monolith closest to the mountain preening his feathers. He squawked and flapped into the distance. Was it a spy? Kayden had to consider that almost any creature could be a potential threat, but there was nothing he could do about it except hurry.

Now that they had arrived, Kayden marvelled at the massive flat slabs of stone that comprised the circle. There were seven of them in all, arranged in a ring not far from where the sheer face of the mountain rose hundreds of meters into the sky. The stones appeared to have been erected into chiseled out grooves, and then backfilled with smaller rocks that wedged into any empty chinks to keep the megaliths upright. It was amazing. Kayden had heard of such things in Europe. He'd even written a school report on the most famous of these prehistoric monuments, Stone-henge on the Salisbury Plain in England, but he'd never been there. Seeing a stone circle up close was fantastic.

He ran a hand along the first stone and shivered. It was like touching a block of ice. Casting long shadows against the mountain, each stone stood like a silent custodian of a bygone age. Were any of the Garde left in this place? Or had they all, like Magda, been driven out by the evil that had taken up residence long ago?

Rosalyn walked into the center of the circle and stopped.

"Quite an achievement, is it not?" She turned slowly about. "I am trying to imagine what it was like several hundred years ago when this sacred place must have been used regularly."

"It's really cool," Kayden responded in hushed tones. He noticed her raise a hand to stifle a smile. "What?"

"It has been a long time since I have heard you use the word 'cool' to describe something." Rosalyn became serious. "Have you not yet received detailed instructions as to the location of the doorway from your friend, the mouse?"

"No. I think she's gone to sleep."

"Then we will locate it ourselves." Rosalyn moved through the circle to the stone where the crow had sat and stood with her back to it, facing the mountain. "According to Magda, the door should directly align with this stone, correct?"

"Yes." Kayden waited as Rosalyn walked forward and began to finger the rock wall in front of her.

"I do not see any sign of a doorway." She lifted her hands in puzzlement.

"I think it'll be similar to the portal I use to enter Erinbourne. It can only be found by using my runestaff." Kayden moved to stand beside her. Lifting the staff, he twisted it until he could clearly see the image of the mountain near the top. He centered his thoughts on what he needed at that moment.

The staff quivered in his hand before warming to his touch. The rune blazed. As Kayden watched, an answering light arched from the rune on his staff to the mountain, landing on a spot above his head. Then, as though he had set a match to a streak of gunpowder, the light sizzled in either direction, sending sparks flying. A jagged line of white flame traced a line across the rock horizontally and then turned sharply down to end on either side of Kayden and Rosalyn. Left behind of the blazing white flame, was the clear outline of a door, brilliant with light. And at the center of the door, a small indentation sank noiselessly into the rock. It was there that Kayden aimed his runestaff and struck with all of his might. The door swung wide.

"*Après vous, mademoiselle,*" Kayden said with an attempt at lightening the mood. He swept his arm into the opening, indicating Rosalyn should precede him.

She passed within and Kayden moved to join her. But before following her down the dark passageway that stretched before them, he paused in the entrance and turned, taking one last look for his friend the hedgehog. Yet, Talbot was nowhere to be seen. Kayden stepped back with a worried frown, and with a deafening thud, the door swung shut.

Chapter Fifteen

It was with a heavy heart that Kayden heard the door seal itself. Talbot was out there somewhere, alone. He feared for the hedgehog despite knowing how capable he was. But they couldn't have afforded the time or risked the danger associated with looking for him. They must keep pressing onward.

It was dark inside the chamber. Kayden took a tentative step, but tripped over the uneven floor and pitched forward. He bumped into Rosalyn, and she caught his arms to steady him. They needed light. He raised his staff and the sun rune shone like a beacon in the darkness.

"That is better," Rosalyn said, sounding relieved.

Weird shadows flickered in corners of the small rocky space they found themselves in.

"What a wonderful variety of uses you find for that staff of yours," she said. "I meant to thank you for your assistance back there. A cougar was most imaginative."

"I can't create anything that isn't a rune on my staff to begin with." Kayden shrugged. He beamed his light down the path. "I guess we'll walk until there's a decision to be made and then I'll wake Millinworth."

"By all means, do not hurry to arouse her."

Kayden looked at Rosalyn sharply. "You don't like her, do you?"

He led the way along a narrow shaft that had been hewn from solid rock. There was only room for them to proceed in single file and, due to the irregular floor, they moved along at what felt like a snail's pace.

"I find her—irritating," Rosalyn said at length.

Gradually, the passage led them down lower and lower, into the bowels of the mountain. As they descended, they passed doors that Kayden thought must be the abandoned homes of the Garde, carved from the rock and fitted with wooden doors.

Intricate runes and symbols were etched into the wood, but there was so much dust they were difficult to make out. A few resembled the animals depicted on his staff, and one or two of them even looked like dragons. He knew from what Durgot had told him on his last visit that dragons were what the Garde of the Araleesh Mountains were known for.

Kayden tried to open a door, but the handles wouldn't budge. They looked as though they hadn't been opened in a hundred years. Thick dust covered the ornate knobs, and, from side to side across the roughly cut openings, cobwebs hung in dirty ribbons. Even the spiders had abandoned their homes. The air was stale and only a slight movement of air from below lent any freshness at all to their breathing.

"It is sad." Rosalyn's voice echoed although she spoke quietly. They were trying to make as little noise as possible.

"What?"

"How the Garde fled their homes and were forced to

join the regular world, because of Respiele and Malahd. This had been their domain since time began."

Kayden had been thinking much the same thing. His own family had lived here. He found himself thinking how well his Gran must have known these corridors. Perhaps one of these apartments had been hers, the home she shared with her mother.

"It is surprising to me that the western portal into your world was not smashed by Respiele or Malahd," Rosalyn continued in her soft voice. "With the Garde gone, it would have been possible to pass through the gates into your world and back again as often as they wished. Respiele could have expanded his vision and made plans to conquer a whole other world. Your world, Kayden."

Her voice trailed off into silence. All that could be heard was their shuffling steps as they made their way across the mountain range toward Malahd's stronghold.

Kayden pondered what she said. The story of how his grandmother had been driven from her home in the Araleesh Mountains, and the remarkable circumstances in which his grandfather came to be in Erinbourne and fight in a war that was not his own, must be fascinating. Mentally, he told himself to ask Gran about it when he returned home.

If he returned home.

To Rosalyn he said, "The path is dividing up ahead. I'm not sure which turn to make, so I think we'd better ask Millinworth."

Gently, he jostled the pocket where the mouse lay sleeping. "Millinworth? Please wake up."

Groggily, the squeaky voice answered without hesitation. "Turn left."

Kayden looked back at Rosalyn and shook his head.

"How can you know that?" he asked the mouse. "You haven't looked to see where we are."

"I know the first crossroads you will arrive at, and which way to turn. The answer is left." The mouse subsided into silence once more, sounding distinctly miffed.

"Do you think she heard me say...you know?" Rosalyn moved up to Kayden and whispered into his ear.

He shrugged.

They came to the fork and turned to the left. There was no variation in the width or size of the passage. Each one had low ceilings, forcing Kayden to stoop as he walked, and they were quite narrow. Granted, the Garde were a small race of people, but didn't they ever want to walk two abreast, or carry anything wider than themselves?

He and Rosalyn trudged on in this way before he held up a hand to stop at another crossroads.

"Turn right this time," Millinworth said. "Then, at the next intersection, take the passage to the left."

Kayden heard the smallest of yawns. The mouse sounded bored.

In the light of his runestaff, Kayden raised an eyebrow at Rosalyn. She gave a non-committal shrug, and Kayden, holding his Runestaff before him, led the way down the right corridor.

"When we arrive at this next turn, I think we should stop, eat something, and talk to Millinworth," he said to Rosalyn. "I have a few questions for her. And I'm hungry."

It took only about half an hour to reach the next fork in the road. Kayden stepped into the small chamber that marked the crossing and motioned that Rosalyn should sit down. He dragged the bow from his back and looked for the food Magda had given him.

Rosalyn lowered herself to the stone floor with a sigh

of gratitude, moved the sword on her back to a more comfortable resting place, and examined her own pack for something edible. Kayden propped his staff against the wall for light and woke Millinworth before helping her out of his pocket. The little gray mouse scuttled off his hand and stood on the cold floor rubbing her eyes and looking about.

"Can I offer you something to eat?" Kayden asked politely in a low voice. "I've got biscuits, several sorts of dried fruit, and a bag of nuts."

"I would like two cashews please," Millinworth said, casting a sideways look at Rosalyn. The mouse hunkered in front of the nuts with her tiny back to the girl and addressed Kayden. "You had questions for me?"

Rosalyn rolled her eyes in the dim light of the runestaff and bit into a biscuit before washing the dry morsel down with a sip of water from her flask.

"Yes," Kayden answered. He swallowed a mouthful of fruit. "I was wondering how far we have to travel through the mountain before we get close to where Malahd lives?"

"Two, maybe three hours, at least," Millinworth said, nibbling on a cashew. "It depends how fast you are. And before you arrive, you will need a strategy and a plan."

She was uncharacteristically brief in her responses and Kayden could only surmise the mouse had indeed over-heard Rosalyn's unfortunate remarks.

"That brings me to my next question," he said. "Have you been inside the fortress to spy on Malahd since he stole the sceptre? Do you know where it is?"

Millinworth's whiskers twitched. Kayden guessed the mouse fancied herself a superior spy and loved to acquire knowledge and deliver news. They were likely the reasons she was good at her work.

She left her cashews on the floor to clamber up his knee and cup tiny paws around her mouth.

"I have most certainly been inside the sorcerer's chambers, yes, yes, yes. His *private* chambers, if you please," she said in a loud stage whisper. "And I am privy to every detail of his actions both small and great since he returned from that—unfortunate incident, we shall call it, in which you lost both the sceptre and the king. Although you did your best, I am positive of that."

"How do you know what I did, or what happened to Ludwig Larkender?"

"I am an emissary of the king," she said, drawing herself up to her full height and sniffing with her nose in the air as though her credibility had been questioned. "I listen, I watch, I take notice of the subtleties that others miss. That is what makes a good spy, and I am the best, best, best."

Rosalyn snorted from the far wall and Millinworth turned her back a fraction further, as though to block Rosalyn from hearing the conversation.

"If I may continue without interruption?" Millinworth said pointedly, looking at Kayden, but raising her voice to mean Rosalyn. "Malahd keeps the sceptre belted to his waist at all times—except…" the mouse paused for dramatic effect, before continuing, "when he sleeps. It lies beside him on his bed, but with my guidance, stealthy manoeuvering, and a bit of luck, it could be secreted away. Drawing upon my expert calculations, we should arrive tonight at just the right hour for this to be accomplished."

She brushed an imaginary speck of dust from her velvety coat and fluttered her lashes.

"*If* you follow my directions to the letter, since I know all of the corridors, including where Malahd's sleeping chamber lies, hiding places along the way, and where the guards stand watch, you should easily be able to escape the castle with the sceptre, and flee to freedom!" Millinworth finished on a high, triumphant note, her arms flung wide to emphasize the success of the venture that she alone would orchestrate.

"That sounds great!" Kayden said. "I'd appreciate your help a lot. Thank you, Millinworth. Now, you'd better finish your lunch so we can continue on our way."

She hopped off his knee and, with a further sniff in Rosalyn's direction, settled herself to finish her meal.

Kayden, Rosalyn, and Millinworth continued to hike along the passageway, only making one more stop to take a drink from the vessel of water Magda had included. This was completed in silence, lest their voices echo along the hallways and alert anyone scouting the passages before them.

As before, there were occasional rooms chiseled into the rock, fitted with broad, short doors. The passageway branched off many more times, sometimes offering three or four different choices. Yet Millinworth did not hesitate in her unswerving course. While Durgot's boussole had been programmed to get them to Malahd's fortress, by taking the mountain paths that Magda had known as a young woman, Kayden felt sure Millinworth knew more about the intricacies of the route they must follow to avoid detection, and how best to reach the sorcerer's bedroom.

As they made their way deeper into the mountain range, Kayden found himself thinking what an amazing place it was, almost like a rabbit warren. He wondered if Durgot's mountain was filled with people, as this had clearly once been. The little man had never mentioned anyone else who might live there.

A faint illumination came from around a bend up ahead. Kayden lifted a hand of caution to Rosalyn and beckoned her come up close behind him. With his pack and weapons protruding from his back, there was barely room for him to turn around, but he managed to angle himself a little and whisper to Rosalyn.

"Take care. There's light ahead."

They inched along the alley. The light ahead took on a soft green hue, as they came to the crook in the path and eased around it. Ahead, Kayden could see that the passageway ended and a wide-open area lay before them. A cluster of spiny-looking bushes grew across the mouth of the cave-like tunnel they were in, sheltering it from view of the outside world. Branches filtered light onto the walls and floor.

How could that be?

Kayden edged up to the leafy fronds and parted them to look out into a huge open space much like Durgot's circular home within the Ildune Mountain. Branches scraping and tearing at his clothes, Kayden forced his way into the thicket and Rosalyn joined him. Soundlessly, they took it all in.

The area before them must have thrived at one time, just as Durgot's did, but it wasn't anymore. It was a larger space than Durgot's home, with several tall, storied houses standing each on a separate hummock in a ring at the center. It was apparent they had once been colourful dwellings, as faded blue, red, and orange paint still clung to their sides. Their windows looked blankly out upon this world.

There wasn't any cheerful sunlight here, as there was for Durgot. Here it was as though storm clouds lay heavy over the life-giving rays of warmth. There was a muted sort of light from above, but it appeared to be having trouble getting in. Grass and weeds had choked out the fertile fields that must have been present once. The houses looked abandoned. The fruit trees, planted in rows to their right, looked barren and shriveled, and a waterfall to their immediate left was only a gurgling trickle of brownish sludge. The disgusting water was probably the only thing keeping the bushes they had passed through alive. Everything else looked dry, dead, and brown.

Kayden pushed further and came out into the clearing on the other side of the doorway. He held the bushes for Rosalyn and then let them spring closed at their backs. He drew in a breath and an overwhelming sadness enveloped him. He looked across at Rosalyn. Pain reflected in her eyes. This was the heart of the Araleesh Mountains, and Kayden knew, from Durgot's similar chamber, that the Gatekeeper would have lived in one of these houses. Who guarded the portals to the outside world now?

But he already knew the answer—no one.

A smell of decay and rotting vegetation filled Kayden's nostrils. This was the birthplace of his family. Anger surged in his heart for all that had been lost thanks to a sinful greed for supremacy. All thanks to his own flesh and blood—his great grandfather, Respiele. On account of him, the corrupt Malahd was given the opportunity to grow in power. And now that the cruel sorcerer was in possession of Erinbourne's Gemstones of Power, he would have ultimate command—the ability to overthrow anyone and rule the entire land of Erinbourne.

The gemstones each represented something different. The Emerald had the ability to heal people, or even a land, but what had Durgot said about the others? Malahd had possessed the Amethyst before. It had the ability to influence people, for good or evil. The Ruby lent physical strength and the Sapphire gave its owner courage. The gemstones had been created at the beginning of this world and gave their owner absolute authority. No one could win against the one who held the sceptre.

But he had to try.

"I *will* stop him." Kayden spoke barely above a whisper, but in his mind, he shouted from the mountaintops to every Garde who had ever lived and died in this place: their homeland—and his. He would not allow this persecution to continue any longer.

Kayden dug his runestaff into the ground at his feet and straightened his shoulders. The domination of this oppressor, Malahd, would end here.

"Millinworth," Kayden said sharply. "Which way do we go now?"

The mouse made several revolutions at the bottom of his pocket before popping her head out the top. Kayden sensed that she was anxious.

"I did not mean to bring you this way," the mouse whined, after gazing at her surroundings for a moment. "We must go back."

"Go back?" Rosalyn snapped. "That is ridiculous. It took a long time to get this far from that last junction. There must be another exit that will advance us further in our quest."

She wheeled on Kayden. "Why do you not use the boussole? It will tell us."

"No!" Millinworth screeched. "I will lead you. A boussole cannot take you to the sorcerer's sleeping chamber or avoid the sentries he has stationed along the way."

The mouse rushed from her hiding place and scurried

up Kayden's jacket, clinging to his shoulder by digging her tiny claws into the collar.

"Aim toward those trees at the far end." She lifted one paw to point in the direction he should go.

Kayden caught Rosalyn's eye. "Well, she does know where the guy sleeps. That alone makes it worth listening to what she says."

"Very well," Rosalyn said, although grudgingly. She lifted her skirts to step over a dead tree that had fallen across the path. "Let us go."

With Millinworth clutching to his shoulder, Kayden struck out across the dry landscape that lay before him. He crunched through brown vegetation at his feet, and dust from the withered plants billowed up, causing him to sneeze.

He focused on the tight group of trees Millinworth had indicated. They were the same strange trees he had seen at Durgot's, with horizontal branches, but these were nearly dead. A few tired leaves clung to the uppermost twigs. It only served to rile Kayden further, and he strode with purpose across the naked land, soon reaching the other side.

"The opening for this pathway is small," Millinworth warned. "You will have to get onto your hands and knees, yes, yes, yes. Although even then you may struggle to wedge your great bulk inside the secret tunnel."

Her prattle stopped without remarks from either Rosalyn or Kayden this time.

Squinting, Kayden could see the sparse remains of bushes that had concealed the entry. Beyond them looked like a dark gap in the rock face only big enough to creep through. With Rosalyn at his side, Kayden dove under the lowest limbs of the trees and jumped into a ditch that must have been a creek bed encircling the formerly fertile space.

He and Rosalyn scrabbled up the other side and stood looking at the hole they needed to pass through.

"I'll go first," Kayden said.

Stripping off his bow and pack, he bent down to clear a way through the brush. The withered plants snapped away in his hands and he tossed them aside.

"Ready?" he asked Rosalyn.

"Ready."

"Wait, wait, wait," Millinworth squeaked from his shoulder. "I will go first. After all, I know these trails best and like it or not. I have by far the most knowledge of this mountain, having lived here much of my life, which by the way made me a perfect candidate to be chosen as King Larkender's spy since…"

"Yes, yes, we get the idea," Rosalyn interjected, and gestured with a mocking bow that the mouse should precede them.

Millinworth's claws gripped the cloth of Kayden's coat, snagging tiny threads as she made her way down to the ground. Then, with a backward glance from her beady black eyes, she disappeared into the darkened cavern.

Kayden, pushing his bow, arrows, runestaff, and pack in front of him, crouched and eased himself into the small cave-like entrance.

Talk about dust. He coughed several times before he could stop himself and paused to listen for any sounds ahead. Thankfully, nothing disturbed the silence that surrounded him. Kayden wondered why the ancient Garde had created such a small space. Even they would have been forced to crawl through here and at six feet tall, he was having a real struggle. Wiggling and sometimes slithering his body along the rough rock base under his hands and knees, he inched along.

"You okay back there?" he whispered hoarsely to Rosalyn, before sneezing loudly again.

"Shhh!" she hissed. "I am alright. Keep going."

Darkness surrounded them. Kayden had forgotten to light the runestaff before entering. Grasping it in his hand, he let his thoughts feel for the image of a sun and the staff warmed and brightened to illuminate the claustrophobic chamber around them.

"Thanks," Rosalyn whispered from behind him. "That makes things easier."

He smiled and shoved everything ahead before pulling himself further along. Light danced on the chinks of rock around him. He raised his head to look for Millinworth, but the mouse was nowhere to be seen. The passage seemed to go on for some distance and he sighed.

Great. Where was that loudmouth mouse?

After about twenty minutes, however, the way began to widen, allowing him to come up onto his knees, sit back on his legs, and stop. He lifted the staff as high as it would go.

There appeared to be a small chamber ahead with another passage leading off it, much like they had travelled on before. What a relief. Only a couple more minutes and they could stand up. As he dropped to his hands, he wondered how Rosalyn was making out in a dress—her poor knees.

There was a slight drop from the tunnel they had traversed, into an open area, and he stumbled over it gratefully and then scrambled to his feet to turn and help Rosalyn. Then, both stood to brush themselves off and look down the next length of under-mountain tunnel they would take.

"Where is Millinworth?" Rosalyn asked quietly, as she

pulled on her pack and slung her sword across her back once more.

"I don't know. Last time I saw her was when we entered the cave." Kayden beamed the runestaff around the room, but the dark stone seemed to suck the light away, revealing nothing but shadows. Thankfully, there was only one way to go from where they stood, so they started along the narrow passage with caution.

The sudden sound of metal scraping against rock had them rooted to the spot. It seemed to come from down the corridor behind them.

"Was that you?" Kayden asked in a fierce undertone, hoping she would say yes, but knowing the grating noise came from farther back than where they stood.

Then the sound came again, only ahead of them this time.

Rosalyn's hand clenched the back of Kayden's coat as she struggled to turn herself, free her sword, and face whatever was coming down the passage behind her, while Kayden lifted his staff and peered ahead. He didn't have the space needed to even reach for his bow and arrows.

Without warning, huge stones were hurled from a cavity over their heads. They were well-aimed blows knocking both the sword from Rosalyn's hand and the runestaff out of Kayden's grasp. Before either of them could react, they were rendered unconscious and buried by a river of falling rock.

Chapter Sixteen

Kayden groaned. He lay on his side, his feet and hands bound in front of him, his cheek resting against sharp edged rocks. He tried to lift his head and open his eyes a crack, but the effort sent his brain reeling with waves of pain that rocketed around his skull, so he sank back down. Coherent thought was nearly impossible, but he struggled to clear the fog and remember what happened.

He heard another moan, but this time it wasn't him. His eyes flew open, dismissing the throbbing ache, and focused on simply breathing in and out before he spoke.

"Rosalyn, are you okay?" His words came out slurred.

She moaned again in response. He sighed with relief. At least she was alive.

Wherever they were, the darkness was complete. He could see nothing.

His runestaff! He couldn't afford to lose the precious staff. In his mind, he reached out to it, despite the pain in his aching head.

"You will not find what you seek." A voice, low and

raspy, came from the inky blackness, and a fiery torch burst into flames nearby.

Kayden shut his eyes against the pain of light, his heart sinking and his pulse racing.

"Who—are—you?" he managed to get out.

"That does not concern the likes of you," the voice said. "But my master will be pleased to know you have awakened. He has been waiting to speak with you."

Kayden heard a scuffing sound and opened his eyes a crack to see a shadowy figure raise the blazing light as it stood. Flames flickered against the walls of the cavern they were in. The figure moved and Kayden watched as the person opened a rounded door nearby, bent to duck beneath it, and stepped through.

With more bravado than he actually felt, Kayden called after the man. "Tell him I have a few questions for him too."

Silhouetted in the doorway, the figure paused. Then, with a click the door snapped shut. Kayden and Rosalyn were alone.

Kayden gulped. What was he going to do?

"Rosalyn?"

"I am alive and awake. Do not worry about me," she said. Her voice sounded rough, breaking the deafening silence in the cave. She coughed. "Do you have your boussole? Can you reach it?"

Kayden struggled to push a hand into the small back pocket of his breeches, thankful he had put the boussole there. It took some manoeuvering, but he sagged with relief when the cold metal of the boussole greeted his fingertips. Bit by bit, he drew it from his pocket, but it was taking too long. Finally, he held it loosely in his hand and was able to flip it open.

A soft yellow glow lit the space. They were in a low-ceilinged, dome-shaped room that had been cut from the rock. Loose stones and shale lay on the floor near the edges. In the center where Rosalyn lay beside him, it was flat and smooth. She looked first at him and then to the doorway.

"We are truly in a bad way," she said. "My sword has been taken. Your runestaff too? And bow?"

"Gone."

"The only reason they are keeping us alive is because Malahd has something he wants to learn from you, right? What do you suppose it could be?"

"I have no idea. But we need to get out of here before he gets hold of us or we're done." While speaking, Kayden had been worming himself toward the wall where the jagged rocks lay in heaps. He snapped the boussole shut and, with difficulty, slid it back into his pocket. It wouldn't do to have that guy return and find the only aid they had left to them.

With his feet pushing and scraping for a toehold on the unyielding surface, he shoved himself back, edging his shoulder and body by tiny increments, and lifting himself to inch backward until he could feel the stones at the cave's edge. With fingers swollen and cramped, he felt for a stone that might sever his bonds.

Ah, found one! With short, steady thrusts, Kayden grated at the ties that bound his hands. The sharp edge also cut at his skin, but he didn't care. All that mattered was to get free before the man returned to take them to Malahd.

He heard Rosalyn also move herself across the room until her back was against the rocks. Kayden knew she was doing the same.

The material was fraying. Bits of it snapped and loosened around his bleeding wrists. A few more moments of renewed scraping and they broke. His hands were free! Kayden pushed himself upright and felt for the same rock to begin slicing at the rope around his ankles. This had the potential to take longer, as the rope was long and had been wound time after time around the length of his lower legs. He couldn't even feel his feet anymore, but he concentrated on cutting just one of them, and was rewarded with a snap as the rope fell to the stony floor.

Although his fingers were stiff, and his head pounding, Kayden lost no time in unwinding the remainder of rope from his lower half. He chaffed his ankles before lifting the sharp rock and feeling his way over to Rosalyn, where he wordlessly began working on her bindings.

Hurry!" she whispered, fear radiating from her body in a palpable wave. "I hear something."

Footsteps echoed from somewhere outside the room. Frantically, she sawed at the rope around her hands and Kayden likewise knelt at her feet doing the same.

Keys jangled at the door.

Rosalyn lay back on the stones, panting. Kayden got unsteadily to his feet, felt for the wall with one hand, and brought up a rock in the other. Stumbling on loose stones, Kayden felt his way along the wall and stopped beside the door. His heart pounded against his ribs. Taking a deep breath, he held it.

A key was thrust in the lock and the door swung open. In the pool of light that entered with his unseen adversary, Kayden could see Rosalyn across the chamber, slumped against the rocks as though unconscious.

"Curses!" The man moved into the room and scanned the area for Kayden, closely followed by two others.

"Where is the boy?" the first man yelled at Rosalyn,

kicking her viciously in the side. She bent over double with the blow and moaned.

With all his might, Kayden swung the heavy wooden door shut from behind, crashing it into one of the men who reeled back through it. Then Kayden leapt at a second man, raised the heavy rock above his head, and brought it smashing down upon the soldier's head. He crumpled to the floor.

Kayden whirled around. He crouched, ready to battle with the soldier holding the torch. The man's eyes glittered at Kayden from several paces away, and torchlight glinted off the dull metal sword he carried.

Then, without warning, the fire was extinguished. The place went dark. Kayden, still holding the rock, his chest heaving as he took great gasping gulps of stale air, feverishly slashed at the air around him. His adversary was advancing on him. Any minute Kayden would feel the thrust of cold steel, he just knew it.

There was a sudden scuffling, a flurry of movement from down low. A deep-throated yell, and someone fell, brushing past Kayden's legs as they crashed to the ground. Then silence.

"Get that boussole of yours open so we might see," Rosalyn said between gasps.

The rock clattered from Kayden's hands to the floor as he fumbled for the boussole and opened it. In the warm, yellow glow he saw her, sprawled on the floor with the last of the unconscious sentries lying half across her feet.

Kayden sprang to her, yanking the heavy body away. "He kicked you in the ribs! Are you alright?"

She slumped against the rocks, her eyes closed, and winced as she lifted a hand to explore her side. Kayden set the boussole on a rock. Its light allowed him to pick at the ropes that still held her legs, finally loosening and pulling them away. Briskly, he rubbed life back into her ankles, all while keeping a close watch on her ashen face.

"I do not think any ribs are broken," she said in a rasping voice. "Help me to stand. We have to leave."

Stepping over the scattered rocks, Kayden eased his hands beneath her shoulders and lifted, before retrieving his boussole.

He looked anxiously into her face. "You tripped that last guy? Or kicked him?"

She gave Kayden a wan smile. "Both. I could not let you be the only hero."

"You're made of tough stuff," he said. But there was no time to linger. Shining the light downward so she could see to step over the prone forms of the guards. Kayden rolled one of them out of the way and wrenched the door open to look out. The other sentry lay unconscious in the hallway. They were clear.

Motioning her to follow, Kayden held the boussole before his face and communicated with the tiny silver object. It only took a moment for its dials to come alive and show Kayden the direction to take.

"Come on."

Looking both ways, *and* above them this time, the pair left the room and edged down the narrow hallway. With the runestaff and their other weapons taken from them, they would have no way to defend themselves if they were found once more.

Kayden led the way, holding Durgot's boussole in front of him as a guiding light, and they shuffled along, hearing nothing.

They came to a divide. Kayden glanced at the boussole

for the correct route. At that moment, a tiny scratching sound came from one of the hallways.

Even though it couldn't possibly be a guard, Kayden and Rosalyn pressed themselves against the wall and Kayden flipped the boussole shut. Holding their breaths, they waited.

"Is that you Kayden?" Millinworth squeaked.

Kayden relaxed and opened the boussole to shine it toward the sound. He stepped into the circular area where the two intersecting paths converged, but Rosalyn stayed in the shadows. The mouse regarded them from the floor. She stood on her hind legs, her beady eyes black and glistening.

"I have been looking for you everywhere!" she said, several tiny tears rolling down her face. "I have been so worried! I only ran ahead to scout things out for you, but of course I neglected to look up. And as I was coming back, I saw it was from there they pounced on you both and knocked you out. I saw it all happen, but naturally I am too small to help in a case such as that so I—"

Kayden held up a hand to stop her time-consuming story.

"I understand, Millinworth," he said, "but it's not wise to stand here talking. We must keep moving or they'll have us again. Once we don't return with those men, more of Malahd's forces will be sent to find out why. Do you know of any other sentries that might be on their way?"

"No, I do not," she answered, looking a bit disgruntled at the rude interruption in her discourse. Wiping away her tears with a paw, she dropped to all fours. "Follow me, I know the best way."

She scampered off in the opposite direction to what the boussole had indicated.

"Hold on," Kayden said. "The boussole says to take the other route."

"It is wrong," she answered shortly. She paused to look back at them. "I am taking you along the back entrance to the fortress. The road you were going to take is swarming with sentries."

Rosalyn stepped forward. "I do not like this, Kayden. Where was she when we first entered this cave? Surely if she had gone first, and if she knows these tunnels as well as she professes, she would have known they were lying in wait, and could have warned us. I do not think she is capable of guiding us."

"I cannot know every move Malahd makes! I did my best to help you. You do not like me, that much is clear. Perhaps you are jealous of my relationship with both the former and—the future—king?" she said with a sly wink. Then she became brisk and businesslike. "In fact, I do know most of Malahd's plans, because I keep my ears open and can disappear at will. But I do not know quite *all* of his plans, and I do apologize that I was not aware of the danger you would come up against."

She followed in a softer tone. "I assure you I am most trustworthy. The Resistance and King Larkender himself put faith in my word."

Kayden considered both Rosalyn and the mouse. "We don't have time to debate. We'll follow Millinworth." Lifting up his boussole for light, rather than direction, he nodded to the mouse, indicating that she take the lead.

Sighing heavily, Rosalyn brought up the rear and they hurried down the path that Millinworth had chosen for them. Thus far, the downward slope had been gradual, but now the corridor began to decline sharply into the bowels of the mountain.

Kayden felt tense. Deep inside him, he recognized that something didn't feel right. What lay ahead?

Millinworth kept up quite a fast pace, for a mouse. Kayden trained the beam of his boussole on her at all times, lest accidently he might step on her, but, in true mouse fashion, she skittered along the side of the narrow alley. After about half an hour she stopped, stood on her hind legs, and lifted a whiskered nose into the air to sniff.

"There is a turn to make ahead, where often I have seen one or more sentries posted. We are very close to the back entrance of the fortress now. It will be watched. Please take extra care to be quiet." Millinworth looked at Kayden for a long moment before scuttling around the corner with Kayden and Rosalyn behind.

Ahead of them, torches had been set into brackets along one side of the chamber, sending eerie shadows to flicker against the roughness of the rock tunnel. Kayden flipped his boussole shut and slipped it into his pocket. His headache was better, but the sudden light still caused him to squint and gently rub the spot where he'd been struck.

They slipped past the first torch and huddled in the gloom between it and the next one, listening. All was silent. They continued toward the second, their senses on high alert, and paused before passing beneath its revealing light. A door appeared ahead of them on the left. Two torches were lit and strapped to the rock on either side with thick metal brackets. But there were no guards on duty. No one could be seen or heard.

Millinworth darted from the cover of the shadows and raced across the floor to the doorway.

"Inside!" she whispered. "Get inside before someone comes!"

She jumped up and down on the floor beneath the

heavy latch of the wooden door. Peering both ways down the corridor for sentries, Kayden caught Rosalyn's eye.

She lifted her eyebrows and twisted her face into a grimace. "No turning back now."

Together they jogged to the door and Kayden lifted up the handle. It slid easily, without a noise, and he pulled it back on soundless hinges. Like phantoms, they slipped inside, and Kayden tugged the weighty door closed behind them. They stood in the gloom, catching their breath. There were no torches this side of the door, so Kayden dug out his boussole again, caught the edge of it with a fingernail, and snapped it open.

A warm glow lit a tiny part of the huge square chamber, about half the size of Kayden's school gym. It was empty for which Kayden was grateful, and he searched the ground for Millinworth, but she was already crossing the room on her way to a similar door at the far end. As he and Rosalyn rushed after her, a glint of something shiny caught his eye and he slowed a little. The room wasn't as empty as he'd thought.

All around the edges of the space, evil looking handcuffs lay on the stony floor, held together by chains that trailed up the wall behind and fastened to the stone with enormous bolts. Kayden held the boussole above his head. As far as the light extended, he could see shackles—waiting to imprison any who dared oppose the ruler of this place. They were in a dungeon of some sort and Kayden's stomach twisted at the thought. What horrible fate had come to the unfortunate souls caged within this cold and unforgiving rock?

Beside him, Rosalyn shivered, and took the lead at an increased pace to get through the room as fast as possible. The space sloped down to a center point in the middle where a small, round hole had been drilled into the rock, no bigger than Kayden's fist. A tiny trickle of steam curled up from somewhere deep below. Both of them gave it a wide berth.

It took a few minutes to reach the other side where Millinworth was already waiting for them. The mouse shifted uneasily back and forth. The latch on the door to exit the room was easy to open as well. This time the door pulled inward, and Kayden stole a look out upon another corridor, wider and dimly lit.

A man hunched against the wall, down the corridor about ten paces to their left. Kayden lunged back inside the room, heart in mouth. Millinworth motioned that he pick her up and when he did so, she jumped to his shoulder and whispered into his ear.

"The sentry is lazy and dozes much of the time. I pass through this hallway regularly. Wait for my signal, cross over to the opposite side of the corridor, and go quickly to the right. You will be fine. There will be another door further down. I will wait there"

"But you're a mouse!" Kayden protested. "Of course, you pass by unnoticed."

As soon as the words left his mouth, Kayden knew it had been the wrong thing to say. Millinworth stiffened on his shoulder and her disapproval radiated outward in waves.

"I mean," he said in haste to correct himself, "it's part of what makes you such a great spy. And you're a good one, it's plain to see, but you're a heck of a lot smaller than we are, so it's not difficult for you to pass by without being seen."

"Regardless of that, it can be done," she said huffily. "And it is the only way from here. Put me down."

Passing through the opening, she scampered to the

opposite wall where she ran along the far edge and was out of sight in a moment. Kayden looked apprehensively at the guard. The man's chin rested on his chest and, even though he stood, leaning against the stone, he did appear to be asleep.

Kayden gestured that Rosalyn should go first. With a nod, she flitted across the alley and flattened herself against the opposite wall, shuffling quickly along in the direction Millinworth had disappeared. Leaving the door behind him open, Kayden went next, reaching the other side and following behind Rosalyn. He paused to listen, but Millinworth was right. The guard must have been asleep.

The rock beneath their feet began to gradually slope up until they were climbing quite a steep alleyway. The next door was not as close as Millinworth had made it sound. Kayden was worried they would meet another guard before they could reach it. Yet, after about ten minutes, the floor levelled out. They rounded a corner and found a staircase cut into the stone. Millinworth was about halfway up, leaping from step to step. Kayden couldn't believe their luck at making it this far without running into more guards looking for them. But Millinworth knew these paths and must truly have brought them a back way.

Without hesitation, Rosalyn took the stairs two at a time behind the mouse. Kayden brought up the rear, both of them catching Millinworth at the top where they took a moment to consider their next move.

The corridor continued upward and was bright with blazing torches, yet ahead of them, the mouse had paused beside a huge door. The stone under their feet seemed well-worn.

Was this Malahd's bedroom? Were they in the main part of the fortress? What lay beyond this door? Kayden had no weapon—no runestaff with which to fight if they were caught. At this point, all either he or Rosalyn had to rely on were their wits.

He was just about to scoop up Millinworth and ask her a few questions, when advancing footsteps and voices from around the corner ahead, roused them into action. Rosalyn flew to the door, lifted the latch, pushed it open just enough to allow her through, and slipped inside behind Millinworth. Kayden was not far behind. With one hand he pushed the door closed and leaned, panting on the wall, in complete darkness.

"I am *so* very glad you were able to join us," hissed a voice, twisted with a lifetime of hatred.

Kayden flinched like he'd been struck. He knew that voice. And as torches were lit by soldiers standing all around the perimeter of the space, he lifted his eyes to Malahd.

Chapter Seventeen

The sorcerer was seated, casually, in a large, ornate chair on a platform at the end of the long room. He was all in black, with a long voluminous cloak draped over his shoulders and down over the back of the throne. His face was shrouded in the cowl of this garment and his body sheathed in black armour. A sword was belted to one side of his waist and, Kayden saw with a sinking heart, the sceptre was belted to the other. It gleamed in the dancing firelight of a fireplace set into the back wall.

Even the sorcerer's hands were covered in black, and Kayden wondered how he had replaced the one that had been severed by Respiele three years ago. While little could be seen of Malahd's face, apart from a jutting chin and a thin red streak of a mouth, his eyes burned like hot coals. Kayden's face flushed under the searing hate of those eyes.

Scraping his enormous chair back, the sorcerer rose, reaching for a thin silver rod with one hand and Kayden's own runestaff with the other. He lifted the latter, pretending to examine the runes etched along the smooth exterior.

"I believe you lost this," Malahd said, the tones of his voice silky with menace.

Without thinking, Kayden stepped forward and called for it, his hand outstretched, but several iron-fisted men seized him before he'd gone two steps, and he was held fast.

A sudden movement drew Kayden's attention to the long table at the center of the room. It was that crazy, self-absorbed mouse!

"Millinworth!" he yelled, fearing for her life.

She scampered along the surface, skidded to a stop before the sorcerer and curtsied, lowering her head with reverence. Then, she turned to look pityingly at Kayden. Rosalyn, who also had been restrained, was dragged forward to stand beside Kayden. It was to Rosalyn the mouse spoke with disdain.

"And you did not think I could be a good spy," Millinworth spat.

"Silence!" Malahd thundered.

He ground his silver staff into the flagstones and the mouse cowered with a little screech as flaming sparks flew.

"Millinworth is my servant," Malahd continued smoothly. "She has done an excellent job of bringing you, like willing slaves to my door."

"I expect to receive my reward now," squeaked the mouse, although there was a tremor in her usually confident voice.

Malahd laughed, if the rasping sound could be called laughter. Stepping from the platform, he swiped his gloved hand across the wooden table, catching Millinworth and sending her spinning with a small squeal of pain out one of the many, narrow windows that had been slashed into the walls to allow light. She disappeared from view.

"Now then," Malahd said, turning to settle himself on

his throne. "Bring these children to me. I have several questions to be answered before they are…disposed of."

The guards who held Kayden in a vice-like grip, dragged him forward. He went silently, watching for some means to snatch his runestaff, but Rosalyn resisted, fighting and snarling obscenities at the guards in another language. Regardless of her efforts, they were both brought to stand before Malahd. The guards dropped their arms and took a step back.

Kayden felt for the runestaff within his mind, reaching out to it as he always had, asking it to return to him, but a black void met his probing thoughts. The staff was beyond his influence.

A powerful aura surrounded the sorcerer. Kayden could feel waves of it washing over him. In his mind's eye he saw it as a red tide, sweeping all coherent thought and resistance before it. He reached out to the runestaff yet again, but it was hopeless. All his thoughts of escape fell like icicles from the eves of a house on a warm winter day. They crashed around him. The only thought that filled his brain now was terror. He fought against it and squashed the feeling before it overtook him.

He would not allow fear to rule him now.

Kayden straightened his back and tried turning his head to send a look of encouragement to Rosalyn, but found he was unable to do even that. He was locked in place by Malahd's fiery eyes. In turn, Kayden's own gaze became riveted upon the being that sat before him. He was fiercely defiant of this usurper.

Malahd, now that he held all the power of the land, was in no hurry. He patted the king's sceptre, mocking the one to whom it now rightfully belonged.

The sorcerer fixed his gaze upon Rosalyn. As his eyes

turned away from her there was a sudden movement. Kayden felt, rather than saw, Rosalyn slump and almost fall, but her captors jumped forward and hauled her upright.

Then Malahd leaned forward, bending the force of his will upon Kayden. It was almost a physical blow. He felt the magician seeking to enter his mind like an obscure, penetrating shadow, but Kayden fought. Short breaths marking the effort it took him, Kayden drove back the sinuous threads of evil that sought to wind their way into his brain.

The sorcerer's gaze broke away and Kayden's body sagged slightly.

Malahd lifted a hand to one of the guards. "You may dispose of the girl. I have looked within, and there is nothing to be gained from her."

The two armed men holding Rosalyn swung around and began to drag her away, kicking and struggling.

"If you take her from me, or harm her in *any* way, I will *not* answer your question," Kayden said, his words slow and measured. It felt like he was shouting, but he knew his voice was barely above a whisper. Enunciating each one had cost him energy. Only now he knew what Malahd wanted to know and how badly Malahd needed his help. Kayden too, had learned something from Malahd's inquisition of his thoughts.

The sorcerer's eyes flickered. Kayden sensed that Malahd had not expected opposition.

The guards reached the doorway.

"Halt!" Malahd barked. "Bring her back. There may be some use for the little wench, after all."

"Give me my sword and we will see what use I am," Rosalyn shouted, as they hauled her back to Kayden's side.

Kayden squeezed his eyes shut, blocking out this place, this scene, and the fear that pressed upon him. He knew it was all carefully calculated to intimidate and coerce. He set his jaw and stared at Malahd.

"You want to open the portal to my world, but you can't —can you?" Kayden asked. His voice was steady with no trace of emotion.

The sorcerer flinched as though he had been stung. His hand dropped away from the sceptre and reached for the hilt of his sword.

"How can *you* know that?" he growled.

Kayden forced a small smile. He would not let Malahd see his fear.

"You need my help, and that of my runestaff, since I don't think it will obey *you*." Kayden met the sorcerer's burning orbs with his own unwavering eyes. The yellow eyes of his grandmother's, the eyes of the race of Garde. "Will it?"

The sorcerer didn't deign to answer. Kayden was gratified to know he had been right. The sorcerer's aura of strength had slipped momentarily, but Malahd gripped his sword tighter and leaned toward Kayden.

"You will open it for me, or the girl will die." Malahd flung himself back in his chair. His momentary lapse was concealed, his power restored.

Kayden shivered. What deadly force would be unleashed upon his own world if he did as the sorcerer ordered and opened the portal? It was unthinkable. He and Rosalyn would die before that would happen. Heck, they were dead already.

"I will help you, if you let her go free," Kayden lied.

The crazed laughter of a madman rang out. "You are in no position to bargain with *me*. We shall make our way to the portal now. Both of you will come. But if you fail, you and your friend will die."

Chapter Eighteen

Kayden watched as Rosalyn was dragged from the chamber, struggling against her abductors. It was useless to fight.

He cast his eyes down and trudged beside the two guards stationed on either side of him. Frantically, he tried to come up with a plan, but all of his ideas included his runestaff, and that was out of reach. Yet, he was the only one who could prevent the catastrophe that would take place if Malahd were allowed to enter the world beyond Erinbourne. There was no one else to rely on or ask for advice. Somehow, he had to stop the deranged wizard.

The door slammed shut behind him as the last of the company exited the room. Malahd led the way.

Kayden knew where they were going. Malahd was leading them down the ancient stone hallways to where they opened into the circular space beneath the mountains of Araleesh. To the dead home of the Garde, that had once flourished with fullness of life and laughter, and to the portal that divided their worlds. Of course, a dictator, like

Malahd, would want to extend his reach beyond the gates of this realm into Kayden's world. It made perfect sense—if you were a megalomaniac.

During the time Kayden and Rosalyn had been tied up in the cell, Malahd must have tried to use Kayden's staff to open the portal himself, thinking the runestaff would obey him. Clearly, it had not, and now Kayden himself was needed. Discovering that his runestaff had not been corrupted was good news, but Kayden couldn't see how he and Rosalyn would escape along with his runestaff *and* the sceptre to boot.

"Think," he muttered fiercely to himself. "Think!"

He stumbled down the long flight of stairs, but didn't fall. His arms were held tight as he was yanked along. Malahd was in a hurry. Rosalyn was just ahead of him, travelling in the same manner.

The troop reached the bottom. Marching with all haste, they rounded the corner and began the steep descent that Kayden had so recently climbed. The space was fractionally narrow here. When one of Kayden's heavy-set guards became wedged against the rock, it became apparent that three of them abreast was too wide to pass. One man dropped Kayden's arm and fell back to walk directly behind him.

During this shuffle, Kayden felt something drop from the ceiling onto his neck, landing between his coat collar and bare skin. He shuddered. What was it? A giant spider, or some other grotesque beast from this place? The thing settled down and hunkered there. Kayden felt tiny claws grasping his flesh for a foothold and shook himself again. The creature grasped a chunk of Kayden's hair and pulled itself to his ear.

"It is I," Millinworth whispered. "I have come back to

apologize and tell you how to get out, out, out of this mess that I must confess is mostly my fault."

After his initial shock, Kayden felt a surge of anger toward the foolish creature.

"*All* your fault," he hissed from the side of his mouth.

"Yes." She sighed into his ear, tickling him, before speaking again. "But listen. You cannot take your runestaff or the sceptre from Malahd. But you have another ally if you will but ask for help."

"What!" He ducked his head and turned toward the mouse. "Why should I trust *you*?"

"You have no reason to trust me, but I must tell you something important that I left out at our first meeting. I overheard Malahd and the captain of his guard talking about who you really are, and your inheritance. Snurler said your legacy lies beneath this mountain, and that if you, Respiele's heir, ever found it, Malahd would be afraid of *you*." The mouse whispered as fast as she could. "I do not know any more than that, but there is nothing to lose and everything to gain if it is true. I advise you to call upon this legacy.

"If you choose to take that chance," she continued, "wait until we are in the dungeon. There is a drainpipe at the center of the room that leads to the deepest depths of this mountain, much further than I have ever dared to go."

Cowering down, the mouse flattened herself beneath his coat. "Good luck to you, Kayden, and to us all."

Millinworth fell silent. Evidently, she felt there was nothing more to say.

But what did she mean, ask for help? Ask who?

The door ahead of them was wrenched open. Kayden, craning his neck as he marched, saw Malahd enter the dungeon. A few guards were next, then Rosalyn and her captors, and then it would be his turn.

'Ask for help,' Millinworth had said. What was he supposed to do? Holler the word? Who was supposed to come to his aid? And who would be powerful enough to stop Malahd?

If Talbot were here, he could take out the guards, but Malahd could not be beaten. None of them could stand against him, especially when he held the sceptre and Erinbourne's enchanted Gemstones of Power. No one stood a chance.

Kayden ducked inside. Ahead of him, Malahd was quickly reaching the center of the room, where it dipped to the drainpipe, and soon he would get to the door on the other side. It was now or never. Kayden had no better plan. None at all, really.

As the area widened, the second guard moved to grasp Kayden's arm. With both men guiding him, Kayden felt able to close his eyes and concentrate. He allowed his mind to drift to thoughts of Gran and what things must have been like in the Araleesh Mountains, before the arrival of evil. He envisioned fertile fields, fruit trees, and crystal clear water bringing life to the thirsty land that looked so desolate today. He could see corridors busy with the comings and goings of the Garde people, and how happy they must have been. And as these thoughts flooded his heart and mind, he asked for help to restore it to how it had once been.

With his head bowed and his heart bursting with love for this land that he had come to think of as his own, Kayden murmured, "I don't know who, or what I'm calling to, but if there is help to be found in this dark place, then I'm asking you—no, I'm begging you—to come and help me now."

His barely audible words seemed to lend strength to his flagging spirit. Kayden lifted his head and hot energy flooded his body. As though his ancestors rose up and spoke through him, Kayden opened his mouth not to whisper, but to yell.

"I call upon my legacy, the Garde of ancient days, and as future King of Erinbourne, to come forth and defend the people of this land who have been, and will be, oppressed," Kayden thundered. His voice echoed off the grim walls of the enclosed space with the power and authority of his fore-bearers.

Ahead of him, Malahd spun around, black robes swirling high into the air as a sudden, rushing wind whistled up from the pipe in the middle of the room. The guards fell back in confusion and the procession ground to a halt.

"*Shut his mouth!*" Malahd screamed.

Gripping the runestaff in one hand, he raised his own staff in the other and aimed it toward Kayden. Flames spewed from the end of his silver staff, shooting into the air like a fountain of fire and tracing a widening path over the heads of his minions. Red fire turned a cobalt blue as it arched high into the air, making its way inexorably to where Kayden stood, sparks dripping like beads of liquid fire onto the people below.

The stillness of the cavern was rent asunder with cries of pain and efforts to scramble out of the way. The captors that held Kayden and Rosalyn fled into the dark corners of the room. Terrified, the guards tried to escape the dungeon, but the doors clanged shut.

The sorcerer rushed toward Kayden. The heat of the flaming river that stemmed from Malahd's staff finally reached him. Blue flames surged, engulfing Kayden with Malahd's scorching wrath, but Kayden did not waver.

Somehow, the flames didn't burn him. Kayden looked through the fiery furnace at Malahd. This fight was between him and the sorcerer now, and he was not afraid to die. Kayden's heartbeat quickened, but his resolve was strong. He spread his feet wide apart and waited.

And then the ground beneath his feet heaved.

The solid rock rippled with sudden movement, and boiling hot steam gushed from the small, round cavity at the center of the room in a blast that extinguished Malahd's flaming assault.

The sorcerer shrieked in fear and rage.

Kayden's runestaff clattered to the floor. Malahd raised his own staff that became a javelin of flame. With his other hand, the sorcerer reached for the Golden Sceptre of Power and withdrew it from the loop on his belt. The gemstones, set into the golden crown at the top, spun crazily in a kaleidoscope of colour, lifting Malahd off the unsteady ground. His hood blew back with the force of the gale emanating from the hole, but he gathered himself, and spoke to the fiery staff before tossing it lightly away. It hovered in the air before the sorcerer, a twirling rod of blue fire. And still, the stone beneath them rumbled with latent promise.

As all eyes were riveted upon the scene unfolding before them, Rosalyn elbowed the guard beside her, who had retained a warning grip on her arm. As he doubled forward, she grasped his sword, slid it free and rammed it into the empty sheath on her back. Then, she darted forward to snatch the runestaff from where it had fallen. She leaped back, clutching it to her chest just in time, as Malahd's spinning javelin began growing in size, crashing into the rocks behind them. Red and blue sparks flew to the furthest reaches of the room like exploding fireworks as the magician's staff twisted and turned, gathering speed and growing into the same swirling twister that had appeared upon the Kalainian Sea. The force of wind blew each occupant back, and they slammed against the rocky walls.

Malahd, rising on the crest of the swirling twister, thrust his arm skyward. Rosalyn's feet skidded away from her as she, and the runestaff, were drawn toward the disintegrating floor. Rosalyn collapsed, helpless, clawing at the crumbling rock with one hand as she held tight to the runestaff with the other.

Kayden lunged for her.

The floor exploded. Chunks of rock flew back from the center, and resounding explosions echoed as cracks ran jaggedly across the rock like the eruption of an earthquake. Kayden snatched at Rosalyn's skirts, refusing to let her topple into the gaping hole exposed by the collapsing rock, and dragged her back from the edge of the floor. The guards around them disappeared, screaming, into the abyss.

Malahd, riding on his whirling maelstrom to one side of the ever-widening gap, pressed closer, reaching to draw Rosalyn and the runestaff into the revolving whirlwind. He closed in on the pair as they scrambled across the disintegrating floor to the safety of the wall. Rosalyn thrust the runestaff into Kayden's hand and they jumped to their feet. Side by side, she and Kayden stood ready to face whatever came next.

In the second it took Kayden to think of what possible rune he could conjure to combat the magician, Malahd was on them. Kayden's feet were whisked away and the runestaff was torn from his grasp. He and Rosalyn were borne into the seething tornado of Malahd's anger and flung into a never-ending loop of dizzying speed.

Kayden was sucked into the very center of the whirlwind and suspended in limbo—a void without sound or movement. Hanging there, he gazed through the exterior of the twister and out upon the destruction of a world he was leaving behind. His heart anguished. There was nothing he could do to fight this fate as slowly he, the hidden Millinworth, Rosalyn, his runestaff, and Malahd spun toward the roof.

Above him, at the highest point of the tornado, Kayden saw Malahd lift the gleaming sceptre, and at his bidding, the rock above them splintered and fell like shards of glittering glass. The sceptre sliced a path through solid granite, and they quickly rose into the night sky above the highest peaks of the Araleesh.

Rosalyn drooped in the soupy mass nearby. Kayden wasn't able to turn his head and look, but he knew she was there, caught in the same suspended animation as him.

Kayden fought the stupor his body felt, and with all the willpower he had left, silently sent one last plea for help.

A voice boomed with a suddenness and strength that shook Malahd's coiling construction.

"I am Alandrial, and I have awakened."

Kayden wasn't sure whether it spoke only in his head, or whether the whole world could hear the tenor and power of the voice. A tear appeared down one side of the swirling grey mass that held them. The heaving twister faltered, and Kayden sensed the sorcerer's unexpected flash of fear. With that, Kayden found he could now move his head, and he looked down where they had been. Below them, the mountain peak had been reduced to rubble in their exit from the caverns, but the wreckage heaved, as though some huge being was forcing its way through.

Boulders the size of houses were hurled aside. The mountains rolled back and shuddered with the force of the one who had risen from its slumber to answer the call.

Kayden watched in stunned amazement as a massive, horned head rose from the ruins and then one arm—no, a huge, folded wing—burst from the rocky debris and leaned onto the rocks to leverage its other wing up and out to freedom. Using both bent wings, the creature dragged itself from the remnants of the mountain and crouched on the summit of the wreckage. Dust from the crushed rock billowed and clouded around it. Debris tumbled from its wings and body. A long, sinuous tail was last to emerge, and it slashed back and forth like that of an angry cat. The beast was scaly and lizard-like, yet glowed with a golden radiance from within.

Kayden couldn't breathe. Could it really be what he thought it was?

The creature lifted its head to search the skies, spotting the twister that bore Kayden away. It flexed its wings. Chunks of rock and gravel flew off his back as Alandrial, the dragon, shook himself and took to the skies.

Within the twister, Malahd's fear was palpable. Kayden could almost taste it. A strangled sound, almost like a whimper, issued from the sorcerer's throat. He struggled to rise higher in the sky, away from the terrifying creature that was now in pursuit. Over and over Malahd thrust the sceptre over his head, beating at the sky with the wildly flashing gems. But they weren't obeying him as they had been.

Without warning, the gems faded in colour and intensity, and with it the solidity of the twister spun away until only a transparent membrane held Kayden, Rosalyn, and Malahd at the pinnacle. They dangled in mid-air for several long moments as the dragon beat his way toward them. Then they plummeted toward the ground in a shower of sparks and blue smoke.

Malahd swung the sceptre forward, his black cloak

streaming behind him. With a sweep of his other hand, he snatched the long silver cane that fell beside him and crashed the two together. The cane took on a different shape. The rumpled feathers of an enormous crow burst into being. The bird extended its wings and ceased its head-long rush toward earth. Malahd leapt astride its back.

Far below, Kayden's runestaff ricocheted off the rocks. He and the others would be next. Wind howled past his ears. Millinworth clung precariously to the cloth of his tunic and Rosalyn sent him a despairing look before closing her eyes to prepare for impact. Yet it never came.

Like a freight train rushing through a tunnel, the dragon sliced along the mountaintop, wings outstretched, gliding above the stone. And just before they smashed into the mountain, Alandrial swooped beneath their flailing bodies. Kayden and Rosalyn sprawled onto his broad back, bounced, and almost tumbled off, but the dragon lifted his wings to check their fall and carried them for several hundred metres before wheeling back to land on a patch of scrub grass growing on the high plain.

Pulling himself together, Kayden slid from the dragon's back. Hope added lightness to his feet and sharpness to Kayden's eyes. He spotted his precious runestaff lying in the grass nearby and ran to pick it up. Rosalyn stayed aboard Alandrial's back.

Alandrial's head was turned so that it could keep both glittering yellow eyes upon Kayden, and when he sprinted back, clutching the staff, one eye winked solemnly. Kayden was overwhelmed. He reached out a tentative hand and placed it on Alandrial's face.

"Thank you," Kayden said, but there no time to waste on further gratitude. He swung aboard the dragon, and Alandrial swept into the midnight sky.

Malahd was not hard to see. The waning moon was high in the eastern sky, but it still cast enough light to see the shadow of the crow, outlined with a faint red glow as it dipped below the many peaks of the Araleesh Mountains. The bird, surreal in size, flapped along a ridge to the north of them before dipping out of sight behind a projection of stone. It was as they dropped over it themselves that Kayden knew where they were. The stone circle loomed before them in the growing shadows of eventide.

What new horror had Malahd conceived?

Chapter Nineteen

The crow had already transformed back into the silver staff by the time they wheeled overtop the standing stones.

Malahd once again held the silver staff and the sceptre. He strode toward the stone circle. Some distance away, since they needed room to land, Alandrial set down on the flat plateau with a leathery rustling of wings. Kayden and Rosalyn slid to the ground and strode toward the sorcerer. Behind them, Alandrial waited.

Malahd had positioned himself at the center of the standing stones, facing the tallest one, closest to the mountain. His back was to them, and his cloak billowed as he planted his staff at his feet, threw back his head, and howled. It was an eerie cry, high-pitched and filled with torment. There were answering howls, echoing from the high peaks all around him. Kayden knew who made those sounds. He and Rosalyn had clashed with them before. They were the Hounds of Enfer. Malahd had commanded their service when Kayden had carried the enchanted Emerald.

As the hounds' claws skittered across the rocks and their hunting cries rang out, Kayden watched as the sorcerer raised both the sceptre and his silver staff above his head, shouting words in an unintelligible language. Then the sorcerer joined the two together and the gems on the sceptre came alive once more. The Ruby, Sapphire, Amethyst, and Emerald shone with a light too intense to look upon. They began to revolve, slowly at first then moving into a rhythm that became a blur of flashing coloured lights.

The sorcerer's staff began to change. One end radiated with a ruddy luminosity that soon changed to an icy blue and leapt with a jagged line of lightning to the stone behind it. Crackling with a charmed electricity, the lightning jumped from stone to stone until it formed a high ring of blue flame that sizzled across the top of the monoliths. Leaping back and forth, the electric charge worked its way down to the base of the rocks, until they too transmuted their form. The standing stones took on the grotesque shapes of monstrous, misshapen men, compelled to perform the purpose of the sorcerer. They quivered in place, as though waiting for the sorcerer's word to enter the battle.

Kayden felt rooted to the spot. Heart pounding, he lifted his runestaff, but couldn't think what to ask of it. What could he create to combat both a pack of bloodthirsty hounds and a troop of stone giants? Yet Kayden knew he didn't stand alone. Beside him, Rosalyn leaped onto a boulder, poised with sword upheld, ready for the first onslaught of hounds that began to pour down the mountainsides around them like a deadly flood. And Alandrial wheeled to face them with a snort, jets of pure golden fire rushing from his nostrils.

Kayden marshalled his thoughts upon the runestaff in

his hand. Yet before he could concentrate on a rune, Malahd rose from the circle in the flaming blue light. His cowl was back over his face and his robes swirled with cobalt flames. Then he also began to transform with the combined power of the sceptre and his own evil magic. He sprang higher than the circle. Threads of lightning, connected to him from each standing stone, crackled and hissed as they fed his evolving shape. Each arm lengthened, widened, and began to slowly beat the air. Then a long, forked tail shot out behind him, curling sinuously around Malahd's legs before his neck swiveled and extended to support a head of gigantic proportions. His entire body widened and grew to become yet another dragon.

Malahd sprang into the air, the sceptre and his silver staff clutched in one scaly claw. His wings beat the air as he rose.

Alandrial screamed a challenge and launched himself skyward. Kayden's heart leapt with fright. He had only just found the dragon, but already their connection was in place.

You need not fear for me, came Alandrial's response. This time Kayden knew the dragon spoke, not aloud, but in Kayden's heart and mind.

Love for the brave young woman standing not far off, also filled his heart. It was a love that tore a cry of pride from his lips as Rosalyn reached for the first lunging hound with her bare hand, held its snarling, writhing form aloft, and plunged her sword through its chest. She cast it aside and crouched, waiting for the next in line to meet its fate. She was fabulous and Kayden bounded to fight at her side.

Yet, he wondered how he would combat the slow, crushing movements of the standing stones. Swaying to and fro, in positions they had held for hundreds of years, the stone men shifted in the sizzling blue light that engulfed them. Each took a clumsy step forward, crunching into one another with an ear-splitting sound as rock ground against rock, stone against stone, and then they turned and marched like automatons toward Kayden.

Kayden thrust his runestaff before his face and squared himself to meet the first giant that lumbered toward him, its cumbersome arms raised. But, what rune could he conjure that would defeat the crushing weight of these adversaries? Animated slabs of granite couldn't be held back or killed as though they were alive. All Kayden could hope to do was break the curse that held them. Backing away from the advancing monoliths, he communicated with the runes upon his staff. If Malahd could create magical fire, so could he. The image of a flickering blaze flooded his mind.

In answer to Kayden's request, a yellow spark licked the bottom end of the runestaff, travelling up its length until the staff was consumed in molten yellow flames. Kayden considered his hand, immersed in the warm sensation the fire had created. Then he pointed his runestaff at the sizzling bolts of blue lightning that engulfed each trudging stone.

Thousands of golden threads, fine as the gossamer filaments of a spider's web, burst from the end of the runestaff and swirled over Kayden's head in a whirlpool of gold. As the shining thread filled the air, they began weaving together, fashioning themselves into a gilded canopy of sparkling light.

Moving with the precision of a military manoeuvre, the stone giants closed in around him, the closest raising a clumsy limb to strike. Kayden could feel the frenetic energy that infused the stones with movement. His skin prickled with electricity, hair standing on end.

Turning on his toes, Kayden swung the runestaff and

the golden mantle over his head and then dropped to his knees, ducking his head and flattening the staff to the ground beside him.

The dazzling canopy hovered over the group of ponderous stone giants, and then dropped, enveloping the enlivened stones. Blue met gold in a dazzling explosion. The runestaff jerked in Kayden's hands as the battling connection between Malahd's magic and Kayden's own authority threatened to break. The ground was showered with the scorching power of the opposing wills. Kayden was yanked forward and dragged around the stone circle, then tossed back, but he bent his force of will upon the curse that lent false life to the ancient standing stones. He bore down, and held the runestaff strong. Time stood still.

By increments, the golden mantle consumed the raging sapphire flames, draping about them and snuffing them out. At last they went dark. Malahd no longer controlled the standing stones.

Then, a soft yellow hue, starting at the base of each monolith, wound up and around each one until they radiated warmth and light. Kayden stood to his feet. With a gentle hand, he set the bottom end of his runestaff onto the rock before him and urged the great standing stones back to the hollows set for them since the beginning of time. A ray of golden light traced a path from the runestaff, across the ground to the megaliths. The stone giants turned as one. Swinging each appendage straight and stiff, they filed back to settle into the ancient grooves beside the mountain.

Kayden whirled about to face the Hounds of Enfer. The golden threads retracted from the standing stones and wove themselves into a thin cord. Kayden slashed his runestaff over his head and the golden cord followed. Gleaming with intensity, it lashed through the air like the thong of a whip and turned its fury upon the hounds that encircled Rosalyn. How she had kept them from attacking him was beyond reason. Yet she had. A mound of carcasses lay in a heap behind the ferocious maiden who wielded a deadly sword.

To Kayden's astonishment, Rosalyn did not stand alone in her battle against the ravening beasts. Another was there: a fearsome warrior with lethal spines covering every centimeter of his coiled body.

Talbot! The hedgehog hurtled back and forth across one side of the rocky plateau, while Rosalyn defended the other. The hounds snapped and growled, but they didn't dare oppose the razor-sharp blades that projected from Talbot's huge form or Rosalyn's shining blade. Too many of them had already met a bloody fate. The hounds drew back, howling their fury.

Kayden looked up, remembering the sceptre. Malahd must be defeated and Erinbourne's Gemstones of Power rescued. He squinted into the lengthening shadows of dusk, straining to see the two great dragons as they clashed, talons rasping across their scaly bodies in mid-air. Jets of flame sliced the moonlit sky with livid streaks. They slammed into one another high above and split the sky with the slashing of their long tails. The very mountains rumbled with the force of their battle.

Kayden acted on impulse. Perhaps it was the blood of his ancestors, running hot within his veins that drove him now. However, before he could even put his request into conscious thought, let alone voice it, he knew Alandrial had heard him call. Kayden watched as the dragon—his dragon —laid his wings against his sides and hurtled from the clouds to meet him.

But even as Alandrial plunged to do Kayden's bidding, Malahd dove after him. The sorcerer was black and huge, the larger dragon of the two, and he dropped like a stone in hot pursuit. The fading moon rose high above the ridge of mountains, and a cold, silver glow lit up the sky. It shimmered on the dragons' scales with each move they made, turning them into dark missiles hurtling to earth. As Alandrial drew closer to Kayden and extended his wings to control his descent, Malahd veered off, disappearing into the shadows of the mountain.

There was no time to be lost. Every minute that Malahd held the sceptre, the fate of Erinbourne was in peril. Kayden grasped his runestaff and poised himself to spring to Alandrial's back. The dragon swooped down to land for only a second on the plateau. Then, just as quickly as he came, he rose, wings beating loud against his body, with Kayden aboard.

Kayden glanced back. The force of their passage drove gusts of wind downward to send Rosalyn's skirts swirling around her legs as she stood below with Talbot and saluted. Any of the hounds left alive had turned tail and run. Just to be sure, Alandrial snaked back along the side of the rocks where the pack had been and covered the hillside in a blast of scorching flame. Then, wheeling about, his tail snaking behind him, he raised his wings, thrust himself into the air, and climbed to a dizzying height.

Kayden hung on. Swiveling on his perch, he looked for the sorcerer, but Malahd had vanished. They could not afford to let evil escape them this time.

Alandrial held his position. High above the mountaintops he lay in an updraft that held them steady until Kayden caught sight of the black Malahd away to the north.

Like an arrow, Alandrial and Kayden were after him. Anger at the cruelty the sorcerer had wrought upon the people of Erinbourne, and against his ancestors, lent motivation to Kayden. He wanted to bring Malahd to justice, and he urged Alandrial to greater speeds as they flew across the peaks. They gained upon the heavier dragon. Malahd turned sharply to the east, where mountain peaks became gentle rolling hills covered in trees.

Ahead of them, a crater came into view. It was shrouded in shadow, completely surrounded by a forest and must have been created by an asteroid. It gave Kayden an idea.

"Alandrial," he yelled into the gale force winds that whistled past his face. "Can you come down on Malahd from above and drive him into that hollow?"

A deep resonant voice responded, filling Kayden with a thrill. "Indeed, I shall."

If only Gran were here to see this now. Alandrial's neck flattened, and he tucked his wings to his sides, making him aerodynamic. Kayden pressed himself against the dragon's back. Like a thin vein of prospector's gold, they shot toward their quarry.

Malahd twisted and rolled in the air, wretchedly trying to avoid their efforts to take him down. He rose higher, thrashing at the air with the desperate moves of one who knows they have nothing to lose. Despite his greater bulk, he was agile. Malahd moved beyond their reach and then flipped about to face them, opening his mouth in a deafening roar that sent fire shooting across the dark sky. The heat of it scalded Kayden's face and hands. He smelled burning hair and knew it was his own.

Kayden and Alandrial wheeled away, but Alandrial returned, answering with a golden fire of his own. Only a thin trail of smoke puffed from the dragon's nostrils as he took a ragged breath.

Kayden realized, with a sinking feeling, that too much was being asked of Alandrial. The dragon had been asleep in a cave for at least as long as his grandmother had been gone from Erinbourne. Sixty odd years was a long time to be dormant. Although Kayden knew nothing of dragons, he could tell Alandrial was tiring. His head was beginning to droop, his evasive movements were sluggish, and the thin trail of smoke continued to stream from his nostrils, rather than fire. Perhaps this was their last opportunity to bring the evil tyrant down and secure the sceptre. At the very least they had to try.

With an effort that Kayden knew cost Alandrial dearly, the dragon rose suddenly, slamming into Malahd's under-belly, knocking him sideways and to the right. Then, Alandrial's long bi-forked tail coiled around the sorcerer from the other side, and yanked, throwing Malahd into a tailspin.

The sorcerer spiralled. Malahd careened through the air, wings thrashing every which way. Despite his tangled dive, however, he retained the sceptre. Kayden caught occasional glimpses of it as Malahd fell. The Emerald, Ruby, and then the Sapphire glinted in the moonlight as they rolled toward the treetops below.

Alandrial hung stationary, watching Malahd's descent. Then, Kayden urged him to follow the flailing Malahd, thinking that one final blast might be all it took now to finish the sorcerer forever.

Just as it appeared Malahd would crash to the ground, he righted himself and soared across the treetops. Malahd wheeled around to shoot a river of flame at Kayden and Alandrial. Kayden didn't think that flames would hurt a dragon, but he wasn't so sure about anything concocted by Malahd. His thoughts communicated to Alandrial.

To avoid the blistering flames, Alandrial fell back on

himself, rearing up and turning away. But his head, neck, and softer underside were aflame, and so was the forest around them. As they fell, the fire became a roaring conflagration that rose to meet them.

It was over. The sorcerer would escape with the king's sceptre and there was nothing Kayden could do to stop it.

Moreover, they themselves were in mortal danger. Alandrial spun out of control, screaming in pain. The burning trees below them shot sparks that seared into their flesh. Though Alandrial fought to right himself and safely land regardless of the fire that burned his flesh, Kayden knew they were doomed.

A mournful cry issued from the dragon's gasping mouth and Kayden felt an agonising pain in his heart. They were going to crash into a burning forest and there, they would die before he even properly met the dragon that was already imprinted on his soul.

Movement caught the corner of his eye. Was Malahd coming back to finish them? Or to gloat?

Kayden lifted his head. He blinked in rapid succession to clear the heat, smoke, and ash from his burning eyes.

There were horses!

White horses, with feathery wings extended as they floated down from the sky like a beacon of hope from above. The Horses of Silpeth soared beneath Alandrial's wings and bore him up on their sturdy backs. It was—unbelievable.

Alandrial was carried over the burning bushes and set down in the soil of a nearby field where the good brown earth extinguished the flames that threatened to overtake the dragon.

Kayden coughed. He slid sideways and almost fell from the scaly back he had clung to. With a groan, Alandrial stood, shifting his posture abruptly and Kayden was thrust upright once more. Both of them looked to the sky.

Line upon line of the flying Silpeth horses surrounded Malahd and held him captive in midair. His scream of rage reverberated off the nearby mountaintops. His long tail slashed back and forth, and he blew endless streams of fire from his gaping mouth.

But where he was clumsy in the air, the Silpeth were swift and light. They prevented his escape without trouble, but they could do no more than that. If Malahd was to be brought down, Kayden and Alandrial must fight once more.

"Are you able?" Kayden whispered. Leaning forward, he held the dragon's neck with both of his hands.

"Yes," came the weak but rumbling answer.

Gathering his powerful haunches beneath him, Alandrial flung himself skyward again. His wings moved slowly, gathering speed as they advanced upon the ring of Silpeth and their prisoner. But this time, Kayden had the presence of mind to ready his runestaff.

At his bidding, the runestaff erupted in flames. Long, golden threads flew out before him and braided themselves into a lone, gleaming cord. Although the natural light of the moon was limited, a luminosity emanated from each Silpeth, guiding Kayden and Alandrial to where they encircled the wizard. The golden flame of the Runestaff blazed in Kayden's eyes as they flew.

This final battle *was* his destiny.

Malahd, furiously angry, flew back and forth between the solid blockades of the Silpeth, breathing jets of fire at his jailors, but they were impervious to his wrath. It was plain to see he was looking for a point of weakness, an exit from the ring of determined horses. However, they held fast, only breaking apart for a moment as they allowed Kayden and Alandrial to enter the arena of war.

Kayden's mind was set and focused. He was not motivated by hatred, or by the thirst for power that had directed the path of his great-grandfather, Respiele. No. During the short space of time he had been in Erinbourne, he had grown to love the land and its people. He felt a kinship with them, a belonging that he had never known in the place he had been born. He fought now to save these people and their world—to right the wrongs set in motion by his predecessor.

Kayden raised the gleaming runestaff above his head and pointed it directly at Malahd, who had made a sudden effort to plunge beneath the layered rings of Silpeth. He was blocked yet again.

Malahd corrected his path and flew, head on, to meet Kayden. He lifted his own silver staff along with the sceptre, each in a gnarled talon of the dragon. But Malahd moved slower now and appeared to be having trouble grasping the implements. His wizard's staff slipped, almost dropping from his claws. Somehow, he recovered and clashed the staff and the sceptre together with might. Crimson sparks leapt from their joining, showering over Malahd, and he flashed with an electric red haze.

The dragon made a large target. Kayden brought his runestaff up like the handle of a bullwhip he had seen his father use. He held it there, the gilded cord curling through the dark sky behind him until they were closer. Then with a sudden movement, Kayden snapped his arm down, sending the golden cord to meet Malahd. With a crack like the report of a shotgun, the golden cord lashed Malahd's massive chest. Malahd reeled back even as he shot a blast of fire to ignite Alandrial and Kayden. Alandrial rolled to one side to miss the stream of flame. The cord recoiled as Kayden raked his arm backward through the air and lashed the sorcerer again. Malahd screeched in pain and fury. He flung himself to one side, vainly trying to escape.

Kayden jerked the runestaff back and struck again, encouraging Alandrial to follow Malahd's every move. They all plunged below the Silpeth sentinels, hurtling on a collision course for the ground. Kayden drew back his arm, the golden cord coiled in the air, and came down with force upon Malahd once again, beating him into submission. This time, there was a sizzling sound, an explosion of scarlet fire, and a cloud of smoke, as Malahd shrank in size and shape, tumbling to earth as a man. But still he held the two sources of his power.

Somehow, Malahd landed lightly on the grassy field below and crouched. The folds of his cloak were smoldering, but otherwise he seemed prepared to continue the battle. Yet there could be only one victor.

Not far away, Alandrial also set down. Kayden slid to the earth. His hand lingered on the heaving side of the golden dragon and then, in the luminous light of the Silpeth, who gathered again in a circle above the two men, Kayden strode toward the sorcerer.

Something scrabbled in his pocket, distracting him, before he realized it was the forgotten mouse. With a frightened squeak, she scratched her way out the top and jumped into the grass. Kayden paid her no further notice. He knew there would be no rune to call upon that could help him out of this situation: no falcon, whale, wolf, or wind. This time it was his own force of will working with the runestaff, against a wizard armed with not only his own magical staff, but also Erinbourne's stolen Gemstones of Power. The odds were stacked against Kayden, but still he marched.

"You dare to believe you are a match for me," Malahd screeched.

"I do," Kayden answered.

Malahd sent a jagged bolt of liquid blue lightning to leap across the short distance between them. Kayden held up his runestaff. An answering golden light streamed from its tip and met with Malahd's. The beams came together creating a blistering arc of light.

As they fought, the sorcerer lifted the stolen sceptre and the jewels began to spin wildly at the top. Before Kayden's eyes, Malahd grew in stature, and the power behind his staff grew stronger.

Kayden felt Alandrial looming behind him and saw the Silpeth close ranks around them.

"The future king stands not alone," Alandrial said, his voice booming.

But Malahd, bolstered by the strength of the sceptre, began to rise on his whirlwind. He smiled at Kayden, tipping the sceptre toward him in a gesture of farewell.

Suddenly, Malahd screamed in pain. He dropped the golden sceptre and toppled to the ground.

The gemstones winked out as though someone had turned off a switch.

Chapter Twenty

Like a flash, Kayden rushed forward, snatched up King Larkender's sceptre, and kicked Malahd's silver staff some distance away. Kayden stared at the crumpled wizard. His grand plans for the domination of two worlds were ruined, and he was reduced to the status of a man, writhing on the ground. Something small also thudded to the ground next to him. It was tiny, and alive.

Millinworth?

But Kayden couldn't waste time with questions. As Malahd struggled to recover himself and scrambled for his weapon, Kayden thrust his own runestaff into the moonlit sky.

Every rune from top to bottom erupted into silver, glittering radiance, cutting through the darkness. Malahd screeched, and cowered in the light. He yanked the hood of his robe over his face.

Kayden tossed the runestaff into the air and it snapped into a hundred tiny pieces, each fragment becoming one of the animals that had stood with the Garde since the beginning of time. The wolf, falcon, cougar, and a host of others all took silvery shape and sprang to the defense of Erinbourne. The ghostlike figures of the animals surrounded Malahd. They were faint and without substance, but filled with power and menace.

Kayden reached into the hidden, inside pocket of his tunic, and brought out the marvelous magic of Magda—the Eluvia. He sprinkled it into the air where it hovered, rustling with the growth of golden vines and leaves. Kayden sent it floating toward the sorcerer and Malahd was bound head to toe with the multitude of vines. Although space was left for the sorcerer to breathe, Kayden made sure to use extra bindings around Malahd's mouth. Then, Kayden reached out his hand to the glowing animal shapes that covered the hillside and called his runestaff home. And, in a blinding flash of light, the long, gnarled staff, worn grey by time, returned to its master.

It was over.

Kayden stood with the milky white Silpeth on the hillside where they had landed and thanked each one personally. They came at the request of Magda, who had reached out to them for help by sending a message on airborne spores from her enchanted flowers. With a final word of thanks, Kayden watched as the Silpeth leapt into the sky, their silver manes and tails glowing against the deepening shades of the night sky. And then they were gone, winging home to the eastern reaches of Erinbourne.

Kayden turned in a circle looking at the ground.

"Where's Millinworth?" he said aloud, though no one was there to hear him. "Don't move until I find her."

Tucking the sceptre into the belt about his waist, he lit the shining sun on his runestaff and held it up as he scanned the area. "I'm positive she had something to do with why Malahd dropped the scepter."

After a minute of searching, he was rewarded with a scurrying movement in the grass near a tree stump.

"I am here," she squeaked.

The mouse scrambled onto the stump and bowed low in the steady light of the rune.

"I must beg your forgiveness," she said with unusual brevity. Her head hung low. "I—it is all my fault and I accept whatever punishment you may inflict upon me."

She held both tiny paws out in front of her as though Kayden would reach down, bind them with chains, and drag her off to the gallows.

He laughed. "I want to thank you," he said, crouching down beside her. "What did you do to Malahd at the end?"

"I bit his hand," she said, but she peeped up at Kayden between her lashes and a glint of her old self came back. "You are not angry with me? But how can that be so? I led you directly into danger, several times. I did not do more to warn King Larkender, and now he is dead."

A tear escaped her tiny black eye. "I am so terribly sorry."

Without another word, she flung herself upon the rough top of the stump and began to weep.

"Some penalty will be given to you Millinworth," Kayden agreed, "but without your intervention, I don't know what might have happened. I thank you for that."

He straightened, scooped up the weeping Millinworth, and popped her back into his pocket.

He walked to where Alandrial stood waiting for him and laid a hand on the dragon's cheek. "Can you carry me one last time tonight?"

"Wherever you wish to go." The deep, steady assurance of the dragon's voice warmed Kayden's soul.

"I'm afraid we shall have one other passenger," he said, swivelling around to eye Malahd, who thrashed on the ground nearby. The wizard was unable to speak, but his eyes threw daggers at them.

"I shall carry him with my talons. He is not fit to ride with you."

Kayden nodded. "Nor should he be given the privilege of riding such a majestic creature as you."

He walked to where he had tossed the sorcerer's silver staff and tentatively touched it. It was ice cold and sent a jarring shock wave through his body. He reared back, but then resolve and anger flooded through him. Reaching out, he grasped the staff with determination. It jolted him again, but he grasped it even firmer.

"Malahd has been defeated, didn't you know?" Kayden found himself addressing the shiny rod in his hand.

The thing subsided, not exactly growing warm, but the feeling of frost receded from the smooth contours of the staff. Kayden brought it back to Alandrial along with his runestaff.

The dragon hunkered low. Kayden swung a lanky leg over Alandrial's neck and settled himself aboard. Then, the dragon walked to where Malahd lay still and rigid in the grass. Alandrial unfolded his wings and rose into the air, just slightly, before reaching out to roll the wizard into his talons. Lifting into the night air, and with an unerring sense of direction, Alandrial took them back to the stone circle where Kayden's friends were waiting.

The dragon dropped Malahd to the rock with a thud and then landed beside him. Kayden dismounted and reached a hand into his pocket for Millinworth. She scampered off a few paces and sat up on her hind legs, clearly worried what Talbot and Rosalyn would say.

With a cry, Rosalyn ran across the space dividing her from Kayden. Talbot didn't run, but he strode toward Kayden and Alandrial with a grin on his pointed face.

Tears streamed down Rosalyn's face as she flung herself into Kayden's arms and unashamedly sobbed. Kayden held her close for long minutes. He nuzzled her hair before whispering into her ear.

"I love you."

With a long sniffle, she leaned back to look into his eyes from the light of the runestaff. She smiled.

Her lips trembled as she repeated the words back to him. "I love you too."

Kayden drew her close and then, taking her hand, he led her to where Talbot awaited his turn.

"My friend," Kayden said, shaking his head in amazement. "How do you always manage to return just in the nick of time?"

Talbot laughed.

Kayden didn't dare hug the enormous hedgehog for fear of the lethal spines that covered his body. Instead, he passed his runestaff to Rosalyn, grabbed Talbot's paw with both hands, and pumped it vigorously. "Thank you for all you've done."

Talbot turned away and Kayden saw him brush a tear of his own away before he met Kayden's eyes and grinned.

"I see you have the culprit trussed like a chicken ready for the stew pot," he said, with an effort at humour. Then he became serious. "When I returned to find Malahd's men bound and left outside the stone circle, I knew you had gone into the mountain. But I also guessed that Malahd would return to this place. There is untold power to be found within the circle of the stones."

With a huge paw, Talbot gestured at the silent megaliths.

"Yes, I've seen a little of it at work," Kayden agreed. "Now, I'd like to introduce you all to Alandrial. Learning of his existence was all that my grandmother said it would be, and the joy I feel at this moment, with my friends and loved ones, is indescribable. Each one of us played a vital part in bringing this siege to an end, and I'm grateful to you all."

"Even me?" chirped Millinworth, hopping up and down.

Rosalyn jumped. "What is that confounded mouse doing here? She led us straight to him!"

Millinworth ducked into a crevice.

"It's all been sorted out," Kayden said. He slid an arm around Rosalyn's waist. "Millinworth was instrumental in bringing Malahd down. I'll tell you about it later."

Rosalyn looked doubtful. "What do we do now? We have no shelter, nothing to make a fire or eat, and we are exhausted."

Kayden turned to her. His eyes crinkled as if with some hidden surprise. "I have a plan."

Giving Rosalyn a final squeeze, he stepped away from her and walked to the stone circle, positioning himself at its center. He looked back at his friends, silhouetted in the shadows beyond the megaliths. Pulling the great sceptre from his belt, he lifted it up in the light of his runestaff, and gazed at the beautiful gems inlaid with elaborate gold ornamentation in the shape of a crown. The Sapphire, Ruby, Amethyst, and Emerald all glimmered, but as he concentrated on them, they began to glow from within, taking on a luminosity of their own. The intricate crown started to revolve. It was slow at first, but soon began to whirl until each gem melded into a blinding kaleidoscope of colour. It gyrated at such a speed, Kayden felt as though, if he let it go, it would lift off and take on a life of its own. But he pushed back these thoughts, closed his eyes, and drew upon the power of the gemstones as he made the most important request of his life thus far.

Lifting both the sceptre and his rapidly warming runestaff, he touched them together. They crackled on contact, jumping apart with bursts of multi-coloured sparks like they were two north ends of a magnet, and then smashing together again as though inextricably drawn together. Finally, they fused as one. Ribbons of red, green, blue, and purple leapt from the gemstones to each of the monolithic stones that surrounded Kayden. The gemstones in turn became conductors for the churning energy that forked from the standing stones and up into the midnight sky.

The bright colours wound together high above and then divided into bolts of pulsating light that flooded the air in wide banners. Weaving up and over the mountain tops they flowed across the sky, flooding it with warmth and radiance. Kayden was aware that Rosalyn and Talbot had climbed onto the rocks nearby. He heard their voices, but he didn't waver in his attention to the work he had set before himself.

"What is he doing?" Rosalyn asked Talbot.

"The Emerald is at work, I believe," Talbot said in an awed whisper. "It is the healer, after all."

A thunderous sound met Kayden's ears. To his great delight, the mountains of Araleesh, levelled by Malahd's escape to freedom, began to rebuild themselves. Stone upon stone, boulder upon boulder, they came together beneath a watchful moon and the united authority of Erinbourne's Gemstones of Power. It was like an old movie, the sort where the film is run backward and something that was broken becomes whole once more. Only this was truly happening. In mere minutes everything was set back where it was supposed to be and the bright lights that arched across the mountain range faded until they went dark and still.

"It's done," Kayden said, stating the obvious. The staff went cold in his hand, and he lowered it before sticking the sceptre into his belt. "We can go in now."

"In?" Rosalyn asked him. "In where?"

"Into the caverns of my forefathers," Kayden replied. "We'll spend this night in the space that was prepared for the Garde at the beginning of this world. But first, something must be done about Malahd."

Rosalyn and Talbot joined Kayden as he left the stone circle and made his way back down to the flat plateau.

In their absence, Alandrial had laid down to rest and keep an eye on Malahd. As Kayden, Rosalyn, and Talbot approached, he spoke.

"There is a cave where I and my kin once slept not far from here along the face of the mountain. In it, I could take my ease for the night, and watch over the wizard at the same time," the dragon suggested.

"That seems like the perfect solution," Kayden said. "Thank you."

When the dragon had gone, taking the carefully wrapped package of Malahd, with him, Kayden opened the stone door with his runestaff and they entered the mountain chambers once more. Millinworth rode with Kayden, and Rosalyn walked close behind, but Talbot maintained his alternate form saying that he was worried Malahd's sentries, now free, might still be skulking about.

Kayden wasn't concerned. He knew the evil that had

dwelt in the Araleesh Mountains for so many years, was now gone, and he strode down the narrow corridors with a glad heart. It took them a short time to reach the small opening into the space at the center of the Garde's old domain.

Kayden pushed back the bushes that covered the entrance and stepped through, taking a deep satisfied breath. In the light of his runestaff, he could see that the brown sludge had disappeared. In its place, good clean water gushed from the waterfall to his left and splashed into a crystal clear pool that then flowed into several waterways. Kayden knew from seeing Durgot's home within the mountain, that these channels distributed water to the entire area. They would branch off in all directions, watering the grasses, trees, orchards, and vineyards that once had been so bountiful as to feed all the people who dwelt here.

"The water...It's back!" Rosalyn murmured from behind him.

With the shining sun at the top of his runestaff to guide them, Kayden led them to the first of the dwellings that squatted in a circle at the center of the space. He took the long flight of stairs two at a time and tried the door. It opened easily.

"Come on in, the water's fine," he said, the light from his runestaff lending a warm glow to the old house. "We'll spend the night here and make our way back to the castle in the morning. Malahd must be brought to justice. Besides..." he paused and became serious, "I want to know what happened to Steve."

Chapter Twenty-One

Sunlight streamed through the grimy kitchen windows of the house where they had spent the night. The place was thick with dust and smelled musty with neglect, but it had been a warm and dry spot to sleep. The house would soon be returned to its former self once the Garde moved back into the mountain.

Rising from the floor, where he had laid with his friends under the thin blankets they had found, he roused Rosalyn, Talbot—who had resumed his small hedgehog shape—and Millinworth, who was curled up on a cushion she had dragged from atop a grubby old sofa.

"Come on," he called to them, folding up his own coverlet and setting it back where he'd found it. "We should go. There's nothing to eat here and the sooner we get to the castle, the better."

Ten minutes later they all stood outside the dwelling, looking in wonder at the changes that had been wrought in just one night of freedom from the curse of Malahd. The vegetation was already taking on a pretty green hue, and water gurgled through the many small streams that fed the land. The crops and fruit trees that had once grown here, would be back.

"Properly tended, the area we look upon fed the entire population of Garde," Rosalyn said. "Did you know that?" she asked Kayden, moving to link her arm with his.

"I've seen Durgot's domain, and wondered why he needed so much food, but I always thought he lived there alone. Now I realize there must also be many Garde in the Ildune Mountains. Just because I didn't see them, doesn't mean they weren't there." Kayden gazed into her eyes that looked trustingly into his own.

Talbot stood up on his hind legs, peering out across the expanse, and addressed Kayden. "You entered the southern portal of the Ildune Mountain and exited by the north, but to both the east and west there are doors leading to corridors, and homes in the rock much like the ones we saw while here. Many Garde dwell there, as they do in each of the mountain ranges. They toil with Durgot, tending the crops and orchards, but they are an elusive folk and their abodes are well-hidden."

"The Garde fled from the Araleesh Mountains when Respiele and the sorcerer took possession of their homes by force." Rosalyn sighed. "And, along with many others, the Gatekeeper was killed. Thankfully, his runestaff was never found, or Malahd would have been through to your world long before this."

"Potential catastrophe averted," Kayden muttered. "But I feel an urgent call from Alandrial. Let's get out of here and find him."

With Talbot in one pocket and Millinworth in the other, Kayden led the way. He and Rosalyn retraced their steps along the corridors and out the same ancient door they had passed through the night before.

There was a difference felt along the hallways now though. They were flooded with light and a sense of hope. From where it came, Kayden could not tell. It seemed to emanate from the very walls around them, although the tunnels were built into solid stone.

"Someday I want to know how they do that," he said to no one in particular.

Soon Kayden shoved open the heavy door and followed Rosalyn into the stone circle. As he thought, Alandrial was waiting for them on the other side. He was crouched on the flat rock, his back to them as he looked off to the east where morning already blazed in the sky.

He was alone.

Kayden marched toward him.

"Good morning, Alandrial," he said, looking around with concern. "Where is Malahd?"

"Gone. And dead, I believe," the great dragon said, turning his craggy head. A full realization of the size and power of Alandrial hit Kayden, and he stopped in his tracks. He had not seen the golden dragon in daylight.

The dragon was as big as two of the Garde's houses. His golden scales shone in the rising sun. His head was huge and rugged with two projections rising from the top, while his long, tapered tail curled around his body. He was amazing and beautiful.

Kayden dragged himself back to what Alandrial had said. Gone? Dead? He could sense what the dragon was thinking and feeling. It hit him like a wall. The dragon felt remorseful that he had failed in his task, yet exultant that at last the reign of the sorcerer was ended.

"How did this happen? Where is he? Do you know for

sure Malahd is dead?" In his agitation, Kayden began to pace back and forth.

"I am getting dizzy," Millinworth complained from his pocket.

"The cave where I spent the night was once the access to a huge cavern we dragons used," Alandrial said. "It is warm and dry, and stretches well back into the mountain. I rested across the mouth of the cave to keep a watchful eye on Malahd throughout the night."

Alandrial paused, lifting his head with a certain air of pride. "Please know, I was not sleeping. I have slumbered for many, many years, trapped beneath the foundations of that accursed fortress, and shall need no more sleep for quite some time—but I *was* resting. I was imprisoned by that vile sorcerer and his bewitched protégé, Respiele. It appears much has happened since then. Where is Respiele?"

"He's dead," Kayden answered with a sigh. "Three years ago. But he was not the one in charge, even back then. It was Malahd."

Alandrial shifted his weight and curled his long tail tighter about his body before continuing." Alandrial closed his eyes. "I would have done something before this, but I was effectively silenced." His huge lids opened and the dragon looked at them again as he continued.

"Just before daybreak, at the darkest moment of the night, I heard Malahd moan. He would not respond to my queries as to his well-being. Therefore, I ignored him. My only interest was to keep him incarcerated, not make him comfortable. It was my aim that he face punishment for his crimes."

"But he escaped?" Kayden broke in.

"What is he saying?" Rosalyn interjected. "I understand certain dialects, but cannot grasp this. Is there a problem?"

"Yes," Talbot whispered, waving a paw to shush her as he hung out the top of Kayden's pocket, listening with rapt attention. "He will relay all to you in a moment."

"In a way, yes," Alandrial answered Kayden's question. "Malahd was somehow able to free himself from the bindings you cast about him. He ran down that corridor, no doubt believing it would lead back into the mountain he was familiar with."

The dragon leaned to one side and scratched a spot on his neck with a talon.

Alandrial settled himself again. "Without light to see, Malahd could not have known that the wide channel ended in a precipitous drop into a pit of lava." The dragon lifted his massive shoulders in a dismissive shrug. "A pool of molten lava may seem an odd thing to have at the back of a dragon's lair, but it warms the mountain. We dragons are cold-blooded, and it was nice to have a little warmth on a cold winter's day. In any case, I chased him through the cavern and heard him scream as he fell. No one, not even a sorcerer, could survive that."

Kayden drew a long, ragged breath.

"Then, it's truly over," he said.

Quickly, Kayden imparted the information to Rosalyn. Her eyes grew wide to hear Malahd had finally met his end.

"What do we do now?" she asked.

"Well," said Talbot, "there is only one thing left to do."

Kayden looked at him with raised eyebrows. "Yes?"

The hedgehog's tiny black nose twitched. "We must return to the castle where you will be crowned king."

Rosalyn's head snapped up and her eyes grew wide. "That is true! In all the struggle to reach Malahd, I had forgotten." Her gaze fell to the sceptre and the sparkling Gemstones of Power, strapped around Kayden's waist. "You could not have used it to rebuild this mountain if you were not meant to be king. Only a true monarch may heal the land."

Kayden shuffled.

"I'm just going to focus on getting us back to Larkender Castle," he said firmly. "I can't think of extra stuff like that right now."

He stared past the dragon and into the east where a fiery sun took ownership of the sky.

"Can you carry both Rosalyn *and* me?" he asked Alandrial, after a long silence.

"Naturally."

"Then let's get out of here," Kayden said.

Rosalyn was first. She placed a tentative foot onto Alandrial's bent front leg and, gathering her skirts, along with the sword she insisted on bringing, she jumped aboard. Then Kayden seated himself behind her, back far enough that Millinworth and Talbot weren't crushed. The great dragon rose to its feet. Uncoiling his tail, he stepped forward a few paces and crouched to launch into the air.

It was exhilarating, reminiscent to the time they had ridden the leader of the Silpeth, but with far more power and strength. Adrenalin rushed through Kayden as Alandrial's wings unfurled and their slow and steady beat took them to dizzying heights.

Twisting from his perch, Kayden took one last look back at the Araleesh Mountains. They seemed at peace, unlike his heart and mind. All this talk about him becoming king had him worried. He couldn't seriously stay in Erinbourne. He had to go back to the world he knew and pick up his life there. And yet, his heart lay in Erinbourne, and in the hands of this blue-eyed warrior that sat in front of him. How could he leave?

Chapter Twenty-Two

No sign could be seen of Steve. Kayden asked Alandrial to dip low over the forest where they had left the whinsomey giant, but the area was deserted. With heavy hearts, they rose into the clouds once more to set a course for the north and the castle that King Larkender had presided over for a very long time.

There was plenty of time to think, since the wind whistled past their ears and whisked away their words before they could be uttered. Rosalyn and Kayden soon gave up trying and sank into their own thoughts.

Questions, ideas, and possible outcomes raged through Kayden's mind. First and foremost was this outrageous notion of him becoming king. How could he do that, exactly? He couldn't very well commute from a ranch in Canada. Nor could he leave his family hysterically searching for him. No, he had to go back.

But what of his feelings for Rosalyn? Now that he was faced with it, he thought of the choices his grandparents had made. They must have felt this gut-wrenching sensation too. But they'd made it work somehow. He saw himself on the same throne that had held King Ludwig Larkender, with the golden circlet round his head, and the Golden Sceptre of Power in his hand. Kayden shook his head to clear his brain. No. It wasn't conceivable. But the thoughts crept back like reoccurring nightmares, offering wild possibilities, but no solutions.

Nothing more had been exchanged between him and Rosalyn either. After him revealing his admission of love, he'd been so busy that now it felt a little awkward to bring it up. He could tell she felt the same too. Her lashes fluttered down to conceal her expression every time their eyes met.

Nonetheless, when they neared the peaks of the Tareele Mountains, shadowing the tall turrets of Larkender Castle, Rosalyn reached for his hand. He squeezed it back, and all the emotion of their struggles and the journey threatened to overwhelm him. His throat closed and he took a deep breath.

They landed on the grass in front of the outer ramparts with a rush of wind and a swish of Alandrial's huge leathery wings. Guards who had been watching from the battlements called to others, trumpets were blown, and scores of people rushed to the top of the walls, jostling one another for a look at the dragon.

A voice rang out above the rabble. "It is the young man who carried the Emerald!"

Voices rose behind the battlements as word spread. There was a loud noise of timbers being flung to the ground and then the huge gates were thrown wide. Throngs of people poured through and ran down the cobblestone entrance to the castle. They filled the grassy verge between the stone fortifications and the Glee River, to stand whispering among themselves, their eyes agog. The last dragon was reputed to have died long ago. No wonder the people were amazed.

Kayden slid from Alandrial's broad back and reached up to offer his hand to Rosalyn. Then both of them stood erect as the crowd parted and Queen Mirabelle walked through. She was dressed in a long flowing gown of the palest blue, edged with silvery lace at the wrists and throat. Her golden hair was braided and rolled into a bun at the nape of her neck.

"Kayden…" she said with trembling voice, "my dearest boy. You have returned with our Rosalyn, and I see, with the brave Talbot and—Millinworth."

She smiled at them all, as one by one, the animals appeared.

"And Alandrial," Kayden added. He motioned to the dragon who bowed his head so low he touched the ground with his chin. "He has been imprisoned beneath Respiele's lair since the time of my grandmother. When the first great battle took place."

"Alandrial," the queen repeated in wonder. "I am so pleased to meet you."

Her lips quivered and shining tears ran down her lovely face. Reaching out, she took Kayden's hands in hers and pressed them warmly. Kayden dipped his knee and bowed his head.

"You have no need to bow for me," the queen said, with a catch of breath as she struggled for control. She tugged Kayden up to stand and searched his eyes. "My beloved husband would have been so proud to see you all here today —and with Alandrial."

She dropped Kayden's hands and lifted a palm to her tear-stained cheek. "I can scarcely believe it. But what news have you?"

Kayden cleared his throat. Stillness fell upon the assembly, and a thousand ears listened to his reply.

"Malahd is dead and the kingdom of the Garde, in the Araleesh Mountains, is restored." He stared steadily into Queen Mirabelle's face and was rewarded with her cry of happiness and relief. Protocol be-darned, she leaped forward and grasped him about the waist.

"What joyous words! Ramson," she called to a young lad who stood nearby, "climb onto the ramparts and shout Kayden's news to the people."

Pandemonium broke loose. There was cheering and dancing, hats were thrown in the air, and people hugged and cried. The black threat to their world had ended.

Kayden, Rosalyn, Talbot, and Millinworth were swept into the arms of the people and carried with honour—and a little embarrassment—into the castle.

A feast of epic proportions was arranged for that same night. Yet before the event, Kayden sat on a plain wooden chair in the sleeping chamber he had been given. He rested his head in his hands, his heart and mind in turmoil. There was a light tap at the door.

"Come in," he said, looking up. His hands fell wearily to rest on the same tattered breeches he had worn throughout the expedition.

It was Queen Mirabelle, and he leapt to his feet, dusting off his filthy knees as he blurted the first thing that came to mind.

"What are you doing here?" Realizing that sounded very rude, he hastened to apologize. "I mean, hello, your highness. Please sit down. What brings you to see me?"

The lady swept into his apartment and seated herself gingerly on the chair that he'd vacated.

"I will not waste time. What I wish to say is important and cannot wait." She sighed heavily and began. "Ludwig's body was found later that terrible afternoon you were attacked on the Kalainian Sea. When he was brought home to me, I experienced the worst day of my life..." She looked steadily at Kayden, her shoulders stiff and her chin held high, but she twisted a lace-edged handkerchief in her hands.

"The love of my life was lost to me, his life taken by the hand of one so vile, words cannot describe the monster."

Standing abruptly, she moved across the room and peered sightlessly out a small, thick-paned window.

"Listening to the accounts of witnesses that day, I understand you did everything possible to save the life of my husband and I want to thank you personally, and in private." She took a deep breath and turned to face Kayden, tears flowing freely down her cheeks. "And I wish to tell you that tonight, you shall be named his successor."

She took a moment to dab her eyes with the kerchief. Kayden opened his mouth to argue, but she raised a hand asking him to wait until she finished.

"As his only living descendant, it is your place to ascend the throne, but doing so is also a burden not to be taken lightly. For myself, I do not believe there is anyone in our kingdom that could shoulder the responsibility this tribute carries, possesses the integrity it requires, or would merit this honour more than you." She walked toward Kayden and placed a gentle hand on either arm.

Kayden was overwhelmed. His own eyes brimmed with tears for King Larkender and the queen, for the people of this land who had lost so much, and for the difficult decision he must now make.

"Thank you," he said simply. "But you know I'm not from your world. My heart feels torn in two."

She held his eyes with her own. "I am well aware of the inner turmoil you must be feeling. You are not from this world—and yet, you are. Whatsoever decision you make, I will respect. You shall be brought to me before the feast begins so we may enter together with Rosalyn and Talbot. Alandrial is a trifle large to enter our halls, but he will be honoured. Millinworth has informed me, at great length I might add, of her part in the course of events. While she shall not be punished, I have relieved her of further service to the monarchy."

The lady smiled a little. Kayden could imagine Millinworth's non-stop dialogue, with embellishment, but he was glad the mouse had been honest.

Queen Mirabelle continued. "From what Millinworth said, I understand crows were dispatched by Malahd to keep him informed of your whereabouts, and that they transported her to meet with you at the stone circle. Does that sound correct? This was in order that she might lead your company to be captured."

Kayden nodded. "That sounds about right. I believe Malahd wanted me kept alive long enough to force me to open the portal into my own world. Only a runestaff could do it, and it would not obey Malahd."

"Ah, then the situation was more dire than I had supposed. We are most grateful to you all." She sighed again before saying more briskly, "Please inform me of your decision before the feast begins, and I shall make the proper announcement."

Her skirts rustled as she walked to the door. Lifting the

latch, she paused. "I have the utmost faith in you Kayden. You would make a fine king."

She glanced back at him once more. Then, pulling open the door, she passed through and closed it softly behind her.

Kayden began to pace. Back and forth across the flagstone floor he marched, muttering to himself and raking fingers through his already rumpled hair. What was he to do? All along he had known this day would come, but the knowledge had been too far-fetched to even consider. Now, the time for major life choices had arrived.

There was another knock. He rushed to it and wrenched the door open, but it was only a young boy, who left Kayden with an armload of folded clothes and instructions on where he was to go for a bath. As Kayden gazed at the richly woven fabrics in his hands and carried them to his bed, his eyes were caught by his faithful runestaff propped against the wall.

And somewhere deep within, he knew what he would do.

Chapter Twenty-Three

The great castle hall was jammed with people, seated at long lines of tables, when Queen Mirabelle led Kayden, Rosalyn, and Talbot—having changed into his huge alternate form as the occasion befit—marched in from a side door, and onto the platform at the north end. Every chair scraped back as the people of Erinbourne rose to acknowledge the queen and her brave companions. A hush fell over the chattering crowd.

Kayden looked out at them, faces happy and glowing with love for their queen in the light of candles placed about the room. Queen Mirabelle walked before him in a trailing gown of midnight blue, strong and purposeful. She carried the Golden Sceptre of Power with the crest of gemstones inlaid in the crown at its top, and a shining circlet was in her hair.

She moved to stand at the large podium and lifted her arms as though reaching out to hold each person close.

"Please seat yourselves," she said with a smile. "My dear people, it is with sorrow I must speak today on behalf of King Ludwig, but with great joy I declare the defeat of Malahd at the hands of several courageous souls who—"

A roar of such clapping and cheering arose that she was forced to delay her speech for many moments. Eventually, she lifted her hands once more and the room subsided.

Indicating each one as she introduced them, she began again with a pause between names to allow for applause. "These courageous souls deserve our praise. Rosalyn Chester, Resistance fighter, personal guard to the king. Talbot, trusted friend, warrior, and fierce defender of Erinbourne, the monarchy, and his companions. In the courtyard outside—for obvious reasons—are two other defenders of this realm. One is Alandrial, a king among dragons, and staunch warden of this land. The other is Steve, a whinsomey giant of no fixed address, but possessing great courage and fortitude..."

As the queen took a breath, spontaneous applause erupted, and she waited patiently for the throng to quiet themselves. Kayden and Rosalyn exchanged smiles. Steve was alright.

"Finally, I present to you Kayden Bramly, grandson of Alainea Ilstyne of the Araleesh Mountains, great-grandson of Respiele Larkender, and great-nephew of our late King Ludwig Larkender. Kayden is a man who, through his own choice, became protector of a people he did not know, and guardian of the most powerful and precious artifact this land possesses."

She raised the sceptre and wild cheering accompanied her gesture.

"These four were aided by countless others—Magda Roudel, keeper of vivacity and all things green, Durgot Flandish, Gatekeeper of the southern portal, and

Millinworth, a mouse of great repute, to name only a few. They all deserve our gratitude."

Further shouting and clapping burst forth.

"But now, before we commence our feast, a moment must be taken to make an announcement that will affect Erinbourne from this point forward, and unto its furthest reaches. I speak, naturally, of the void left by the king upon his death." She took a deep breath. "As descendant of Respiele and of King Ludwig, there is only one who is in direct line to ascend the throne and become our leader and chief. I speak of Kayden Bramley. Yet, to become king requires more than birthright. It requires a love for the people and creatures of Erinbourne, a clear sense of duty, bravery, integrity, and a humbleness of spirit. As well, the next king must also show himself worthy to wield Erinbourne's Gemstones of Power. It is my belief that Kayden has demonstrated each one of these qualities. Yet, this momentous choice is Kayden's own to make."

She looked, searching, out into the faces of her people. The only sound that could be heard was a gentle snore from the platform at Queen Mirabelle's feet where the tiny curled-up form of Millinworth rested.

Queen Mirabelle raised her voice and lifted the sceptre. "If he chooses to become our king, will you accept his rule?"

There was a moment of silence in which Kayden looked out upon the gathering, his heart caught in his throat. And then, the people flew to their feet, stamping, banging the tables in front of them, whistling, applauding, and waving their hats in the air. Queen Mirabelle turned to Kayden and motioned that he step forward.

"What say you to this overwhelming response?" she asked.

Kayden stepped to the edge of the platform, but in his mind, he was sitting at Durgot's table, watching with wonder as Talbot transformed into a warrior; he was riding a pure white horse as it spread its wings and flew him across Erinbourne, a land he'd come to love in such a short period of time. And he was walking hand in hand with Rosalyn, the beautiful dark-haired woman who had fought at his side, her eyes the colour of the Kalainian Sea.

"It is my deepest wish to serve you, the people of Erinbourne, and become your king, but…I cannot do so without a queen."

Reaching across the space that divided them, he took Rosalyn's hand and felt her warmth seep into him as he pulled her gently to stand beside him.

She looked lovely. A dress of shimmering violet draped gracefully over her body and brushed the floor at her slippered feet. Her rich brown hair was freed of its braid and cascaded across her shoulders in a mass of long curls. Lowering himself to one knee, he gazed at her, love such as he had never known flooding his heart. His face flushed and he watched as her eyes widened and her lips parted into a breath of surprise.

"Rosalyn," he said, his voice cracking with nervousness, "will you honour me by consenting to become my wife… and my queen?"

"Yes," she answered simply.

Kayden rose to tumultuous applause and, stepping into one another's arms, they shared a kiss that sealed a lifetime of happiness.

They stood together then, hand in hand as Queen Mirabelle crowned Kayden king, and with both hands, passed him the Golden Sceptre of Power with which to rule his people and his land. Then ensued such gladness and festivity as the castle had never seen before. Talbot embraced them both, carefully, and even Millinworth woke up long enough to wish them well. Yet there were two important guests who could not be present, and they walked out beneath the glittering stars to share the news with Steve and Alandrial.

And so, although Kayden did travel back to Canada to see his family from time to time, and to ask Gran to finally tell her own thrilling tale of adventure, he was content to ever be...the King of Erinbourne.

vinci-books.com/thesecret

In a world of magic and monsters, an unlikely hero rises to fight.

Charles Bramley never expected to be a hero—until dragons swept him into Erinbourne, a realm on the brink of ruin. With fierce warrior Alainea, he must recover the Gems of Power before darkness consumes all. As evil closes in, Charles must unlock his own magic—but can an ordinary man defy a sorcerer's wrath?

Turn the page for a free preview…

The Secret: Chapter One

The air outside of Larkender castle was filled with the beating of leathery wings and voices raised in anger. A shadow fell across the two arched windows of Kayden's library, blotting out the afternoon light. He laid down his pen and raised a hand from the heavy sheaf of papers on the worn desk before him. Rubbing the tiredness from his eyes, he pushed back his chair to peer at the narrow opening cut into the thick stone walls.

The space was small and sparsely furnished. Only his desk, pushed against the outside wall, several cozy chairs, an end table set between them and a heavy tapestry hanging over the fireplace, adorned the room. He assumed the momentary lack of light had been caused by the passing of his dragon, Alandrial. Although it was unusual for him to set flight before sundown. The blue sky had deepened with shades of late afternoon. All light would soon be gone.

The hollering continued. *What was all the commotion about?*

He didn't need to worry. His friend and warrior, Talbot,

was there—and of course Alandrial. If there was trouble, which there hadn't been for two years, ever since Malahd had been defeated, his friends would deal with it.

Gathering his papers together, Kayden slid open a drawer, dropped the pen he'd been using inside, and stood. The wad of paper in his hands and several pens were the only two luxuries he'd brought into the land of Erinbourne after having visited his family in Canada a short time ago. Although most Erinbournians knew of the four great portals—one of which led into the alternate place called Canada, where Kayden had grown up—it would be difficult to explain the differences between the two lands, and so he kept his paper and pens hidden.

Kayden stretched his hand to ease the cramps he'd gained since beginning this self-appointed task. The manuscript was complete and now all that was left was to read it through and ensure everything was written correctly. He tucked the papers beneath his arm before moving across the room to pull a heavy old chair, belonging to his predecessor, King Ludwig Larkender, closer to the hearth.

A fire crackled its invitation and a thick candle lay ready to be lit on the small table nearby. Settling himself within the soft depths of the armchair, Kayden laid the manuscript on his lap and smoothed his hands over the top page.

Telling the story from his grandfather's point of view had been more emotional than he'd expected, but he couldn't think of any other way to do it. It was easy enough to put himself into his grandfather's shoes and imagine how bewildered and disbelieving he must have been, because Kayden had felt that way too. He'd also entered Erinbourne under strange circumstances, roughly five years ago.

Yet, Kayden was only twelve when his grandfather,

Charles, had passed away, and writing about him—actually *being* him, as he wrote his grandfather's story—had been difficult. Thankfully, Gran had given him the journal his grandfather had written of his adventures in Erinbourne. Kayden had never felt closer to his grandfather as he did when lost in the yellowed pages of Grandpa Charles' old notebook.

A few faded pictures accompanied the diary. Kayden treasured them and picked one up off the table now. It was a photo depicting his grandparents on their wedding day and he gazed into their happy faces.

Charles had looked particularly handsome in his dark suit on that occasion. He had longish, sandy-coloured hair, as was the style back then, and laughing blue eyes that had crinkled at the corners even when he'd been young. A tall, broad-shouldered man, he stood proudly beside Gran with a protective arm around her waist. A livid red scar on his left cheek was quite prominent in the picture and now, after all these years, Kayden knew how his grandfather had gotten it.

Grandad had always been evasive when it came to that scar.

Gran's hair was a rich auburn and was piled high atop her head with flowers threaded through the coils. She was fair skinned with a scattering of freckles across her nose and had the light-coloured, amber eyes that were a sign of Garde heritage. A tiny woman, but Kayden knew she'd been a force to reckon with back then.

He set the picture back on the table. There were other photos as well, always showing the two together: one of Grandad wearing his customary cowboy hat while posing at the Calgary Stampede, and another of them beaming at the camera with their first and only child, Chris. Kayden turned his attention back to the manuscript.

After translating his grandfather's spidery writing, Kayden had learned a few details he didn't think his grandmother had ever been told. His grandfather wrote that he'd protected her from information he felt would cause her more grief. Gran hadn't read the memoir, not wanting the pain of loss it would evoke.

Kayden was the only one to whom the secret was revealed and felt he would have to share it with Gran, next time he was home. For now, it raised some interesting questions in his mind. Of course, Gran's detailed account had also helped when piecing events together. He'd faithfully copied down her every word. He was sure everything was accurate.

The story would have been quicker to write if he'd been able to use a computer, but such technology did not belong in this world. Instead, he'd penned the tale of his grandparents' adventures in longhand.

A sigh escaped his lips. He laid the title page aside and bent his head to begin reading. It was important for each detail to be exact as far as Gran had told him. Thankfully, she had an excellent memory.

A roar of rage penetrated the thick stone walls of Erinbourne Castle, but Kayden was oblivious to the possible reason for Alandrial's fury. The sights and sounds of the ranch he knew and loved in the foothills of the Canadian Rocky Mountains drifted over him as he read the opening page, and Kayden became lost in the story of how twenty-year-old Charles Bramley found himself in the alternate universe of Erinbourne…

Charles gathered the reins and drew his saddlehorse, Champ, to a halt as he crested the ridge. Beneath him, where the Bramley land butted up against the tallest mountain of this particular range, stood his father's missing herd of cattle.

"Finally!" he said aloud, taking off his cowboy hat and dragging a sleeve across his dripping brow. It had taken all morning to find this bunch, and not a moment too soon. He glanced at thunderheads rolling over the mountains.

The group of thirty-five cows, calves, and the young bull that accompanied them nestled in a lush green gully just before a sheer rock face reared into the air. They were protected against the prevailing winds, and lay together lazily chewing their cuds.

Charles smiled as he returned the damp hat to his head. Couple the imminent storm with the scorching heat of a mid-July afternoon and he was glad to be heading home. Right after he assured himself the calves were all healthy and accounted for, of course. Responding to the pressure of Charles' legs, Champ moved forward. They wound their way down the rise on a parallel path to the resting animals, lest the cattle be spooked and run.

Charles reined up again as a cow lumbered to her feet. She watched him warily, swishing her tail against the flies, her mouth continuing to grind. He counted each body and leaned back in the saddle, satisfied they were all there. He and Champ could turn their attention toward home, which was at least another three hour ride.

A sound like a crack of thunder, so powerful it rattled his teeth, split the heavens.

Charles ducked. His horse bolted and Charles scrambled to hold on. Only he was unseated and flopped back across Champ's hindquarters. They topped the hill again in a headlong rush for home before he could pull himself forward enough to grasp the saddle horn and haul the runaway horse to a stop.

The animal pranced uneasily as Charles twisted around to look back. The storm was still a good way off. What had made that fearsome sound?

A movement caught Charles' attention. Holding a hand to shade his eyes, he squinted toward the tallest peak. Something black was hurtling through the sky. It was huge.

Was it a plane, crashing after hitting one of the mountain tops?

No. As it grew closer, it looked like an eagle tumbling end over end as though shot from a cannon. But this thing was far larger than any bird Charles had ever seen. It rolled toward him through space at a remarkable speed, soon reaching a spot almost directly overhead.

Charles was mesmerized. Although his horse strained to sprint away, he held Champ still.

As he watched, the bird's wings shot out at right angles to its body and, with difficulty, it righted itself and checked its headlong flight. The enormous bird flapped unbelievably long wings and began circling as though looking for something. A snake-like neck protruded from the body at one end and an equally lengthy tail unfurled from the other. The tail slashed at the air.

Charles' attention turned back to his horse and he slackened the reins. Champ was right. They needed to get out of here.

The horse lunged forward, needing no encouragement to run. Charles flattened himself across Champ's neck as they streaked down the knoll and across a meadow on the other side.

They were nearing a forest of pines when, without

warning, a sack dropped into Charles' line of vision and thudded to the ground in front of them. Champ shied violently to avoid it, lunging to the right. However, Charles didn't. With a heavy thump, he hit the ground. He lay on his back, winded and listening to the sound of Champ's receding hoof beats as he thundered for home.

Great.

Charles opened his eyes to look for the winged creature above him, but it was nowhere to be seen. At least that was one thing to be glad of.

What in the heck had fallen, and where had it gone?

Rolling onto his knees he stood, reconciling himself to a tiresome trudge back to the ranch, with a massive storm at his heels. He didn't even have a coat, because it was tied to the saddle. Walking over to pick up his hat, Charles rammed it on his head with disgust.

He might as well take a few moments to find the thing that had caused the problem. His eyes scanned the area.

There it was. He walked through the grass to the brown cloth bag, as long and narrow as his arm, tied at the top with bindings that ran from one end to the other. He picked it up and was shocked at the weight.

Deftly, he loosened the ties and slid the bag away, revealing an intricately designed pole about the length of his arm and the thickness of his wrist. Awed, he turned it over in his hands to examine it. It was heavy as though made from real gold, with indentations and various markings engraved along its length.

On one end, three gemstones, each the size of a hen's egg, were inlaid into an elaborate setting of gold. A ruby, a sapphire, and an emerald all flashed with rich, brilliant colour. They were hypnotic, and he gazed at them for some time, feeling unworthy to touch such beauty.

Yet, one gemstone was missing. The claws that should have held it in place had been pulled back and the stone was gone.

Charles scanned the earth, thinking it might have dislodged and been lost when it fell, but he couldn't find it.

He turned his attention back to the kingly item and reached out a hand to trace the glimmering stones. They were cold as ice. When his fingers passed over the gems they lost their sparkle, turning as lifeless and dull as the chipped stones along his driveway at home.

Where in the world had this thing come from?

He slipped the pole back into its protective covering, fastened the top together, and drew the cords over his head and shoulder to lie across his back. He couldn't just leave it lying there. It must belong to someone.

He set off walking and was just nearing the first scraggly pines when a gust of wind almost blew him off his feet. He staggered and grabbed for his hat. Tall grasses swirled and flattened with the force of the gale, and a few of the smaller trees snapped off and whirled into the forest.

Had the storm gained on him so quickly?

He twisted his head around to see that the white thunderheads, their dark underbellies filled with the promise of rain, were still hanging threateningly over the mountains. So what was causing the extreme wind? He hurried for the sanctuary of the sturdy pines, bent almost double in an effort to stay standing.

A dark shadow surrounded Charles, growing blacker by the second. Something was bearing down on him from above. He looked up, one arm shielding his face from the blast of wind and the other holding his hat.

Huge talons, each one as sharp and deadly as a spear, sprang from the end of a claw opening directly over him.

Above that, all Charles could see was a bank of armoured plates, appearing to have been carved from stone.

He ran, but was seized as easily as a hawk snatches a mouse from the prairie grass and lifts it writhing into the air to be consumed.

The Secret: Chapter Two

Charles had been taken by a dragon. He wasn't sure how he knew, or how it could possibly be so, but he knew the thing that had flown above him in the sky was a dragon.

He dangled from the beast's claw with his arms and legs pinned, unable to move beyond a little useless squirming. He knew about dragons, of course. They were mythical beasts from fairy tales and fantasy books he read in his spare time, but how could one be real?

"What are you doing? Let me go!" Charles screamed, but his words were torn away by the wind. The only response was the slow, steady beat of the dragon's wings as the creature bore him toward the mountain.

Charles' mind reeled and his head drooped as he watched the landscape disappear behind him. With every thrust forward, Charles travelled further from the safety of his home.

What was happening? What did this creature want with him? Would it land on the mountaintop to eat him? Would he be picked apart like some flapping fish on the bank of a river, or swallowed whole and his bones ejected later as owls did with their prey?

He lifted his eyes. Their speed was increasing. Charles could feel the beast tense with the strain of moving its wings faster and faster, pulling at the air until they were hurtling toward the highest peak of the mountain range. He looked back. Behind him, like tiny ants, the cattle he'd struggled to find lay placid and content, oblivious to the turmoil over their silly heads.

It was unbelievable. Not thirty minutes ago, life had been normal…Almost boring. Now, here he was, held in the talons of a dragon and careening to certain death against the side of a rock. Closer and closer they came to the mountain, their speed increasing exponentially.

"Don't you see you're gonna hit it!" Charles yelled.

His words had no effect upon the beast, and Charles closed his eyes, stiffening himself, involuntarily preparing for impact—and a painful death.

The world exploded around him. A searing pain flew up his body from one end to the other. Where the golden rod lay across the middle of his back, the pain was worse. It scorched Charles' flesh like a white-hot flame. His mouth opened in a scream of agony, but the sound of his cry was swallowed into the explosive din of their impact with the mountain.

The world went white.

Nothing existed apart from the collision. It was like the report of a cannon shot beside his head. When finally he became aware of his body, it felt thin, stretched like a rubber band, and wracked with throbbing pain, as though he had been wrung out by huge, unseen hands and tossed aside to die. He floated in a sea of sightless pain until he could neither feel nor hear anything.

Charles awoke still dangling from the claw of his captor.

Am I in Heaven? No. If I was in Heaven, I'd be free of this monster carrying me. But how did we escape death?

His body hung limp. He ached from the punishment he'd been put through, and from the talons that still bit into his flesh. His mind could not accept what had happened and struggled to make some sense of his fate.

Opening his eyes just a crack, he looked down. They were flying high above snow-capped mountains. He shivered. Once, when he and his mother had flown to see her parents on Vancouver Island, he'd looked down at the tops of the mountains in just this same way—with a few distinct differences. Peering at the lofty peaks out the window of an Air Canada jet was clearly not the same as soaring over the mountains in the clutches of a fire-breathing dragon.

Fear gripped him. His stomach churned and he was sick.

Don't look down again. You have to figure out what's happening to you and how to get away.

But Charles knew there was nothing he could do at this point, and likely nothing he could do when he was released either. What *did* one do when captured by a dragon? Did dragons eat people? The whole situation was too farfetched to even contemplate. Maybe it was nothing more than a bad dream.

Charles squeezed his eyes shut and then opened them halfway again, hoping somehow it would all be gone. Nope. He lifted his face, his hair slick against his head in the great wind created by their flight, and tried to focus on where they were going. At this altitude and speed, he was freezing cold, but somehow the temperature helped to bring him back to his senses.

Another huge creature leaped from atop a peak to the left of them. A second dragon! Swiftly it rose to meet them in the sky.

A person rode astride its back, raising their sword into the air. The shiny edge glinted before it was lowered to indicate they continue on the same course.

To his right, far into the distance where the mountains gave way to flat countryside, there appeared to be farmland. Tiny checkerboard patches of varying colours glowed in the afternoon light. Charles considered how long they must have been flying. That was odd. There shouldn't be that much open area yet. Not when you flew straight west of Calgary toward the coast.

Ahead of them, the mountain range curved to the right in its never-ending sweep across the land, and lowland followed the bend.

The dragon dropped lower as he tilted his wingtip toward the earth. His long scaly neck stretched in front of him. The beast was staying closer to the peaks now, skimming over their tops.

Charles tried to calculate the time of day or how far they'd flown, but it was hopeless. He had no idea how long he'd been unconscious. The sun was to his left, although lower than it had been. So, he might say it was about six o'clock, but he couldn't be sure. And as for how far—who knew how fast a dragon could fly?

Then he had a horrible thought. What would his parents think when Champ returned to the ranch without him? They would be filled with fear. Charles imagined his mother crying and wringing her hands with worry. They'd likely organize the neighbours to search for him and tirelessly scour the foothills near their home. But he was far beyond their reach. *He* didn't even know where he was.

He snapped out of this inner turmoil as he caught sight of a waterfall tumbling down the side of a steep outcropping of jagged pinnacles ahead. When they were closer, he determined the pinnacles of rock were actually the points of some sort of castle or fortress built into the side of a mountain. Openings along the face of the rock looked like windows and a wide ledge ran horizontally several hundred metres below.

The dragon sailed past the face of the mountain fortress and began a slow spiraling descent toward the ancient-looking structure. Charles caught his breath. They were landing on a circular area hewn from the top of the mountain home. Soon, he would learn the purpose of his abduction.

The dragon extended his wings and flapped against the air to slow their arrival. Dragons must land here all the time. He watched as the one they'd met in mid-air settled onto the rock, folded its wings, and crouched to allow its rider to dismount before taking again to the air. The rider joined three other people who had clearly been watching for them.

Rock rushed to meet Charles. The stern faces of the waiting group disappeared in a blur of tears as his eyes adjusted to the lack of wind. Wincing, Charles averted his face and prepared himself to be crushed, but the dragon released his steely talons and dropped Charles from a height above the onlooker's heads. It made his landing painful, but not life-threatening. His body bounced and his head rocketed off the stone.

He was so cold that he felt brittle, as though his limbs would shatter when they hit the rock. Only they didn't. He came to rest on his back, eyes closed, and struggled to catch his breath. Stars danced behind his closed lids, and he was close to blacking out.

The sound of footsteps strode toward him, followed by a man's voice, low and furious.

"Who is this? What happened today? I take it you failed?"

Someone jumped onto the stone near Charles' head and he realized there'd been a rider on the dragon that had carried him. Feeling nothing could be gained by sitting up and demanding answers, Charles lay still, listening to his fate and struggling to concentrate after the blow to his head. Besides, he didn't think he could move at this point.

"We found Ludwig, as you thought we would, and there was a battle," a woman said. "Thankfully there were two of us and we were able to ambush him before he could use the sceptre. He was easily defeated. He and his dragon are dead at the foot of the Ildune Mountain range."

"And the sceptre?" the man asked.

"That is why I brought *him*," the woman answered, prodding Charles with the toe of her boot. "During the battle, Nagilla and I were driven through the periphery of our world and into the next. I was unaware such a thing was possible, but it seems under the right circumstances, and with enough velocity—"

"What!" the man interrupted. "You crossed over to the other side—and returned? Without using the portal?"

"Yes. However, the trauma of violating that border and considerable pain of entry caused Nagilla to drop the sceptre. Before we could retrieve it, this…person picked it up and strapped it to himself. I had no option, but to bring them both. I feared the tear in the border between us would close and we would be trapped on the other side."

"Yes, yes, spare me the details. Where is the sceptre now?" The man's voice grew impatient and thick with greed.

The toe of a boot edged into Charles, and he was flipped onto his stomach. He felt a knife slice through the leather thong across his shoulder and the bag was lifted away.

"Excellent work, Laveza." The man's voice was no less sinister, but became buoyant with glee. "Give it to me! You and Nagilla shall be rewarded."

"And the young man?"

"Kill him. I have no use for such a hindrance. Nothing else matters now that I have the sceptre."

Footsteps marched away.

Hands grasped Charles under his arms and dragged him across the stone. As banged up, cold, and disoriented as he was, Charles could do nothing to prevent it. Yet before they reached the edge of the cliff, Laveza strode past him and spoke to his captor in a low voice.

"Take him to the dungeon, Armon. He has no idea where he is and would have no place to go if he escaped. I have a few questions for him before he is flung to the ravens."

"Yes, ma'am."

As strong hands dragged him away, Charles sank into oblivion.

Charles awoke in semi-darkness. Experimentally, he moved each leg and then his arms. Nothing appeared broken, but his hands were shackled and chained to the cold stone wall at his back.

A meager flame spluttered from a torch fixed along the wall where he slumped, and he wondered where he'd been taken. He was even colder than before, if such a thing was possible. His teeth chattered, and his bones felt as though they'd turned to ice. The jeans and thin cotton shirt he'd worn for the heat of a July day were no match for the frigid temperatures he'd experienced since his abduction. And now to be flung into a dungeon! What was this, the Middle Ages?

There was a noise somewhere to his left, and Charles snapped his head up. At the far end of the enclosure, a door was illuminated by light and two figures passed through.

He stiffened. The light revealed how huge and empty the space was, and the small round grate at the center of the room where a thin stream of steam arose.

The two made their way toward him. The smaller of them was a young girl carrying a tray set with dishes and a candle. Beside her strode a tall woman dressed in light-coloured pants and a long tunic belted at the waist. Boots reached her knees and a sword was slung over her back so that the hilt was just visible over her left shoulder. Her face was severe and pinched, and her dark hair cropped into short untidy tufts. She exuded authority and menace. When she spoke, Charles recognized her voice. She was the rider who had brought him to this awful place.

"Put the food beside him. And unlatch his hands." Laveza crouched in front of Charles, and narrowed her eyes as she searched his face. "You will tell me what I wish to know, but not tonight. Tonight, you shall be left to…settle into your new lodgings."

With a mocking smile, she stood.

"You are fortunate. My master does not often take prisoners and you would have been executed by now if not for me. However, I feel you may be useful. Information of the world beyond our borders would be most enlightening." She wheeled about and addressed the person at her side. "Stay with him until he has eaten and shackle him again. If he gives you any trouble, use your knife and kill him. He is not *that* important to our cause."

Laveza turned on her heel and strode away.

The girl knelt to place the tray and a blanket onto the floor, keeping her eyes lowered. She then reached behind Charles and fumbled with the metal bindings. They clattered to the floor and Charles moved his hands to his lap, hoping to chafe some life back into his aching wrists.

He tried to speak, but his throat was raw and he only croaked. Painfully, he swallowed. "Thanks," he said. He had plenty of questions, but didn't know where to begin and kept his head bowed.

"What is your name?" the girl asked softly.

Charles looked up as she pushed the tray closer and nodded, urging him to eat. She was a slight young woman, of perhaps his age of twenty, with long straight hair pulled tightly away from her face. Other than that, all he could make out was that she wore a skirt made up of a mixture of holes and patches. It was held up with a belt from which hung a pouch. He had no doubt that within the pouch there was a lethal knife. He had no wish to see her use it.

He smiled at her in the flickering light of the candle, hoping to reach out to her for help in some way. Still, she did not meet his eyes. "I appreciate the food. But more than anything I'd like to know where I am, who these people are, and what's going on. Am I going to be killed?"

Elegantly, she shrugged. "It would cost my life to tell you who they are and what their plans entail."

He sighed, yet felt a glimmer of hope. She seemed

different than the others he'd met so far. He grabbed a lump off the tray that turned out to be a bread of some sort, tore a piece off with his teeth, and chewed.

"My name is Charles," he said around the mouthful of bread. "Not sure what point there is in telling you that since apparently I'll be dead tomorrow."

He tossed the bread back onto the tray with a clang. "And I don't even know what this place is or why I'm here! I have parents at home that'll be out looking for me. They'll be worried."

"Please, try to eat something…" the girl said. She hesitated. "I can tell you that you are in Erinbourne, and my name is Alainea. I have heard their recent conversations, since they believe me to be of no threat to them or their plans. It seems the dragon and its rider breached barriers that were set in place since the beginning of time. These barriers have remained to prevent any knowledge of, or travel between, our worlds. However, somehow they passed through and brought you back with them."

She stole a glance back to the doorway where she and Laveza had entered. Lowering her voice to barely a whisper, she leaned closer. "And I shall tell you that my father is Respiele Larkender. He is the master of this castle and will kill anyone who angers or opposes him—and that includes me."

"He would harm his own daughter?" Charles said in alarm.

She did not respond.

"Do you oppose your father? And can you please explain more about this place I seem to be in? Or how I can get home?"

Alainea scrambled to her feet and laid a warning hand

on the pouch tied to her belt. He gathered what that meant and fell silent.

Alainea said nothing more. Charles sensed she was worried she'd already said too much. Feeling as though a dry biscuit and a cup of water was a poor meal to offer a man facing his execution, he ate reluctantly and in silence. The second he placed the cup back onto the tray, she clamped his wrists back into the chains and whisked up the tray. Her skirt swished as she bustled away without a backward glance.

"You can't just let me die," he called after her. "I haven't done anything to deserve death. Please help."

The door to the cavern swung shut with a thud and she was gone.

Charles slumped against the stone wall. None of this made sense. He went back and forth over the bizarre events since he'd found the herd of cattle, but his mind churned endlessly in circles without coming to any conclusions. He'd never heard of Erinbourne. And these people looked like they'd stepped out of the 1400s.

Plus, dragons? He shook his head as if to clear the dreamlike situation he found himself in.

At least, when the girl re-fastened the metal bracelets around his wrists, she'd left his hands in front of him. Awkwardly, he dragged the blanket over himself and shivered. It wasn't much against the chilling cold, but it was something. His head drooped as he dozed, his sleep filled with dreams of swords, dragons, and beheadings.

A tiny scratching noise awakened him. He remained still, but listened attentively. The fitful flame in the bracket nearby had all but gone out, leaving a sour smelling smoke to flood his nostrils.

The scratching came closer, accompanied by a snuffling

noise. Something small bumped into his foot. It was too big to be a mouse.

Charles lifted his lids and found himself looking into the sparkling black eyes of a rat.

"Hey there," Charles said. "You're stuck in this dungeon too? I bet there are some crumbs up here if you want to look."

His response surprised him. Rats were dealt with harshly back home, not welcomed. Yet, as he awaited his doom, it seemed only right he should be glad of some company, whatever it was.

The rat sat up on his hind legs and regarded Charles. Small round ears wiggled and his long, hairless tail curled around his feet. The animal wasn't afraid, which Charles found strange. It cocked its head to one side and stroked long, translucent whiskers with a paw. It was twice the size of any rat Charles had ever seen. Yet he felt no concern, despite being unable to defend himself.

The rat dropped to all four feet and moved alongside Charles, his nose snuffling out the few crumbs that had fallen. The rodent nibbled them, not ravenously, as Charles would have expected, but thoughtfully as though it was accustomed to much better offerings elsewhere.

"Well, suit yourself," Charles said. "I know it wasn't a gourmet meal."

The torch sizzled and its light grew dimmer.

"We'll be in darkness soon. Sure wish you could chew through these chains. I bet you know how to get out of this place too."

He looked at the rat and it sat up on its haunches again, twitching its ears. Although the rat faced away from him, Charles got the feeling it was listening intently to his voice.

"The name is Charles," he said. Under other circumstances he would not have considered talking to a rat in a gloomy cell while his hands were bound to a wall, but the little fellow felt like the only friend he had. "My parents and I have a ranch in the foothills near Calgary. Ever been there?"

The rat shook his head.

Charles stopped dead and stared at him.

Okay, that had to be a fluke.

"Anyway, today I was out checking cattle and this stupid *thing* fell out of the sky. Why did I have to go pick it up? I should have just minded my own business, but oh no, I had to go grab it. It was the dumbest move I've ever made too, because look where it's brought me."

Charles raised both hands with a clatter of chains and brushed the hair from his eyes. "I'd just like to go home. Somehow, I have to get there."

His voice sounded bleak, even to his own ears. He was fast losing faith that he'd ever see home again.

The last vestige of light wavered and was gone, leaving him and the little animal in complete darkness.

Charles sighed. Tiny pattering sounds told him the rat was making his way to the grate at the center of the room and disappearing. Alone with his thoughts once more, Charles wondered how he could possibly escape this prison and the unbelievable world he appeared to have been dropped into. It seemed hopeless.

The Secret: Chapter Three

Charles dozed fitfully throughout what he supposed was the night. Unable to sleep any longer, he sat staring sightlessly into the darkness.

Silence surrounded him, enhancing his fear of what the day would bring. Despite that, when footsteps echoed in the hall outside the room, and the flickering light of a candle appeared, he allowed himself to hope all of this had been a terrible mistake. He leaned forward, willing it to be the girl, Alainea, and when she alone walked through the door, he exhaled with relief.

She placed a tray on the rough stone floor and reached up with the candle to light the torch closest to where Charles lay. Then she stuck the candle back in its dish, picked up the food, and walked toward him balancing everything carefully. Their eyes met, and even in the dim light, Charles fancied he saw pity in her glance. Perhaps he could convince her to set him free, although he had no clue how to get home.

"Thank you," he said with a heartfelt smile as she

approached. As before, she placed the platter beside him and crouched down to remove the shackles. Released, he rubbed life back into his hands before attempting to eat.

"You are welcome. I brought you food and drink. Something more nourishing this time." She plucked a cloth away from a bowl of hot cereal, a wedge of pale cheese, and two slices of bread. After the trek through frigid corridors, the porridge was only mildly warm, but it looked wonderful. He tore into the meal.

"It's great," he mumbled.

She regarded him a moment, and then spoke. "Obviously, we cannot keep cattle for milk or cheese on a mountaintop, but there are farmers in the valley below who have been—convinced to sell us a few things."

She seemed to be volunteering information, and Charles looked at her over the bowl as he spooned food into his mouth. He nodded encouragingly. The porridge warmed him a little and at least served to fill the gnawing ache in his stomach.

"Are you a prisoner here too?" he asked it with hesitation, as he reached for the cheese, but it was a question he'd started to consider during the night. Alainea seemed unhappy, burdened with a heaviness he could certainly understand if she lived in a place like this against her will.

"In a way, yes." She stood and moved to settle herself more comfortably some distance away. "There are prisons of many sorts."

He glanced at her, trying to read her expression, but her face was hidden in shadow.

She added, "I have spoken to Maurice."

The statement sounded momentous. Maurice, whoever he was, must be a person whose opinion and worth bordered on divinity. She did not look at Charles, but directed her speech to the wall beside him as though unwilling to meet his eyes again.

"Is that a good thing?" Crumbs dribbled from his mouth as he spoke, but he was too hungry to care.

"Maurice is an astute judge of character," she said as though he hadn't spoken. "He and his family, along with my mother and I, are the only Garde left in this fortress. The others were either killed or driven off before I was born. No one else is trustworthy. However, Maurice seems to think you could be. And that you need our help."

"Help?" Charles mumbled around his bread and cheese, which, to his surprise, was quite delicious. He reached for a battered tin mug of water to wash it down before trying to speak again. "I have no idea who Maurice is or how he could know anything about me. No one has been in here or spoken to me since you and that other woman, last night. But yeah, I need help and lots of it."

Again, Alainea continued without paying the slightest attention to him.

"Maurice also believes I need as much help as you do. He says I should confide in you." She looked up and searched his face. "Indeed, you will not last long here, and time grows short. May I trust you?"

Charles met her unwavering gaze. Despite his lack of understanding, he felt a kinship with this girl. Whatever it was she needed, he would help.

Besides, he wasn't getting out of here without assistance.

He sat up straight. "Yes."

She held his eyes, as though looking through to his very soul.

"I believe you." She twisted her hands together in her lap. "We must move quickly."

Charles swallowed the last morsel of bread and grabbed the cup to drain its contents.

"I'm going to need to know a few details," he said. "Life has been pretty strange since I was picked up yesterday."

"Of course! I do apologize." Alainea glanced back at the open door to the dungeon with a frown. "It must be a short version, though, as Laveza will wish to speak with you as soon as you have eaten."

"Great," Charles said, following her gaze. "I can hardly wait for that."

Alainea leaned forward and tapped his boot with her fingertips. "Listen carefully. The reason you were brought here was because you were somehow in possession of, the Golden Sceptre of Power. There was a great battle yesterday. I do not know all the details, but the king was killed and this artifact was taken from him. The sceptre bestows immense power upon whoever possesses it. Now that my father, Respiele, has it, he will increase in strength and might, affording him the ability to take over our world. That must not be allowed to happen."

Whirling around, she put up a warning hand, squinted back out the doorway from where she had come, and listened. Satisfied no one was coming, she continued in a throaty whisper.

"The power comes from the gemstones, but you may have noticed that one is missing. My father himself removed the Amethyst, many years ago, before fleeing from King Larkender and secluding himself here. If the Amethyst were to be joined with its brothers on the sceptre, they would form an absolute power. There would be no stopping Respiele."

She took a long breath and plucked at a tear in her garment. "Fortunately for us, the Amethyst was taken away several days ago. Each gem carries a power independent of the others and this person wished to have it in his possession as a powerful ally. He went to gather forces in the north. At present, the Amethyst is in the clutches of one more dreadful than my father—the sorcerer, Malahd."

"So, you want help with what exactly?"

"I am not sure you are capable of helping. But before Malahd returns tonight with the Amethyst and the additional troops, I must secure the sceptre and escape this fortress. I shall take you with me."

"You're kidding." Getting themselves out of here seemed tricky enough, but she wanted to take that strange sceptre too? The whole scheme sounded like a pretty tall order. From what he'd seen already, these people didn't mess around. He and Alainea could both be killed for the smallest misdemeanor—she had said so herself—let alone if they were caught trying to steal the most prized possession in the land.

"If we succeed in getting the sceptre," Charles said, also watching the doorway for the dreaded arrival of Laveza, "how in heck would we escape? There must be a lot of people here, an army maybe, and we're halfway up a mountain."

"That is of no consequence." Alainea brushed his concerns aside with a wave of her hand. "I have—"

She leaped to her feet and reached for her knife, swivelling her head to the doorway where a light was bobbing along the corridor.

"Pretend you are still groggy from yesterday," she hissed. "Tell her you have a headache or concussion. Say as little as possible."

At the other end of the dungeon, Laveza entered, holding a crude-looking lamp.

"Is he shackled?" she barked at Alainea. When the girl shook her head, Laveza waved a hand. "Do it then. Immediately!"

Alainea scrambled across the floor to Charles, her back to the advancing woman, and met Charles' eyes as she bent to fix his hands behind him once more.

"I will send Maurice for you. Follow him," she whispered in his ear. She picked up the tray without another word, straightened, and dipped her head to Laveza. "Is there anything more you wish of me?"

"No. Leave us."

"The boy remains dazed," Alainea said, hovering nearby. "It might be best to let him rest longer."

"I do not recall asking for your opinion. Get out." Laveza's gravelly voice sliced into the chilly air.

Alainea turned and hurried away.

Charles felt as though the one hope he had was fast disappearing down the hallway, but he didn't allow his glance to betray her. He determined to do as Alainea had told him—to appear ill and unable to answer Laveza's imperious questions. With a heart as chilled and despairing as the rest of him, he subsided against his chained wrists and allowed his head to drop to his chest as though holding it up was too much of an effort.

"Look at me," Laveza demanded.

A metallic, sliding sound told Charles she had unsheathed the sword strapped to her side. Before the razor-sharp tip of it was pressed beneath his chin, his head lifted.

"I want to ask you a few questions," she said. "Whether you choose to answer will determine the outcome of this little chat."

Charles lifted his lids a crack, pretending it was hard to open them for long. He moaned.

"What is this land you come from? Who is in charge of it?" Applying pressure to her blade, Laveza pushed his head higher. "Is it defended, and if so, how well? Do they possess gold or other riches?"

The edge of the blade sliced into his soft flesh. It stung.

"Answer me."

His body strained to follow the angle of her sword and save him from a more serious injury. He was fearful she would end his life here and now if he didn't volunteer some sort of information, but if he moved his jaw he might cause her sword to pierce him further.

"I can't talk," he said between compressed lips, staying as still as possible.

As she removed the sword, she drew the razor-sharp edge along his cheekbone. Pain seared along the mark, and warm blood trickled down his face. He shook his head. Droplets flew away and splattered the stone floor. Laveza smiled.

"The land…" Charles started and then stopped to clear his throat of the lump of fear lodged there. His head sank to his chest. "The land is called Canada."

Throughout the night he had pondered why this person wanted knowledge of his homeland. There were no *good* reasons for it. She sought information with the hope of invasion, and he had to deter her somehow.

"It's a land of warriors," he said. His voice sounded weak. Good. "There are armies placed along the mountain borders and we have advanced methods of warfare…"

Purposely, he made his voice trail off at the end and he slumped lower, his head lolling.

Laveza kicked him in the side with enough force to throw him sideways, the chains following with a loud jangle. He cracked his head on the stone. The air was expelled from his body in one loud groan of pain. He thought he might pass out. Struggling to catch his breath, he took a deep gulp of air. His lungs felt like they were in a vice.

"You are lying. Think very hard about what to say when I return." Laveza snarled above him. "If you will not talk, it is not worth the effort to keep you alive…I suggest you find the answers to my questions."

Wheeling about, she strode from the dungeon.

Grab your copy…
vinci-books.com/thesecret